Paul N. McMahon

The K-7 Directive

ISBN 0-7414-2313-8

Published by:

INFINITY
PUBLISHING.COM

1094 New DeHaven Street, Suite 100
West Conshohocken, PA 19428-2713
Info@buybooksontheweb.com
www.buybooksontheweb.com
Toll-free (877) BUY BOOK
Local Phone (610) 941-9999
Fax (610) 941-9959

Printed in the United States of America

Printed on Recycled Paper

Published January 2005

I dedicate this work to my parents.

"All that is required for evil to prevail is for good men to do nothing."

— **Edmund Burke**

The K-7 Directive

Prologue

June, 1955- Kermervo, Kuznetsky Region, Russia

Gregori was feeling a little bit worse than usual that morning. He often harbored a cold, but that day was different. He sat on the edge of his bed for what seemed like half an hour. There was an abnormal tightness gripping his legs; his throat was raw, and his breathing labored. His wife lay sound asleep next to him; it wasn't time for her to get up and head for her job at the garment factory. The night before, like most nights, Gregori had met his comrades at the bar for drinks, cigarettes, and the requisite complaining about life and work in the coal mine. The forty-nine-year-old had worked in the coal mine for most of his adult life, as did his father, his uncle and, now, even his twenty-year-old son, Pavol. His father had died of black lung disease, and he imagined its death grip may have gotten hold of him.

"Fuck it," Gregori moaned. He had to get to work or the party would give him the real shit assignments, or, worse, take away the perks he had accumulated in the last twenty years. He turned on the light next to his bed and reached into the drawer for his cigarettes. Lighting one, he took a long slow draw, holding it in. Coughing harshly as he exhaled, he stood and felt the harsh Russian tobacco take hold of his brain, reinvigorating it, if only for a moment. His stomach, in knots, was churning and gaseous. Releasing a loud belch, Gregori went into the kitchen. He couldn't eat breakfast, but grabbed the lunch his wife had prepared for him the night before. Hanging next to the door to his room were his work clothes, gloves, helmet, and head lamp. He dressed and headed for the door.

Feeling that his nose was running, he reached up to wipe it. As he grabbed the doorknob, he noticed some blood on his right hand. "Fucking dry air always gives me nosebleeds," he said.

Gregori stumbled out of his house and headed for the bus stop for the mine company bus. It was still dark, cold, and drizzling. Gregori leaned against the signpost and lit another cigarette. He barely had enough strength to strike the match against the strike board. The bus came; he boarded, and then it headed to the mine. By this time, sweat was beading on his forehead. He felt a throbbing pain in his lower body. Trying to get through the pain, he noticed his co-worker, Ivan, slumped in the seat next to him and kicked his leg.

"Ivan, the vodka wasn't that bad; get your ass up," Gregori barked.

"Gregori, my friend, I have one hell of a hangover, and I don't remember drinking that much. The fucking bartender must have served us wood alcohol," his friend replied.

The bus pulled through the gate to the mine, next to the elevators that led down the shaft. They disembarked, lit cigarettes, and got onto the elevator platform. Typically, there were at least fifteen other workers who would come at the same time in the morning as they. This day, it was just the two of them. As the sun began to rise over the horizon, they descended into the dark, cold shaft. Aside from the other workers missing from the morning shift, they should have also seen the first group of workers from the night shift coming up as they went down. They must be late, Gregori thought. The mine was two hundred and fifty meters deep, with two main vertical shafts and three horizontal tunnels that extended through the main coal deposit. There were two shifts, and the mine was essentially in operation twenty-four hours a day. Ivan and Gregori worked the day shift in the newest tunnel.

"Ivan, what's going on?" Gregori asked. They both looked over at the vertical bucket lift that carried the coal to the topside of the mine. The lift was moving, but the buckets, normally topped off with coal, were empty. Also absent was the noise of the miners, as they tunneled through the coal, which would fill the mine with a muffled hum. And there was no harsh, acrid smell of Russian cigarettes as the workers lit up near the top of the elevator shaft.

"The fucking night shift has always been full of lazy shits," Ivan groaned. Reaching the bottom, they headed toward the new tunnel. Still no noise, but there was an unusual odor hanging in the air. It was a smell Gregori remembered from the collective farm where his wife's father worked. A smell that, at times, made him lose his appetite when he thought about it. On the days when they slaughtered hogs at the farm, the one thing he remembered most, aside from the screaming of the pigs, was the smell of blood and feces. As the pigs were slaughtered one after another, the acrid blood smell would emanate from the abattoir, intermingled with the smell of their entrails. "Blood?" he thought. That smell hung in the air along with the humidity of the mine.

Outlined in the light of their head lamps they saw a figure on the ground in front of them. They moved forward to it to see who it was and looked at the badge—it was Pavol, Gregori's son. Gregori wanted to pull him up from his slumped position, but, in a panic, yanked on the brim of his helmet. Pavol's head came back, and the helmet slid off with a noise that sounded like feet walking in thick mud. At the same time, the skin on his face, neck, and head sloughed off and dropped at Gregori's feet.

"Fuck!" Gregori yelled. Instinctively, he jumped to the side to get out of the way and slipped in the pool of blood that had accumulated around Pavol's body. Gregori came to rest against a coal car, facing Pavol's body. Pavol's eyes were missing, and where his head should have been was a bloody skull.

Ivan moved to help him up, but stopped short and grabbed his chest. Looking down at Gregori, his eyes wide open and his mouth open as if to speak, Ivan spewed a stream of blood on Gregori's face and body. The hot ejecta contained not only blood, but also chunks of muscle and organs. Ivan fell to the ground, shaking violently, blood coming out of his eyes, nose, and mouth. After twenty seconds or so, he was still.

Gregori, terror stricken, felt a warm mass in his pants and thought he had shit himself. He tried to yell out, but all that came forth was blood. He choked and continued to vomit while still sitting upright in the place where he had fallen. As with Ivan, shaking followed shortly thereafter. The last thing he felt was his gut heave, bubble, and erupt as his bowels evacuated again. Like Pavol and his friend Ivan, Gregori lay dead at the bottom of the mineshaft.

Aralsk, Kazakhstan, in the former Soviet Union

Andrei Statnekov sat at his desk going over the results from yesterday's experiments. The twenty-five-year-old Russian had thick dark hair, glasses, and a curious and inquisitive nature. Young and ambitious, he had already created waves at the research facility. The facility was an effort by the Soviet Union to consolidate its top scientific talent and use their knowledge to create weapons of terror.

Andrei had showed early promise in the biological sciences as a teenager and had progressed rapidly through school. He was asked to come to the facility by one of his university professors, a party member with connections to high-ranking officers in the Soviet military. Even though he had not yet earned a Ph.D., he was given privileges and access to research projects believed by most to be beyond his twenty-five years. Regardless of what the other researchers thought, Andrei believed he had proved himself and was still doing so. He had not only developed more efficient ways of culturing viruses, but also had developed ingenious ways of mass production and the creation of dispersal systems. He had conducted many open-air releases of weaponized pathogens at Vozrozhdeniye Island, the test site for the Aralsk research facility.

His skills went well beyond his biological training and

crossed into many disciplines. He had all of his father's practical engineering skills, picked up while working with his father repairing trucks and tractors on the collective farm near where he grew up. Perhaps this was why some of the other researchers, who considered themselves experts in their specific fields, and were, therefore, limited to that specialty, were, at times, jealous. Most just didn't have his ability to adapt to new problems outside their respective realms.

After Andrei finished up the last report, he started to design the experiments for the next day. He and his co-workers were experimenting with a cocktail of pathogens, using sheep, cattle, pigs, goats, and, most importantly, monkeys as test subjects. He began to write, but was interrupted by the ringing of his phone. Deep in thought and trying to concentrate, he was hesitant to answer, but reluctantly reached over and grabbed the receiver as the seventh or eighth ring sounded. "Andrei," he said.

The voice from the receiver was intent and serious. "Andrei, this is Dr. Milovidov."

"Yes, I am going over the results right now and will have them—"

"Andrei," the doctor said, cutting him short. "We have something we have to take care of. There has been an outbreak of some sort at a mine near Kermervo. Ninety miners are dead; the army has it sealed off," Milovidov said.

"A mine? What is it?" Andrei asked.

"They can't really say, some sort or infectious agent, virus, or bacteria perhaps," replied Dr. Milovidov. "We need to get your team together and meet at Building Five."

"Right away, I'll get everyone assembled. Give me twenty minutes," Andrei said.

Dr. Milovidov had not given many details, which was strange; he was typically much more loquacious. The tone and curt manner were enough to let Andrei know something terrible had happened. "What had killed the ninety miners?" he wondered. Walking out into the hallway, he went from room to room and gathered the ten-member team. Most of them had experience working with the military to help deal with outbreaks, some of which had been perpetrated by the very research facility in which he worked. These were all, of course, research projects for the greater good, that being the communist cause. These outbreaks were typically mild strains of the flu. The flu virus was used to test dispersal system designs for other more deadly viruses.

The team assembled outside the building and headed over to meet Dr. Milovidov at Building Five. Building Five had specially equipped vans that contained mobile labs with containers and freezers for tissue preservation. Some of the vans also contained systems for decontamination of the facility's workers. Still other vehicles had devices for the sterilization or cleansing of large areas, including fuel-air bombs and other such ordinances. Andrei was only concerned with the mobile labs; the cleansing systems were the responsibility of Dr. Milovidov and the military. Once, Andrei had witnessed the cleansing of a village that had suffered a natural outbreak of anthrax. The bomb was quite impressive, as well as effective.

"Andrei, I have enclosed a description of the scene and a layout of the mine," Dr. Milovidov said when they met. "Get there fast and collect as many samples as you can. We will be right behind you to take care of the cleanup." Andrei simply took the envelope and nodded.

It was mid-morning, the same day that Gregori had died. Andrei and his crew boarded one of the mobile labs and drove to a military base nearby to board a cargo plane for the three-hour flight to Kermervo. They could only bring their decontamination suits and materials for collecting the infectious agent. The other trucks were loaded on trains and would meet them there the following morning. He had a mission: Collect the bug and get it back to the lab to find out what it was.

On the flight, Andrei wondered if this outbreak was an accidental release from some other research facility in the Soviet Union. No, it couldn't be, he thought, and besides, Kermervo is remote and not particularly close to any known labs. He carefully read the report. It didn't contain much more than he already knew. There was a list of the miners' names and instructions to make sure they were all accounted for. It also contained a detailed layout of the mine. With about thirty minutes left in the flight, Andrei and his team partially dressed in their biohazard suits, donning all but the gloves and head covers. Andrei briefly addressed his team. "We have a large number of deaths from this thing; I want everyone to be particularly careful. We have no idea what it is."

Soon after, the plane landed at a civilian airport in the town. Andrei was anxious to get to the mine; the plane trip had been a little rougher than he liked. The team off-loaded the equipment, loaded it into a military truck, and headed toward the mine, about fifteen minutes south of town. Approaching the mine, they were stopped by a soldier, wearing a military-issue, biohazard suit, which was part of the unit that had surrounded the mine. The soldier's job was not so much to keep any survivors from leaving as to keep the curious, suspicious, and grieving family members from entering, if there were any. Reports were coming in that most everyone in the town was dead or dying.

Before opening the window of the truck, Andrei and the others put on the remainder of their suits. Andrei, riding up front, spoke with the soldier. "I am Andrei Statnekov. Dr. Milovidov has spoken to your commanding officer."

"Yes, I am aware. You may enter, but..." the soldier said.

"Yes, soldier?" Andrei asked.

"It is nothing, I am sure you are use to such things," the soldier replied.

"Have you been inside?"

"No, sir, but there is a supervisor—he is the one who found them. He's still inside because we think he may have been infected. He's in the second building on the left."

Andrei asked, "Are there any other survivors?"

The soldier called over to his commanding officer. A tall lanky man with a serious look approached and said, "I am Colonel Petrov. You must be the scientists."

"Yes, are there any people in the town that are infected?" Andrei asked.

"We know that many, maybe twenty-five men, didn't come to work today," the colonel replied.

Andrei gathered his team just inside the gate of the mine. Eventually, they would have to check on the other miners who didn't come to work, but first they wanted to talk to the superintendent. They walked over to the building where the mine superintendent was waiting. He opened the door and saw a small, frightened-looking man with his head in his hands leaning on a desk, a cigarette dangling from his mouth. Startled, the man looked up and seemed even more frightened when he saw Andrei and his team.

"Fuck my mother, am I going to die?" he said as he sat up in his chair, dropping the cigarette to the floor.

"What is your name?" Andrei asked the man, trying to speak as calmly as he could. He didn't want the man to come at him and put a tear in his suit. Just in case, two of his men had sidearms, but they were difficult to use in the bulky protective gear they were wearing.

"My name, my name is Yuri... and please tell me I am not going to die like those men I saw," the administrator replied.

Andrei, again trying not to alarm the man, said, "We are here to help and will get you to a medical facility and get you treated. We need you to look over the list we have and tell us who did not come to work today."

"It's awful. I came in late; I saw that the belts were working, but there was not any coal. I tried the telephone, but there was no answer. I don't go down into the mine. I work up top. It is not something I like to do anyway, but I had to see what had happened. There was no explosion, no smoke—the mine was fine. The first man I saw, it was as if he had melted. I found one more and then ran; I ran to the elevator and came up and called the local garrison."

Andrei left two of his men with Yuri and headed toward the mineshaft with the rest of the men. They went down to the lowest portion of the mine, per instructions from Dr. Milovidov. The suits had their own supply of air, and, as such, the team members could not detect the odor of blood that had so alarmed Gregori.

They headed into the shaft with their headlamps ablaze. Within the first fifty feet they spotted the bodies of ten miners. Beneath their feet was a river of coagulated blood mixed with flesh and organ parts. Andrei and his team had never seen anything so horrible. In his lab and at the laboratory facilities, they had every deadly pathogen known to man, but none that demolished a human body in the manner this disease did. He looked at one of the men and Yuri's words came to mind: "…it was as if he had melted." Andrei and his men set about the task of collecting samples. He knew what they had discovered would be of great value to his work and the work at Vozrozdeniye Island.

CHAPTER ONE

May, 2003- Balad, Iraq, North of Baghdad

Mohamed Al-Jaffar had been working in the Iraqi bio-weapons program for almost thirty years. Balad was the latest location for this work; they constantly moved around to avoid detection by the CIA, Mossad, and MI6. He and a staff of over twenty people worked to develop systems of mass production and dispersal for the deadly diseases Saddam Hussein had in his arsenal. Early in his career, he had been quite enthusiastic and worked long hours to please his superiors, but these days he usually put in an average day, eight or nine hours, and did just enough not to get reprimanded by them.

Al-Jaffar had studied biotechnology in France and Russia, completing his postdoctorate education in biochemistry at the Pasteur Institute. This was quite an accomplishment when compared to some of his more senior co-workers. He was a short man, unkempt and not particularly attractive, but with a Ph.D. he commanded a lot of respect and had garnered interest from many women when he was younger. With a Ph.D., he was able to earn a substantial living and have access to many resources, all because he was willing to do the dirty work of the Ba'ath party. In a country that had been at war or under sanctions for more than twenty years, it was important to be connected to the right people. As he sat in front of the fume hood, Al-Jaffar paused and thought about what he had been through in the last two years. He put down the pipette and the bottle that contained a culture of bacteria. He was plating out a newly acquired strain of anthrax. He stopped and sighed. Despite his connections, despite his position and even his knowledge of biology, his daughter, Amal, had died of rhabdomyosarcoma.

Rhabdomyosarcoma is a type of cancer that attacks primitive

muscle cells in the body. He spent a great deal of time, money, and effort trying to secure the drugs he needed for his child, but he had failed her. He could only watch as she slowly withered, life fading from her body. She was his only daughter and was so bright, so curious, and so proud of her father. He was thinking how talented she was, how Amal had played the piano, and how good she was at math and science. He sighed again, and one of his co-workers at the next hood looked over. "Mohamed, are you ok?" his co-worker asked.

"Yes, yes, just tired, you know the drudgery of lab work," Al-Jaffar replied. His co-worker nodded and went back to work. He tried to continue working, but, again, he stopped short and began thinking about his wife, Mina, beautiful, stunning Mina, the joy of his life, a gorgeous, vivacious, intelligent woman whom he had met in France while she was in medical school. He thought back to the day he had first met her. He was working at a fume hood that day as well. At times when he worked, he would take his glasses off and set them aside on the lab bench next to him. He caught the fuzzy form of Mina walking into the lab; she was there to talk to his advisor. Even without his glasses on, he could tell, or maybe he just felt, what a stunningly beautiful woman she was.

Mina had died as well, not long after they lost their one and only daughter. Mina had not died from a faceless disease like Amal. Mina had suffered a fate many others in Iraq had—she had spoken out and expressed her anger at what was happening to so many children in Iraq because of the Ba'ath party's persistence in holding them hostage, using their oil money for their own gains. She was a pediatrician and had seen, firsthand, the malnutrition and suffering that children were enduring because of the Iraqi regime. She would use her own money and buy medicines and take them to the worst parts of Baghdad to help the sick and poor. Al-Jaffar loved her even more because of that. It was in the true spirit of Islam.

She became even more outspoken after their daughter had passed away. Perhaps she was trying to put the anger she felt over Amal's death to some good. Despite his warnings and his pleadings to her not to attract too much attention, she continued, going so far as to write an article for an Arab newspaper in another country. One evening, the Republican Guard took her away from him. He was spared only because of his extensive knowledge of biotechnology and his proven abilities. They did interrogate and torture him, toying with him by showing pictures of his wife they had taken while torturing her. They even joked about how there was plenty of medicine for the cancer his daughter had, but she was not deserving enough to have been given it. He begged them to kill him, but, despite their cruel and sadistic nature, they let him go.

To punish him further, they limited his access and essentially made him a laboratory technician. His duties were far less glamorous now, limited to making reagents and sometimes cleaning lab equipment. He was still called upon to assist in data analysis and experimental designs at times, but others were reluctant to deal with him for fear of reprisals.

For a few months after the death of his wife, he had considered suicide, but couldn't bring himself to do it for religious reasons. He now wanted to leave Iraq. He thought about revenge, but that was out of the question. He needed to get out, but needed more money to do so. There was nothing left for him here. With his wife and child gone, his life and career were over. Al-Jaffar's parents had both died many years ago, and his only sibling, a younger brother, never spoke to him.

His thoughts were interrupted by a nudge to his back. It was his supervisor, Ahmed. "Mohamed, what's wrong with you? We need to get this finished by the end of today." Ahmed had been Al-Jaffar's technician before his fall from grace. How humiliating it was to have this ignorant, uneducated thug telling him what to do.

He grunted and said, "Yes, sir, I am just a little tired. I will get it done as requested." Ahmed looked at the co-worker at the fume hood next to Al-Jaffar, and they snickered as he got back to his repetitious drudgery.

Later in the evening, around seven, Al-Jaffar finished his work, hung up his lab coat and walked out to the center of town. He ate dinner at a small outdoor stand, eating grilled vegetables with some grizzly meat and drinking some tea. He then went to a park, sat on a bench, and waited. He waited until Ahmed, that arrogant little shit, locked the lab and went home. Once he was sure Ahmed had left, he went back to the lab. By this time, dusk was approaching, and he had to work fast to get to the lab and back home before it was too late. He didn't want to be caught outside and arouse suspicion from the local police, Republican Guard, or any militia groups. Despite the nature of the research in the lab, it had only one guard, but he was a friend of Al-Jaffar's and willingly let him inside. Having only one guard was probably an attempt to not attract attention to the facility, which allegedly produced dried milk. Regardless, it suited his purposes because there was no way he could accomplish what he wanted to do at a more secure site.

Approaching the entrance, he saw the guard milling around the outside of the lab. "Abdul-Wahed, how's it going? It's me, Mohamed." Al-Jaffar spoke in a somewhat muffled voice as he walked toward the lab, coming out of the shadows of a dim street lamp.

"Al-Jaffar, what brings you back to the lab? Did you forget something?" the guard asked.

"Yes, in fact, I did. I bought a book the other day, and, well, I really want to get back to reading it. I left it in the break room," Al-Jaffar said.

"Ok, what does it look like? I can go in and get it for you."

"No," Al-Jaffar said abruptly.

"No? Of course, it is no problem; tell me where you left it

and—" the guard asked.

"Well, actually, I think I left it there, but it may be elsewhere."

A bit suspicious, but knowing Al-Jaffar was somewhat anxious at times, the guard said, "Ok, it's probably better that I stay out here anyway, in case one of my supervisors comes around to check up on me."

With that, he turned and walked the short distance to the door with Al-Jaffar walking a few paces behind. "How long do you think you will be?" the guard asked.

"That depends, not more than thirty minutes, I suspect," Al-Jaffar replied.

Abdul-Wahed opened the main entrance, and Al-Jaffar entered the building. The door slammed shut behind him. Knowing he didn't have much time, he moved as quickly as he could toward the area where they kept the pathogen stocks. While not state of the art, the area did have multiple rooms with increasingly protected work areas. There was a video-surveillance system, but it only had tapes and was not being watched by anyone in real time. He knew they rarely reviewed them anyway.

He entered the first door and donned a biohazard suit. He went through the first airlock and ran over to a chest freezer that was in one of the corners. A few weeks back, he had secured five vials of a virus in a case in a liquid nitrogen storage freezer. Since he was the one doing the inventories now, another one of his lousy assignments, no one had noticed. Normally, the vials would be stored in a more secure area, but he had moved them to this freezer to save time when he came for them. In the freezer, he had also hidden a small canister. The canister looked like a small thermos, silver with a screw-capped lid. The lid had a small hole, about six millimeters in size, that let the nitrogen vent from the container; a sealed container would build up pressure as the gas warmed. It was about eight inches in length and three inches in circumference.

He removed the lid and placed the plastic vials from the freezer inside. The container had slots, as many as eight, not unlike the layout of a six-shooter pistol. He topped it off with liquid nitrogen, secured the cap, and headed for the exit. He used the decontamination shower and put the suit back in its place. He was not concerned about infecting the assholes in the lab; he wanted to protect himself. Though rapid, the shower was sufficient. He had thought that as part of his great escape from this hellhole he would infect everyone with some little nasty creature he had helped develop, but, again, the risk of infecting himself was too great. He didn't want to get sick and die as he was heading for freedom and a better life in France.

He went to his desk and pulled a small leather satchel out of his drawer and, oh, yes, a book. The book was a guide to the Provence region in France, written in French, his second favorite language, after Arabic. He and Mina had vacationed in Provence while studying together in the early years of their relationship. He had started to daydream about the trip and Mina and told himself, "Mohamed, stop! No time for that now." It had taken him close to the thirty minutes he had said it would take to find the book. As he turned to leave, he was startled by the guard, who was heading toward him from the door to the laboratory.

"Did you find it yet?" the guard asked.

"Yes, yes, I did. It was in one of the meeting rooms. I had left it in a pocket of a lab coat. I have it, so we can leave," Al-Jaffar said.

"What's in the case? You didn't mention a case."

"I have some papers that I want to go over. They are in English and it takes me longer to read them these days. Reading them at home in bed helps me get to sleep," Al-Jaffar joked. Damn it, he thought to himself, I should have planned for having to deal with the guard, but what could I do against him? It's not like I could wrestle or fight with him.

The guard didn't quite get the joke about the papers, but let out a short laugh. "Sure that's all that's in there? It looks heavy."

"Yes, just papers," Al-Jaffar replied. He was getting nervous and thought he should have mentioned he had a drink container, just in case the guard looked into what was in the satchel. He was sweating, and his heart had begun to beat even faster. This entire event had invigorated him. Despite his nervousness, he actually was enjoying the subterfuge; he wished he had made an escape earlier in his life, when Mina and Amal were still alive. Adrenaline surging, he began to move toward the exit.

The guard hesitated at first and then smiled. "Fair enough, Mohamed, I'll let you get home to your reading so you can get to sleep." He turned and headed for the exit.

Once outside the door, Al-Jaffar bid the guard goodbye, thanked him again, and headed into town to get a taxi. The nitrogen in the canister was good for eight days. In the morning, he would deliver it to his contact, who would take him to France and freedom.

Bozeman, Montana, United States, Montana State University

Despite the cold weather, with slight winds and sleet, a crowd was beginning to gather at the entrance to the Renne Library. The short dark-haired man, with glasses and a conspicuously large nose, was standing on the steps shouting and gesticulating, attracting more and more attention. The man was an imposing figure, with a very broad chest, heavily muscled arms, and thick powerful legs. About thirty students were at the bottom of the steps, shouting back. Surrounding the man were fifteen to twenty young men, all

16

wearing camouflage outfits. To some they probably looked like National Guard members or ROTC. Their hair was neat and short. They scanned the crowd like a Secret Service detail for the president. Some had nightsticks with them, threatening some of the angry students, trying to keep them at bay.

The man's name was Michael Olsen, sixty-years old, a former rancher from Idaho, who had made quite a sum of money and was now living nearby on another ranch in Montana. Olsen, however, had another more notorious affiliation. He was the outspoken leader of the Aryan Front, until recently a little known white supremacist group headquartered in Montana. The events of September 11th, 2001, did wonders for his group and they quickly grew from ten to more than sixty-five members, riding the surge of prejudice against foreigners. He had set up cells in Indiana, Michigan, upstate New York, and South Carolina. They were working on cells in Florida, Texas, and New Mexico. He drew his membership mainly from the uneducated and the unemployed, who felt their livelihoods were threatened by Hispanic immigrants and others.

Olsen was charismatic, intelligent, and well-read. He used his skills very effectively, manipulating vulnerable people into following his path. He had even attracted the support and sympathy of some more well-off, educated people and that made him particularly happy; he needed their money and connections. The climate of hate had apparently affected the thinking of many people. Today was not a recruitment trip. He knew the student body and professors were quite liberal. It was simply a way to attract attention to the group and try and provoke some people into foolish acts. He quite enjoyed being a provocateur, and it only added to his growing feelings of invincibility. Over the roar of the crowd his booming voice could be heard, without the aid of a microphone.

"These stinking, diseased, and psychotic Mexicans come to

OUR country, take jobs away from whites, and send all the money back to their mistresses to feed their fourteen bastard children. And you tell me this is good for OUR country."

A small dark-haired girl in the crowd was fuming and yelled, "Fuck yourself!"

He caught her glare, stared back at her. "Go back to the Guatemalan whorehouse where you were born. Nobody wants your nasty Hispanic venereal disease here." He continued with racist jibes at Hispanics, African-Americans, Asians, and Middle Easterners, coming to the ultimate conclusion that it was a Jewish plot to undermine the success of white Americans.

"The filthy Jew bastards, after taking the banking system in the United States after World War II, are now trying to gain control of American businesses by sanctioning the importation of their heathen cohorts—Mexicans, Nicaraguans, African Niggers, and the damn Chinese! And now, they are so deeply rooted into the American government in Washington DC, those Jewish devils are running the US from Tel Aviv! Something needs to be done to remove the filthy Jews from power and restore the reign of the Christian white man."

Of course, all this was nonsense, and most people would shake their heads and walk away, thinking that denying him an audience for his distorted views was the best course of action. Still, the young students let him provoke them, just as he had wanted. He paused and looked over the crowd, struck by the distorted, tortured faces shouting back at him, spit coming from their mouths and the steam from their breaths making them look like some of the farm animals he had slaughtered at his ranch. Feeling satisfied about arousing the crowd and provoking them, he was about to leave; he could see a small detachment of university and local police heading toward the library.

As he gestured to his lead bodyguard that it was time to

leave, two men from within the crowd, accompanied by the small dark-haired girl, came rushing toward them. His subordinates began to form a protective circle around him, expecting to have to subdue the three individuals. That never happened. Someone in the crowd, a thin man looking to be in his mid-twenties, cut them off. He drew a knife, and, with a slashing motion, cut the arm of one of the men. With another quick thrust, he drove the blade of the knife into the man's chest. The injured man fell forward, thrashing at his attacker. He dropped to the ground as the girl came to his aid. The man with the knife stood his ground and held the knife straight out, hoping someone else would come at him.

Olsen didn't recognize the man with the knife, but knew he did have some support among the locals and possibly among the college students. The stabbing incident gave Olsen and his group sufficient time to make their way toward the three black Chevy Suburbans they had parked nearby. The students split off into factions, mostly anti-Olsen, and a riot ensued. The police, more concerned now with the injured student and breaking up the melee, let Olsen go. They had had run-ins with him before and knew where his ranch was.

As Olsen headed west, away from the town, he laughed and thought to himself that, while he enjoyed these little games, he had bigger objectives and they had already been set into motion. This little diversion would not affect those plans in any way. Even if he was thrown into prison for what had happened today, there were others of a like mind who would see that his plan was completed. And, when they did, he would be freed from prison and allowed to continue his campaign.

He looked over at the burly young man driving the truck and laughed. The man returned his laugh and said something about what a great speech he had given. Olsen said, "Thank you; of course it was." He took out a laptop from behind the seat, booted it up, and dialed into the Internet with his remote connection. He clicked his list of favorites in the Internet browser and pulled up a site called The Jewish Defense Council.

Washington D.C., The new Department of Homeland Security

He only had a few boxes, mostly filled with books about foreign lands and maps, and one box was full of pictures. His files would be brought over later by his new assistant and by some GSA workers who took care of the move. Not that he really needed them; most everything he needed was accessible via his computer. His new job was completely different from his last. Francis D'Abruzzo had just joined the Department of Homeland Security after six years in the Navy. His new assignment was to coordinate efforts by the various underlying agencies within Homeland Security to develop systems to detect biological attacks. While he wasn't an engineer, he had worked with the military in developing similar systems for field operations. He was a doctor, having received his B.A. in Biology from the University of Virginia and his M.D. from Johns Hopkins. Tall, with neat short curly hair and a slightly olive complexion that belied his partial Italian origin, he was fit and happy to finally have a job that would allow him time to pursue some of his personal interests.

As a doctor in the Navy, he had been stationed on an aircraft carrier and was constantly shipping out for long periods at sea. While he loved the Navy and the opportunity he had to travel to exotic places, he was looking forward to a more settled existence. Looking at some of the pictures of his family in one of the boxes, the first one he saw was a picture of his father, a widower who lived in Wilmington, North Carolina. His father's smiling face reminded him that he would have to call him and give him his new office phone and e-mail address.

There were other pictures, many of his girlfriend, Marina,

who unfortunately, or maybe fortunately, considering the problems they had had lately, had returned to her native Turkey to work at the new Turkish Forensic Institute at Istanbul University. "Hell, these days foreign contacts can be a liability anyway," he said to himself. Even so, he still loved her deeply and knew she felt the same about him. He glanced at the pictures of him, his deceased mother, his father, and his twin brother, Nick, with whom he hadn't spoken in about a year. He had no recent photos of his brother, at least none more recent then their college years. He paused and wondered where he was and felt guilty about the lack of contact. He had decided recently to try and locate him and work things out.

At that moment, his new secretary walked into his office. "The movers are here with your files. Where should they put them?"

He smiled and stood up from his kneeling position next to the box of pictures. "They can put them over there by the window, and make sure they get something for their efforts—some candy, snacks, something."

"Sure," she said grinning, impressed with his seemingly generous nature, unlike many of the other bosses she had worked for in the government.

As the movers came into the office, the phone rang. He hit the speaker button and said, "Francis D'Abruzzo, Homeland Security." Saying that phrase felt odd, but he felt a surge of pride through his body, knowing they had important work to do. "Frank..." the voice came softly through the speaker.

"Marina?" He had sent her his new extension, at first regretting it, but now thankful.

"Yes, Frank, it's Marina. Do you have me on speaker?"

He went to the phone and lifted the receiver. "Marina, we're no longer on speaker. What time is it over there?"

"It's not important. I couldn't sleep, and I wanted to hear

21

your voice. So you've started the new job?" Marina asked.

"Yes, I'm just moving some stuff in and I was... looking at pictures."

"Pictures of me, I hope?"

"Of course, we took some really nice photos together... there was the one of us in London," Francis replied.

"Frank?" Marina began. Only Marina called him Frank, and he loved the way she said it, with her slight Turkish accent. "I know things were not that good between us when I left, but I wanted to know if you still had the ticket."

Before Marina had left her job at NIH to go back to Turkey, he had planned to go to Istanbul to spend a few weeks with her. At first he thought maybe a clean break was best, but damn it, he hadn't ever felt about a woman the way he felt about Marina. "Yes, I still have the ticket and the time off as well. I told my new boss I had plans for a vacation before I took this job, and he agreed to let me go. I was going to exchange the ticket and go someplace warm. Mexico or maybe Hawaii. Why?"

"Well, I want to see you. I... need to see you. Do you think you might still want to come?" Marina said.

Francis paused, feeling his face flush and his heart race. He knew he was in love, but was still angry she had left so suddenly, especially since they had been talking about marriage.

"Frank, I think it may have been a mistake to come back. I have been talking with my old bosses and, well, since my mom is back in the United States and... I just feel more American than Turkish. Can you come over? I really need to see you."

Francis stood still; he didn't speak; he did want to see her since he hadn't changed his vacation plans. "Marina, you know I'm still mad at you for leaving me here, but I want to see you as well. Ok, I could never say no to you, anyway. I

22

can come over like we had planned, except I may have to push it back a week, or at least a few days," he said.

"Wonderful, I will meet you at the airport. Call me before you leave," she said. They said their goodbyes and Francis looked down at the box of pictures again, continuing to unpack.

Athens, Greece, Internet Café

Nick D'Abruzzo was stirring the thick black coffee he was drinking with the small wooden stirrer the waitress had given him. He had checked his e-mail, but there were just ads and old e-mails he hadn't deleted. Seemed like these days he only ever heard from one or two people, and they usually just sent him those bullshit jokes everyone sends out. It didn't matter; these days he really preferred to be alone anyway. He reread an old e-mail from his father that he hadn't replied to. His father, despite their strained relationship, had always tried to keep him up-to-date on family matters, especially his glorious younger twin brother. Sometimes he felt like his dad was just rubbing it in, but deep down, he knew he meant well. But did he have to constantly hear things like, Francis got some damn award, or Francis got another fucking degree! Francis is a god, and you are a big disappointment! Even though they were identical twins, he sometimes felt like they had a completely different set of genes. He had always played catch-up with his younger brother. Even though he was the older twin, he was shorter and wasn't as athletic as Francis. He had always tested high in intelligence tests, but when it came to translating that intelligence into high marks and scholastic accomplishments, he continually came up short.

By their college years, he had decided he needed to get as far away from Francis as he could. While Francis stayed close to home and attended the University of Virginia, Nick went out west to the University of Idaho. He had started out as premed, thinking that if he got into medical school, he could finally get some respect from his father, and maybe he would get the first line of the annual Christmas letter his father sent out. But, again, his efforts fell short—he tanked on the MCATS and his chemistry grades were abysmal. He ended up having to stay an extra year and finished a degree in Animal Science instead. Thinking back, though, that year was probably one of the happiest years he had ever had; he met some great people and had a blast, but his happiness was short-lived. For the next ten years, he jumped from one miserable job to another while Francis continued outclassing him. He looked at the e-mail again and closed it, not deleting it because he knew he would have to come back to it again. Hell, there was nobody else around to beat the "Francis is God" bullshit into his head but himself.

He took a sip of coffee, lit a cigarette, and typed www.jewishdefensecouncil.com into the URL locator of the browser. "Damn slow connection," he muttered as the page loaded. He hadn't checked the site in days, but expected there would be some new instructions for him. A smile came to his face as the pages finally came up. If some random person were to read and believe the lines of text on the site, he would think it was a group of well-to-do Jewish businessmen who provided financial assistance to Jews who had suffered alleged hate crimes. He laughed, and the young girl at the computer next to him looked over. He glared at her, and she turned away. Nick thought this was one of the best things he'd ever done. Not even Francis could have conceived of such a brilliant scheme.

The Jewish Defense Council was a front he had created; a portal whose main purpose was as a communication platform between Nick, Olsen, and other members of the Aryan Front. Olsen was very pleased with the idea and gave him, as a reward, a number of guns, including a German Luger. What pleased Olsen even more was that some unsuspecting fools had even sent them money and made donations through the website. Not bad, using the Jews' own money to destroy them. It wasn't much, but it did help pay for the upkeep of the site. Hell, if needed, they could max out the credit cards of the donors, but they didn't want to attract too much attention to the site and detract from its main purpose as a communication portal.

Nick selected the link that had the requisite photos of the Holocaust and some survivors. He looked at the twenty or so JPEG images and scanned them to see if there was a recent posting. Yes, there was a picture of someone with the caption Saul Stanski, Holocaust survivor. He selected the image and hit a combination of keystrokes, launching a prompt box for a password. He typed his password and a text window was opened. The message was brief, but very detailed, describing the location, the man he was supposed to meet, and the phrase he was to use when he met him. He closed the site, cleared the computer cache and history, and logged off. He left some money for the coffee.

As he stood and put on his coat, he didn't noticed the young woman following him with her eyes. As he left the café, the girl picked up her cell phone and made a call. Nick was dressed in casual clothes, posing as a vagabond hippie traveling through Europe. As he stepped out onto the sidewalk outside the café, he hailed a cab. Throwing his large backpack into the back, he said to the taxi driver, "Eleftherios Venizelos." The airport was northeast of the city and not too far away, only thirty minutes or so, when traffic was good. The taxi driver nodded and pulled out into Leoforos Amalias Street.

As the taxi made the right turn onto El Venizelou, a small white car with two passengers cut in front from the left lane. This was not an abnormal experience for the taxi driver, and he successfully avoided the car, which had come to an almost complete stop. Nick looked over at the car as his taxi driver braked and skillfully maneuvered his vehicle to the left and sped past. The men in the car, which seemed to be stalled, were shouting at each other and pointing at the taxi

Nick was riding in. Feeling shaken, but anxious to get out of Athens, Nick took it in stride. He had experienced similar bad taxi trips in his travels around the world and this one had not been that bad so far.

Nick settled into his seat, closed his eyes, and sighed. As the last bit of breath was leaving his lips he heard a boom. The rear window of the car exploded, showering the inside of the taxi with glass. Turning to look back, Nick saw the white car that had cut them off was close behind. The passenger had a small firearm dangling out the window and fired another shot. Considering the speed they were traveling and the constant changing of lanes by the taxi driver, he was amazed the bastard shooting at them could get off such a good shot. "Shit, who the fuck would be following me?"

The driver was pulling the taxi to the side of the road, and Nick, ducking down and reaching between the driver's seat and the passenger seat, grabbed his shoulder and said, "Five hundred Euros if you get me the hell out of here." The driver was not aware they were being shot at, thinking maybe someone had thrown a rock at the window, and was babbling angrily in Greek. Trying to pull the car off the road and give an answer to Nick at the same time, he turned to glance at Nick and saw the small explosion of blood from the back of Nick's right shoulder as a bullet hit him. Wincing, Nick jerked back, and motioning with his left arm into traffic, said again, "Get the fuck out of here!" The driver hesitated for a moment, then pulled back into traffic and sped off.

Nick, crouching in the back seat, removed a Mac 10 from his bag. He had intended on disposing of it the night before, but was glad he hadn't. He quickly jammed in a magazine. "I don't need this kind of attention, damn it," he muttered. He felt a burning in his right shoulder, but knew the wound was not that bad. Another shot smacked into the top left portion of the back seat. He rose and let out a small burst of gunfire. The driver of the white car swerved to avoid the shots successfully. Nick rose again and pointed the gun at the driver. He anticipated the driver might react in the same way and let out a small burst to try and get him to react. The driver made the same slight turn to his right and Nick, matching the motion of the car, let out another burst.

"Yeah!" he yelled, when he saw the windshield of the white car explode. The driver was able to maintain control of the car for only a moment, then edged slightly into the far right lane and clipped a car that had just made a turn onto the street. The right front tire of the white car hit just enough of the fender of the smaller car it had just hit and ruptured, sending the white car into a clockwise spin.

As the taxi driver continued to drive, Nick said, "There's a hostel near Strefi Hill, take me there." He heaved a roll of hundred Euro notes into the front passenger seat. The driver, upset and nervous, smiled, took the money and headed off toward Strefi Hill.

CHAPTER TWO

Balad, Iraq

Al-Jaffar had not slept much that night, which was not unusual, but his sleep seemed to be even more restless and disturbed than usual. Maybe having the canister from the lab in his house made him nervous, but he couldn't say. He thought leaving Iraq would make him happy, but he realized he still had a long way to go before he realized that dream.

As he stood to dress, the dreams he had when he did manage to sleep began to flood his brain. He had been in Provence, at a café. He smiled, but began to recall more of his dream. The person sitting across from him at the café was, at first, Mina, but she transformed into some sort of mythical beast, Anzu perhaps. Al-Jaffar had studied ancient mythology when he was a child. In Sumerian mythology, Anzu is a demonic being with lion paws and face, and eagle talons and wings. He thought it an odd, inexplicable dream.

He went into the kitchen of his small two-bedroom apartment to have the last meal he would be eating there. As he prepared coffee, bread, and cheese, the dream again came to mind. He remembered the beast had dined with him and thanked him for freeing him from captivity. Then the beast walked away, attacking all he came into contact with. Some he bit in two with his massive jaws, others he would slice with his large heavy talons. Al-Jaffar shook his head and quickly downed the coffee, bread, and cheese. He went back to his bedroom and picked up a small bag. Not wanting to attract attention to himself, he had packed only a few things and some food. He thought if he were stopped, he would need an alibi and had planned for that as well. In a larger bag, he placed the satchel he had taken from the lab.

It was nine a.m. by the time he had everything ready. He left a light on in the kitchen and headed for the door. It was

Saturday, and it was not unusual for Al-Jaffar to head off on some excursion, so neither his neighbors nor the local police would be surprised to see him drive off. The Republican Guard was a different matter. Since no one at the lab would be aware anything had been taken and the guard who had been on duty that night would not be back until the following Wednesday, Al-Jaffar felt relatively sure no one would know he was gone until he failed to show up for work on Monday. Even then, they would probably not be alarmed. He had been intentionally missing days and showing up late, creating a pattern of behavior that would help conceal his departure.

His car was one of the luxuries he still had from his former life, although luxury was an exaggeration. A 1989 Mercedes, the engine was fine, but the chassis had many bumps and bangs from the duty it had seen driving through the busy streets of Baghdad and other cities in Iraq. At one point, after Mina's death, he had lent it to a friend who had used it as a taxicab, a common practice for many out-of-work Iraqis.

Carefully, Al-Jaffar set the bag behind the driver seat. He looked to make sure the lab canister was sitting upright and that the bag fit snugly. He didn't want it to open or get banged around, just to be on the safe side. He had included some cans of tea and a few lemons in the satchel as well, so, if stopped, he could pass it off as a thermos of hot water for his tea. He sat in the driver's seat, put the key in the ignition, sighed, and said a prayer to Allah asking for a safe journey. He started the car and began to head out of the city. The streets were busy with many people headed to parks and markets. It took him about twenty-five minutes to get out of the city and on to the main road heading north. He started to feel more comfortable when he was able to drive a bit faster.

After about an hour of driving, he came to the first, and he hoped the last, roadblock. He prayed it was the local police and not the Ba'athist militia, but, as he got closer, he saw the distinctive uniforms and the Kalisnikovs rifles. The guards were busy hassling a truck driver. Two guards had him up against the side of his truck, while another was in the truck bed looking through some containers of what looked like vegetables. Al-Jaffar hoped this would be a distraction and they would let him pass. He was about five cars back from the truck.

They're taking their damn time he thought. They seemed only to be checking the papers of each of the drivers of the cars in front of him. He reached over to the passenger seat and grabbed his documents, preparing to hand them to the guard. Only one car left in front of him now, and it had a family—a mother, a father, and two small children. One of the children was waving at Al-Jaffar from the back seat and smiling. He hesitated, but then smiled and waved back at the child. Other than the death of his wife and daughter, the other thing that made him sad these days was to see so many children in his country hungry and without proper medicines. So many beautiful children had been lost.

The guards waved the family by and signaled to Al-Jaffar to move up next to them. He obliged and handed the guard his papers. The guard took the papers, glanced at them and back at Al-Jaffar, not saying a word, turning back as the truck driver who had been stopped began to speak loudly and nervously. He turned back to the car, looking at the front seat and then the back. "Where are you headed today, Dr. Jaffar?" the guard asked.

Al-Jaffar tried to remember the script he had practiced over and over the past couple of weeks. "I am traveling to see my nephew. He has a soccer match in Ash Sharqat. It is at twelve," Al-Jaffar said.

"Soccer?" the guard asked.

"Yes, he is a good player and very fit, always exciting to watch," Al-Jaffar said.

"Yes, exciting. I see that you're a doctor. May I ask you a medical question?"

At this point, Al-Jaffar was anxious to get past the post and he had not anticipated such a personal question from the militiaman. "Oh, well, you see, I am not a medical doctor, I am a researcher, but maybe I can help," he replied.

The truck driver was again speaking loudly, and this time his anger was met with the butt of a rifle from one of the other guards.

The guard speaking with Al-Jaffar turned to look at the scene by the truck and then said, while still looking away, "No, no, it is ok. Here are your papers; you may continue."

Al-Jaffar drove off, thinking he had made a mistake. Hitting the steering wheel with his fist, he knew he should have just said he was medical doctor. Damn it, he could have faked an answer. As if an ignorant militiaman would know any better. "Idiot!" he said. He had gotten too nervous. He wondered how he could not have anticipated that. He hoped the truck driver provided enough of a distraction that he would not be remembered. Refocusing on the tasks at hand, he concentrated on his driving and began to recite a prayer he had learned as a child as he headed up the sloping terrain toward the area that was inhabited by the Kurds.

Washington, D.C.

Francis had finished unpacking and settled into his chair. He picked up the phone and dialed his dad's number. The phone rang, but there was no answer. His dad never liked answering machines and that always bothered Francis. He hung up the phone and was about to send him an e-mail when one of his new co-workers poked his head in the door. It was the tall, lanky, bespeckled man Francis had met at an orientation meeting. Jim, he thought, yes, his name is Jim. Jim had come over from APHIS at the USDA. "Francis, they're having a demo in the Electronic Command Center down on the fifth floor. You want to go? It's supposed to be pretty cool." Jim was a bit of a dork, but he was pleasant enough.

"Sure, let me grab a cup of coffee first," Francis said. After Francis had poured himself a cup of coffee, the two of them walked to the elevators and took them down to the fifth floor, exchanging small talk about old jobs and the new office. The command center was pretty impressive. Looking through the doors, they could see a room packed with top-of-the-line PCs, all with new large flat screens. They were told at an earlier briefing that the room was shielded against electromagnetic pulse and had its own power systems and environmental controls.

About twenty people were at the front of the center and were standing by a massive screen. The screen had multiple displays, and one of the people in the group was pointing at the screen and talking. Francis was impressed and walked with Jim toward the group. "What we have in this part of the screen is a link to a similar command center at the CDC in Atlanta, and here you can see our Geographic Information System that is tied into the DOT and the FAA," the guide was saying. There were other displays showing simulations of terrorist attacks including a graphic display of a plume from a dirty bomb. There were at least ten links to all the major national and international television networks, all playing simultaneously.

Francis stepped back from the group, and the guide's voice faded. He sat in one of the big padded chairs in front of one of the many PCs; Jim was still over by the group asking a question. Francis looked around, taking it all in. Jim walked over and said, "Man, this is cool; I'd like to have one of these at home."

Francis laughed and shook his head. The computer's screen saver was the Homeland Security terror level alert indicator, currently on yellow. He touched the mouse, and the desktop came up. There was a portal page open on the computer, and he started reading some of the links. The portal had a number of frames, including one in the upper right-hand corner displaying a list of news feeds from various news agencies.

Francis scanned them briefly, taking note of a few of the more interesting headlines. He read them as Jim was still jabbering away.

"German police arrest three Turkish men of suspicions of drug trafficking."

"One hundred grams of Cesium 137 unaccounted for by Swiss Radiological Institute in Bern."

"Simon Wiesenthal Institute suspects growing connection between al Qaeda and Neo-Nazi groups in Europe and white supremacists in the United States."

"Terrorism not suspected in gun battle in streets of Athens."

The one about al Qaeda and the Neo-Nazi groups seemed odd to him, but he reasoned they both had similar goals, including hatred of Israel and of the United States government. It seemed to him that such an alliance could produce some devastating terror assaults on the US. It only made his job, and the job of his new co-workers, that much more difficult, yet important.

Jim had walked off to joke around with someone else he had just met, leaving Francis in his aloof and contemplative state. Francis thought about the trip to Istanbul and considered cancelling it. As he stood up and took in all the technical gadgetry, he hoped the people using it were just as impressive. His cell phone beeped, and he looked at the text display—one missed call. He looked at the number: his father.

Athens, Greece

The taxi Nick was riding in attracted some attention as it pulled up to the curb in front of the Acropolis Hostel near Strefi Hill. Riddled with bullets and without a back window, it looked more like a car seen in war-torn parts of the West Bank or Greece's North Balkan neighbors, the former Yugoslavia, during the ethnic troubles there. Nick, with a round red circle of blood on his back right scapula, didn't help, but he wasn't concerned with the small group of people who stopped to look; he wouldn't be here that long. He gave the driver more money, more than enough to repair the car, and with a firm voice told him not to talk to the police and to get as far away as he could. Nick slung his black bag over his left shoulder, wincing at the stinging pain he felt in his right, as he raised his arms to lift the bag. A passerby offered to help, but he brushed him aside and headed into the hostel.

Walking up to the desk, he was greeted by an attractive young Greek woman who didn't notice Nick was injured. "Can I help you?" she asked, smiling.

"Yes, I need a room. The rooms have their own bathrooms, right?"

Taken aback by his somewhat abrupt response, she replied, "Yes, they all have bathrooms, but we won't have anything open until this evening."

Nick, shaken up by the events on the taxi ride, not knowing who it could have been who tried to kill him, was calmer now that he was inside the hostel. The woman was still polite despite his abruptness, and he found that refreshing. Lying to the woman he said, "Are you sure? I called earlier, and the man who answered the phone told me that you weren't very busy. I really need to take a shower."

She glanced at the registration book again. "We do have a room with a shower. Maybe you can take one there." Nick didn't intend to spend the night. He really needed to get out of Athens, considering people were taking shots at him.

When he didn't reply, she added, "One of the managers lives there, but he's out of town. I'll let you use it for ten, no, fifteen Euros."

Realizing she was trying to make some extra cash, Nick replied, "Fine, where is it?"

The young women grabbed a key and motioned for Nick to follow her. They walked through the office behind the front desk to a door. She unlocked the door and said, "The shower is past the kitchen to the right. Take as much time as you like, but only for showering. I mean, don't go to sleep or anything. Let me know when you're done."

"Yep," Nick said as he walked past her. He shut the door behind him and went into the bathroom. Stripping off his clothes and throwing them onto the floor near the shower, the first thing he wanted to do was take a look at the gunshot wound. Nick had been shot before, while training at Olsen's ranch, but that one was much worse, so he was not unaccustomed to the feel of a gunshot wound. He even smiled, thinking back to how he pummeled the little shit who had done it. Despite the man's apologies and pleas not to, and despite having a bullet in his leg, Nick beat the crap out of him while Olsen looked on. Olsen didn't care, and, in fact, encouraged him, thinking the other man was incompetent anyway. As for his current situation, he knew the bullet had just glanced off of him, possibly from a ricochet. He was glad he didn't have to pick out any glass or dig out a bullet. The wound was superficial so all he needed to do was wash it out in the shower.

Showering quickly, he dried himself off and stuffed his old clothing into a garbage bag he had in his travel bag. He pulled out his shaving kit and set to work. He had bleached his hair before coming to Greece and needed to change his appearance once again. He had bought some dye and had intended on dying his hair once he got to Ankara, but considering recent events, it was probably better he do it now. He didn't have much hair, so it didn't take long.

Once finished, he changed into clothes that were casual, but different from the hippie vagabond look he had used before. With khaki pants and a nice white button-down shirt, he looked more like a frat boy now. "Can't go to the airport; I'm sure my friends from the CIA, or wherever, have that staked out," he muttered. He wasn't worried; he had arranged for an alternative travel route just in case. He checked his bag and found the tickets he had purchased for a cruise ship. He still had the gun and would have to depose of it before he left Greece, but he thought until he was on board the ship he would hang on to it, just in case he drew any more unwanted attention. He had plenty of time to get where he was going, but obviously he would have to go via a less conspicuous route.

He left the room and walked out past the front desk. The receptionist did a double take, surprised by the change in his appearance, but, after hesitating, she asked, "Did you still want a room?"

Glancing back over his shoulder, he waved and said, "No, thanks for the shower, though."

He walked out onto the sidewalk, went up a half a block to the intersection, and hailed a cab. The traffic in the city had gotten worse. Nick instructed the driver to take him to the Piraeus Port Authority. Arriving at the port, Nick paid the driver, grabbed his bag, and headed for a café across the street. He needed to get rid of the gun and decided now was the time. He walked into the café, looked for, and found, a back door. The door was stuck, so he leaned into it with his left shoulder and it opened. Scanning the area behind the café, he saw what he was looking for and tossed the gun into the trash can along with the remaining magazines. He had propped the door open and walked back through and out again through the front door. Nick stopped to wait for some large cargo trucks to pass and crossed to the ramp leading up to the ship. The ship would take him along the coast of Turkey all the way to the port of Mersin. Nick wouldn't be on board for the return trip.

He looked into his bag, grabbed the ticket and the fake Irish passport he had. Today, he would be Sean Fallon from Waterford, Ireland. The ship did not appear to be too crowded, which suited Nick just fine. Passing through the security checkpoint with his fake passport was not a problem; he headed for his room and some much needed sleep.

CHAPTER THREE

Washington, D.C., FBI Headquarters

James Reynolds was reading over some reports that had been coming in from the various police departments and security agencies he was working with to track the activities of white supremacist groups. Reynolds had worked for the FBI for fifteen years, having come over from the New York City Police Department. He loved his job. Fighting criminals was what he had been born to do. Even when he was a child, he was always interested in law enforcement. Every Halloween, he would venture out in the same costume, a police uniform his mother had made for him. The best part was he had a real hat that had been given to him by a police officer in Brooklyn, near the Bedford-Stuyvesant neighborhood where he grew up.

He had joined the New York Police Department early and rose through the ranks rapidly. By the age of twenty-eight, he was a detective, but he wanted to do more. He had taken advantage of every opportunity for advancement afforded him because of his minority status as an African-American, not that he really needed them; he was a highly intelligent and motivated man. Like many police officers, Reynolds didn't really care for the Feds, though it became obvious to him that to do what he wanted to do, he had to consider making a move to the federal government. He had earned a bachelor's degree in Criminal Justice in the evenings from the City College of New York and had started a master's. At age thirty-four, he made the move, and he and his wife and kids headed south, down Route 95, to Washington D.C. Today he was co-coordinating various groups' efforts in investigating the recent rise in supremacist organizations. After the Oklahoma City bombing and the siege at Waco, the government had really cracked down, and there had been a dramatic decrease in problems involving some of the hundred-plus active organizations, some big, some small.

Reynolds had personally noticed, however, that after September 11th there seemed to be a renewed effort by some of the groups to reestablish their networks, probably thinking that the Feds were concentrating all their efforts on foreign terror organizations, like al Qaeda. This was, of course, incorrect; the FBI was focusing on all suspected terror groups.

He read the first memo in the stack. It contained select passages from a report by the Simon Wiesenthal Institute in Los Angeles.

> "In the beginning of 2003, our research has indicated that Neo-Nazi groups in Europe, particularly parts of the former East Germany and Holland, have been entertaining a number of suspected representatives of al Qaeda. We have confirmed evidence that two meetings were held on the island of Cyprus in April of 2003. While no arrests were made, these contacts have been confirmed by the Cypriot police and by Interpol. The nature of the meetings can, of course, only be assumed to be related to a potential alliance and cooperation between these organizations in their efforts to reign terror over free-thinking individuals."

Included in the report were transcripts from intercepted phone calls and one letter from a suspected al Qaeda terrorist living in Algeria. The letter, while cryptic, did include some vague references to the contacts. Reynolds continued reading; the end of the report mentioned the possibility that one American citizen, not of Arab descent, was present at one of these meetings. While they provided a description, his identity was unknown. Reynolds was incredulous. He couldn't imagine what the white supremacists or Neo-Nazis would hope to gain from this relationship. He could only infer that perhaps supporting the terror efforts of al Qaeda would help destabilize the government and further their twisted agenda. He could just picture the meeting between these groups; he figured they despised each other.

He had worked on cases involving skinheads who had randomly attacked anyone they suspected of being of Arab or Middle Eastern descent. It just seemed so incongruous to him. Still, if true, it could present some real problems for the war on terror, especially if the level of cooperation rose to conducting joint terror attacks. Much of the efforts in counter-terrorism had targeted men of Middle Eastern descent, and, while not an easy task, they represented a relatively small percentage of the population. If al Qaeda could contract out their work to average-looking American men, it would increase their work twenty- or possibly even a hundred-fold.

He looked at the next report and growled, "Olsen! I thought we had you under control." In his hands was a memo about the incident in Bozeman. He wondered why the FBI hadn't been brought in yet, but it looked like the local police couldn't connect Olsen directly to the murder of the college student. They had the kid that did it, but he denied any connection to Olsen, and they had nothing to indicate he was lying. Still he thought they could bring him in for inciting a riot. Olsen was a smart man, brilliant, some said. Reynolds had run into him before; he had even interrogated him about the murder of a prominent Jewish businessman in Denver. Again they could find nothing to connect him directly and he was set free. There was a lot that pissed him off about Olsen, not the least of which was his profiting from his machinery of hate.

Olsen had written two books, and, while you couldn't buy them on Amazon or at Borders, they were in print. Reynolds had seen one once in a bookstore while vacationing out west and even approached the bookstore proprietor about it. The bookstore owner said he sold what the people wanted and, if that was what they wanted to read, then he would sell them and nobody could tell him not to.

Ignorant bastard, Reynolds thought. While he supported free speech, he still thought jerks like Olsen had given up that right. He thought maybe he should call the police chief in Bozeman and see what they could do to get Olsen, once and for all. With the reports he had just read, he feared that Olsen could have some connection to this disturbing new alliance.

Olsen Ranch, approximately 80 miles west of Bozeman, Montana

Olsen had been preparing for years for a confrontation with the Feds. He did not think the problems at the university would bring him any heat, and he was right. They had tried to tie him to the murder and were unsuccessful. They had tried to bring him in with inciting a riot, but had fallen short. Olsen had local connections that served him well. He was willing to spend whatever it took to obtain the services of whatever local officials he could. There were some who did not completely agree with his philosophy, but were, at times, sympathetic to his cause. He had an expansive ranch, over forty-thousand acres, which bordered on a national forest. There were many dwellings on the spread: the main house, two smaller guesthouses, a number of structures for the animals he raised, and a small compound used by the ranch hands. He also had a shooting range and a training area for his cadre of men. Remotely located, the facility was comparable to many in the US military.

There was one new facility Olsen had been working on recently. This one was different from anything else he had. There was a small ridge running north/south across the northwest corner of his ranch. This ridge was accessible only on foot after driving up a rutted, worn-out fire road. The end of the road was a good twenty miles from the ridge. The only other way to get there was by air. That was not a problem for

Olsen; he had two helicopters. The ridge had a natural cavern, one that could accommodate a structure the size of a small camper. The cavern floor was level and dry. The entrance was only about four-feet high and opened into a long passage that led downward at a slight angle to the cavern floor. Here Olsen had constructed his command center. Its height and the view of the surrounding landscape made it a perfect natural fortress. Olsen had even given it a name, The Bear's Den, since his bulky frame was not unlike that of a bear.

In many of the other smaller caves and caverns, Olsen had installed small anti-aircraft and artillery batteries. He even had mini-guns, a modern day Gatling gun, and 50 caliber machine guns set up at the ends of the ridge to provide enfilading cover fire. His men had dug out and widened some of the natural tunnels that connected the main cavern with some of the smaller ones. Inside the main cavern were computers, a power generator, food stores, and more armaments. This was where Olsen had planned to hunker down when the Feds came to get him. Only he and the few men who had built it knew of its existence, and they had all been sworn to secrecy on threat of death. Olsen had even killed one of his higher-ranking associates to guarantee the loyalty of the others.

He had attempted to acquire the technology to tap into the new Homeland Security command center in Washington, D.C. and had been unsuccessful in his attempts, but it didn't keep him from continuing to try. To accomplish his goals, he knew he would need technology as well as military muscle. These days, police scanners were not sufficient. Today, Olsen and three of his lieutenants were running tests on the new command bunker. Olsen was sitting in a chair that had a small computer monitor mounted on one of the arms. In front of him was a screen with multiple displays, including links to traffic camera networks across the nation. It was the one system Olsen's group was able to hack into. The displays were on Central Park in New York City at Columbus Circle.

Others showed downtown Atlanta near Peachtree Plaza. One window included various displays of the Mall in Washington, D.C. Olsen asked his associate, "Are all the systems up?"

"Yes, sir. We're testing the secondary Internet connection right now," the man said. Using a small satellite uplink, Olsen's techs had tapped into a wireless Internet provider located in Montana. As a backup, they could link into one of two other providers located in the western United States.

"Good, call up the com site," he said. The tech sitting to his left clicked on his browser icon and the window displayed www.jewishdefensecouncil.com. "Ok, click on the link for photos of the alleged survivors of the Holocaust," laughing as he said the word Holocaust slowly, emphasizing the word. "Ok, go to the last photo and select that one." The subordinate did as instructed, and, after Olsen hit a combination of keystrokes, a prompt box asking for a password was launched. Olsen, working from his computer, typed in a password, and the communication program was launched. He took note of the list of messages and links in the display and saw Nick had read his last set of instructions. "Good, right on schedule."

As he closed the window, he heard a group of people entering the cavern. He turned and saw his main group of commanders. "Gentlemen, good to see you. Let's get to work," he said. Leaving the technicians to their work, he and the group of men left the command center and settled in a meeting area set up just outside. Once seated, Olsen addressed the group. "I have just had confirmation that Nick has initiated the next phase of our plan. He's on his way to meet with the contact in Turkey," Olsen said. The men's expressions remained unchanged. "Within the next few weeks, we will have the bug and will begin the third phase. I expect to hear from him in about a week and a half."

The group remained silent, waiting for Olsen to finish. "The rest of you have been given your assignments. Once I hear from Nick, you can move out to your designated positions. Check with the techs to get your passwords. I also have packages for each of you that contain further instructions." With that, Olsen took a handful of manila envelopes out a briefcase in front of him and tossed them out onto the table.

CHAPTER FOUR

Washington, D.C.

Francis left his first day of work, having taken care of most of the things he had expected to get done. Administrative stuff mostly, new forms to fill out, including a form designating an heir for his accidental death and dismemberment annuity. He always put his father as the heir, since he had no children and never heard from his twin brother. When he was filling out the form, he first wrote Marina's name. He guessed she was on his mind again. Funny thing, he thought, if she had stayed here she would have to be the designee— they were on their way to the altar.

Thinking about all the boring admin business made him remember his father had tried to call him. He would call him later when he got home. He was headed to class, one he hadn't been to in awhile due to all the recent changes in his life. He needed to go tonight; he was feeling anxious about hearing from Marina. Francis studied Aikido, and he was quite good. Aikido, the modern Japanese martial art, had appealed to him from the start. In the military he had been exposed to many different martial arts— Jujitsu, Tae Kwon Do, Judo, and boxing, but they were always too competitive for him. While he didn't shy away from competition, he thought some of the techniques he learned were only for show or to impress others at the competitions, and he didn't really care to showboat. That's what he liked about Aikido; it seemed to be less concerned about impressing others and more concerned about practical techniques. Being a doctor, he also liked that it was meant to subdue an opponent without causing unnecessary harm and injury.

He was first exposed to the art while traveling in Japan. Having built up some leave when his ship was in port at Yokohama, he decided to travel by train to the island of

Hokaido. Along the way, he stopped at many different towns and visited mountain shrines. He had stopped to visit the Shinto shrine on Atago Mountain before heading to the Senju-ga-hara Forest Reserve. In the town, a small farming community named Iwama, they were having a festival called Tai Sai. Always taking an interest in the cultural activities of other countries, he decided to hang out, take photos, and enjoy the festival before getting back on the train. There were musicians, Buddhists, and Shinto monks performing ceremonies, and martial arts demonstrations, one of which was given by the local Aikido dojo or school.

Francis had been taking pictures of the festival and stopped as he watched the graceful, rhythmic throws, rolls, and defense techniques against knives and swords. He became so engrossed in the display he neglected to take any photos of the demonstration. He did manage to talk to one of the foreign students studying at the dojo and obtain more information about the style. Based on the student's recommendations, he was able to find a school back in the United States and began training soon after returning from Japan.

In the Washington D.C. area, there were many schools to choose from, and he finally settled on one in Arlington that was founded by someone who had trained for many years in the town where he had first seen Aikido. Back then the school was small, about twenty students, mostly in their mid to late twenties with only a few black belts. Now there were about thirty students and more black belts, Francis among them.

He walked into the small church and headed toward the basement where the school was located. He was early, but there were a few students laying down the training mats. He helped them finish, changed into his gi, and knelt down on the mat in the Japanese kneeling style and bowed toward the front of the room. Tonight they started off, as usual, with some techniques designed to teach one how to move like an

Aikidoist. From that, they went on to techniques that were based on the fundamental kotegaeshi technique. Francis loved this technique, and it exemplified almost everything there was about Aikido that made it a very effective self-defense style.

Lining up facing his practice partner, a young high-ranking white belt, Francis waited for him to make his move. His partner, mimicking a knife thrust to the mid-section, came at Francis from about two to three feet away. Francis stepped forward and to his left as his partner had initiated the technique with his right. This was the part Francis loved; it seemed so counterintuitive, but, when performed by a skilled Aikidoist such as himself, it was a thing of beauty. With his left hand, Francis shielded his body and grabbed the arm of his partner near his wrist in a downward motion as he stepped off to his side, ending up in a position looking in the same direction. He extended his partner's arm so it was in front of his body and perpendicular to the original line of attack. With a motion toward the back of his partner, he raised the arm, and, using his other hand, clasped it over the back of his partner's hand, finding just the right angle so he could take his partner's balance effectively and with little strength.

They repeated this technique over and over until the motion and correct positions were embedded in their muscle memory. Feeling much more relaxed after training for two hours, Francis changed back into his street clothes and headed for his new house in Oakton, Virginia.

Mediterranean Ocean along the coast of Turkey

Nick had spent most of his time on the ship in his room, feigning a cold, leaving only a few times to eat, and never venturing to shore when they stopped at Marmaris and Antalya. He was never particularly sociable, and was happy the cruise was full of mostly older Germans and other assorted Northern Europeans, though he admitted to himself that, given a choice, he would much rather hang with these people than the people he was involved with. Nasty Middle Easterners, he thought, as he lay in the bed in his cabin, looking up at the ceiling. Olsen had chosen him for this duty because, unlike many of his cohorts, he had actually traveled outside the United States, mostly when he was working for Vanguard Corporation, a company that made and exported veterinary pharmaceuticals. At first, he thought it was unnecessary, that they could rely on the Arab guys, but eventually he agreed with Olsen that they needed one of their own to guarantee delivery.

The ship was about thirty minutes outside of Mersin, a port on the Turkish coast near the border with Syria. Nick didn't know much about the city, but he had some time to use the business suite on the ship to print some maps and get the names of cheap hotels. No more hostels for him since he was no longer traveling as a hippie. He also found some information about the bus and train schedules to Habur Gate, the main border crossing between Turkey and the Kurdish area of Northern Iraq. He hadn't told Olsen of the change in his path to Turkey since he was confident he could still make it to the next point where Olsen was expecting to hear from him in two or three days. He also thought, at first, that he wouldn't tell him about the life-threatening taxi ride in Athens. They seemed to have lost his trail, but maybe it was the CIA or even the Israelis, and Olsen should probably know about that. Using the portal, he posted a brief message to Olsen: "Ran into some heat in Athens, was able to elude, still on schedule to make it to the Gate."

Packed and ready to go, Nick jumped out of his bed when he heard the voice over the loud speaker announce they had arrived in Mersin. The ship would be there for only one night, but that didn't matter to Nick; to be safe and to not attract any unwanted police interest, he had told the purser he was going to stay and take another ship back to Athens. They even gave him half his fare back, which was unexpected.

Nick exited the ship and hailed a cab. "Can you take me to a telegram office?" he said to the driver. The driver nodded and sped off rapidly. It took about twenty minutes to get from the pier to the telegram office. Nick had to send a message to his contact in Ankara; he had originally planned to meet him there and then they would drive together to the Habur Gate. The message was simple and in code, a code Olsen had devised and had finally convinced the al Qaeda cell to use for any communications via telegram. Olsen had created a front company for which Nick allegedly worked. The company was called Atlas Genetics International and was set up as a company involved in the breeding of farm animals worldwide. Nick had even gone on a few trips to Japan to collect semen for Kobe beef cattle, to Brazil to provide semen for a breeding program for Brahma bulls, and to Argentina for more bull semen to add some legitimacy to the venture.

He handed the note to the telegram office manager, who read it aloud in English. "Goat semen samples to be collected at Habur. Meet at local office." The words "Goat semen samples" actually referred to Nick, and he thought it was kind of funny. "Local office" meant the central post office in Habur. The manager had a quizzical look on his face and said to Nick, "You sure this is what you want?"

Nick smiled and said "Exactly. Address it to Mehmet Albarik." He gave the man the address for the telegram, handed him four million liras to cover it, and headed out the door.

It was mid-day, and he had to get to the train station and buy a ticket. According to the map he had printed from the Internet, the train station was only five blocks away, so he decided to walk. The streets to the train station were lined with shops selling spices, cloth and food. The food smelled good to Nick; the smell of roasted meat was not unlike what they would cook on Olsen's ranch when they were training.

He shook his head and tried not to breathe in the aromas.

These people made him ill, and he certainly didn't want them to handle his food. He would have to find a grocery store, a modern one, not one of these nasty little stalls run by people whom he thought were less than dogs. He started craving McDonald's, of all things. He had eaten pretty well on the cruise ship; the staff did not offend him as much as these people. He had taken some food with him, and it was probably enough to last until he got to Habur, but he would have to find some bottled water.

Glancing at his map, Nick could see the train station was on the next block over, so he turned down a small street to his right. The food smells were replaced by the stale odor of cigarettes and the overwhelming smell of vomit. As he rounded the corner, he stepped on the foot of a junkie who was shooting up next to some trash cans. The junkie, already succumbing to the heroin, looked up with a blank stare, but fell immediately back into the haze of his high. Nick turned as he felt a hand grab his left elbow. He jerked his arm free from the grip, looking at the sad emaciated woman who had touched him. Her teeth were black, some were missing, and she was speaking in Turkish. She was old and had a worn-out body, a prostitute. God, he thought, fucking train stations. No matter where you are, they always have the nastiest people.

Saying, "Get lost," as he turned away, he was approached by a man coming from out of a doorway to his left. Nick continued to walk, and the man came up to his side, speaking in English. "Sir, sir! You obviously are a man of taste. Sir," he said again, "she is no good for you, but I have better, much better, and they are virgins."

Nick kept walking, trying to ignore the man, but his path was impeded by another group of junkies stumbling up the street. As Nick waited for them to go by, not wanting to touch them, the man caught up with him, and, before he could leave, said again, "Sir, please, you need sex. I have better. Russians, Bulgarians, a seventeen-year-old Ukrainian virgin."

Nick turned and confronted the man, angry, fuming, and not wanting to be bothered. The man, with short, dark hair, was very neat and well-dressed and held out a card. Nick thought about hitting him, but was taken aback by his appearance compared to all the other filth in the alley. Nick couldn't get any words out, and the man started talking again, calmly. "Listen, I have top quality, all very clean, some just come this week. You call this number, they will meet you at your hotel, take it, go on." His accent was not Turkish, and Nick suspected it might be Russian or Ukrainian. He didn't know, and he didn't care, and took the card so the man would leave him alone. He walked off without saying anything and crossed the street to go into the train station to purchase his ticket, pocketing the card.

The only ticket he was able to get was for the next morning at 9:00 a.m. He had hoped to take an overnight train, but nothing was available for that evening. Having seen a three-star hotel back near the telegram office, Nick decided to go there, making sure to avoid the street he had taken to get to the station. He found his way back to the hotel, avoiding any encounters with junkies or nasty prostitutes this time. He checked in and went up to his room, feeling he had to shower after his trip through the alley.

After showering, he ate some cheese and bread he had brought from the ship, drank some bottled water he had bought inside the train station, and laid down on his bed wearing nothing but the white towel he had used. The ticket was still in his pants pocket, and, getting up from his bed, he pulled in out. The ticket, some Turkish money, and the business card the Russian had given him were all there, and he glanced at the card again and set it down on the nightstand with the ticket and his passport.

Washington, D.C.

The drive home on Route 66 always bogged down right

between the Route 29 exit and the Dulles toll road. The tension-reducing aftereffects of class had faded away as the competitive drivers of Washington D.C. started to annoy Francis. Even with traffic slowed down, there was always some asshole switching lanes, as if it would make a difference. Eventually, the bottleneck cleared, and he was cruising at top speed on 66 West past the exit to Interstate 495. His new townhouse was no more than five minutes away now. Last summer, Francis and Marina had looked for houses together, and she had convinced him to buy in Oakton, thinking it was more convenient for his job at the Pentagon. Francis hadn't cared and was worried about her hellish commute across the Cabin John Bridge to Bethesda and the NIH. She had assured him she would take the Metro and that she had suffered worse commutes. It turned out she was already thinking of leaving and was really thinking of what would be best for Francis without her around. Thinking back on it now, it was pretty considerate of her, even though it really made no difference to him one way or the other. He had to go downtown now, and the commute from Bethesda or Oakton was pretty much the same.

Pulling up to the townhouse, he checked his mail and entered the garage. The house had three stories, with four bedrooms, two and a half baths, and a large expanded kitchen. He and Marina both loved to cook. It all seemed much too big now, and he considered putting it on the market and moving to a smaller place closer in, maybe Clarendon. Francis climbed the stairs to the second level and went into the living room. Sitting down on one of the black leather couches, he grabbed the phone and hit the second number on his speed dial; the first was still Marina's old apartment.

"Dad?" he said, as his father answered the phone.

"Francis, did you get my call earlier today?" his father said. His father was Joseph D'Abruzzo, widowed and living in Wilmington, North Carolina. "Francis, I wanted to see how your new job was and how the house was. We haven't spoken in awhile." They had just spoken last week, but to his father that was awhile. Even though he had lived alone for quite some time, he still got lonely.

"Everything's fine. I got everything sent over and met a few of my co-workers. Nothing special, paper work," Francis said.

"And?" the elder Mr. D'Abruzzo asked.

"Went to a demo in the Electronic Command Center, pretty impressive. I bet they don't have anything like that at the CIA." Francis joked. Francis was just ribbing his father, a career CIA man. His father was skeptical of the new Department of Homeland Security, thinking it was really the job of the CIA. He had tried to get Francis to go there instead, but reluctantly agreed it was a good opportunity for him.

"Francis, have you heard from your brother?" Joseph hadn't talked much about Francis's twin brother lately since he knew their relationship was strained, so it was a surprise for Francis.

"No, no, I haven't, Dad," Francis said.

With concern in his voice, his father said, "I sent him an e-mail and he used to reply, but he hasn't replied to my last four e-mails." Francis didn't reply, thinking that he didn't even have his brother's e-mail address. "Well," his father continued, "all I know is he has a new job. Atlas Genetics, I think it's called, something to do with large animal breeding, I think. I don't have an e-mail address or phone number for him there, and I tried to get him to send me one. Heck, I'm not even sure where he's living now. You'd think an ex-spook like me would be able to find his own son."

Francis always laughed when his father called himself a spook. Growing up, he and Nick never knew what their father did and were always told he worked for the govern-ment. It was only when all the other kids in the neighbor-hood whose mothers and fathers worked for the government began to find out, one after the other, and spread the word, that they asked their father, and he still insisted he was simply a government employee.

His father continued, "I was thinking that maybe, well, maybe in that 'better than the CIA' Electronic Command Center at Homeland Security, you might be able to get some more information on Atlas Genetics and find out where Nick is these days. I'm getting old, and I want to straighten things out with him. I feel sort of guilty about the way I've treated him at times." Francis felt ashamed as well, knowing he had always been his father's favorite, and, like any sibling, he milked it to the maximum. "Yeah. No problem, Dad. I'll see what I can do. I was sort of wondering myself. Listen, remember I told you I was going to Turkey and then not? I heard from Marina today. I'm going there after all, in two weeks."

"She's a wonderful woman, son. I was sad when she left. Good luck."

"Thanks, Dad. I'll see what I can find out about Atlas, and can you send me Nick's e-mail address too?" he said.

"Sure, love you, son," Joseph said.

"Love you, too, Dad," Francis replied.

Mersin, Turkey

Nick had fallen asleep, and, by the time he awoke, it was almost ten p.m. He reached over to the nightstand for the glass of whiskey he had left there and noticed the business card again. He picked it up, rolling it between his fingers like a poker chip. He hadn't been with a woman in awhile. The last time he had a girlfriend was probably four years ago. Picking up the phone, he dialed the first four numbers from the card and then hung up. Again he picked up the phone, but just held it until an operator came on the line and he hung up again. Man, I need to get laid, he thought.

His mind meandered back and forth between thoughts of revulsion and intrigue. He had never picked up a prostitute himself, but at the ranch, Olsen had supplied some for his men after a hard day of training. Many of them were East German or Polish, having been arranged for in Chicago. Despite being foreign, Olsen considered Northern Europeans brothers. Poles were a stretch for Olsen, but he didn't want to turn away good pussy. Nick remembered how the man in the alley had described one of the prostitutes: a seventeen-year-old Ukrainian virgin.

Nick hadn't gotten laid for the first time until he was twenty and had only been with women one or two years younger than himself. The thought of a pale-skinned Ukrainian woman was appealing, even though he knew there were a lot of Jews in the Ukraine. He picked up the phone and dialed. It only rang twice before being answered, possibly by the same man from the alley. The man answered in Turkish.

"Hello?" Nick said.

"You English man?" the voice on the phone answered back.

"Yes, yes, I'm Irish," Nick said, not even trying to put on an accent, thinking all English-speaking people probably sounded alike to the guy. "I have a card and—"

"You need woman. Tell me where you are, what you want," the man said.

"I am at the Loraza Hotel. I was told you had seventeen-year-old Ukrainians," Nick said.

"Sure, sure, very nice, you have dollar?" the man said.

"Of course."

"Fifty bucks for two hours, one hundred all night. I give you special. You want only one?"

"Yes, just for the two hours," Nick said.

"Ok, I bring her by in one hour. Tell me your room," the man said.

"301."

"One hour."

Nick hung up the phone. An hour and a half passed before there was a knock on his door. Nick open it and saw the man from the alley and a young redhead standing next to him, looking nervous. The man smiled and said, "You the man by the train station. I knew you needed some of my help. Ok, you got two hours. You pay me up front."

Nick had grabbed the fifty from the nightstand when he heard the knock. He folded it lengthwise and handed it to the man. The man put his hand to the small of the woman's back, said something in Ukrainian, gave her a peck on her forehead and led her into the room.

Nick closed the door behind her and said, "Do you speak English?"

She nodded, but did not speak. She looked younger than seventeen, maybe fourteen or thirteen. Nick went over to the window and made sure the blinds were closed.

He had put on a robe before answering the door and still had the towel on underneath. He took off his robe. The girl began to undress herself, but Nick stepped forward and said, "No, let me do it." He had always liked to undress the women he slept with. He didn't know why it just turned him on.

The woman smelled like she had just showered, and he was surprised she didn't have the smell some of the other prostitutes he had been with had—a mix of cigarette smoke and the smell of the Christmas-tree air fresheners in cars. He finished taking off her shirt and the pants she was wearing. The redhead didn't have on a bra, only some small black panties. Her breasts were ample, large B cup, Nick thought. He touched her, but even though she smelled good, he didn't want to kiss her or any part of her body. He never had with any of the prostitutes.

She leaned forward, knowing from his hesitation to touch her

55

what he wanted. The towel around Nick's waist slipped to the ground, and she moved closer, opening her mouth and taking in his erect penis. He stood as she knelt on the bed. Her shyness had subsided, and, by the way she was performing, Nick knew this woman was not a virgin, at least not her mouth. It had been too long for him, and it didn't take long for him to come. She continued to suck even as his penis lost its erection, having swallowed his sperm without hesitation. Man, no other prostitute had ever done that. They all insisted on using condoms.

When she finished, she didn't say a word. Only ten minutes had passed since she had entered the room, and they still had another hour and fifty minutes. He used up the rest of the time with a massage, and they smoked a few cigarettes. Finally, when he was able to get it up again, she gave him another blowjob. It was not quite as good as the first, but better than anything he had experienced lately.

CHAPTER FIVE

Washington, D.C.

Francis got into work early the next day, driving Route 66 before the High Occupancy Vehicles, or HOVs, were in effect for the rush hour. His office was all set up, and the first thing he did was check out his new computer. It was a nice new Dell with a large flat screen, DVD, read/write CD, and zip drive. There was a training class that day, but he was pretty comfortable with computers. Booting up his machine, he came to a splash page that displayed the latest Homeland Security Advisory Level. It was yellow, or "Significant Risk of Terrorist Attack." After talking with his father the night before, he began to think more about mending his relationship with his brother. They were best of friends until about the age of thirteen, and after that, it was never the same.

His clearance allowed him access to many private databases that contained personal information about just about everyone in the United States. He could find information about credit ratings, track license plate numbers, fingerprints, and even access the criminal DNA databases maintained by many states and the FBI's National DNA Database. Since his co-worker Jim was more experienced with government databases, he thought about giving him a call eventually.

Francis had a meeting at ten, a conference call with some other government agencies he was working with coordinating the bio-terrorism counter-measures. He had about two hours until then. He thought for a first cut he would simply do a Google search. He typed in "Atlas Genetics" and got only five hits, none of which had anything to do with animal breeding. Next he checked the Standard and Poor's Index database of company names. He opened their website and did a search for "Atlas Genetics," again nothing. He figured searching on EDGAR would be of no use then, since it was probably a privately held company. Ok, he thought, they must have a SIC code for this type of business. He searched www.siccode.com. Nothing again. What a way to do business he thought. How do people find these guys? I guess by word of mouth. He laughed, wondering if there was a matchmaker website for breeding large animals, something akin to Match.com. Maybe, AnimalMatch.com. Frustrated he typed that in and found that it was registered, but only displayed "Coming Soon."

He had been searching for about half an hour and finally thought it was time to give Jim a call; he had worked at the USDA and maybe he knew some people or some other databases he could search. One more Google search, he thought. Typing in "animal semen" he received about nine hundred hits, including one that mentioned APHIS, Jim's old group. Francis also knew he could check the IRS, but didn't have access to their databases yet. He called Jim, but there was no answer.

Taking a break, he checked his e-mail and saw a message from his father, which he opened. His father again expressed his concern for Nick and his happiness that Marina had called. At the bottom of the message was his brother's e-mail address. He clicked on it and added it to his address book. As he was starting to write a message to his brother, Jim walked in with his omnipresent cup of coffee. "I saw you tried to call me. Had your number displayed on my phone. What's up?"

"Hey, I have a favor to ask you," Francis asked.

"Sure. What's it about?"

"I'm trying to find information about a company my brother is working for, but I haven't been able to get any. I need an address, phone number, or maybe an e-mail. They don't have a website, and I've searched in some business registries and came up empty."

"Sure. I have a meeting in about five minutes and then a few more after that, and then I have to go back to APHIS to finish up some things. What's the company?" Jim asked.

"It's called Atlas Genetics. They're involved in animal breeding," Francis said.

"I'll see what I can find out and get back to you tomorrow morning. If I get anything before that, I'll send you an e-mail."

"Great, see you later," Francis said. Turning back to his computer, he wondered, if I'm sending Nick an e-mail, what do I say after all this time?

He clicked the address and opened an e-mail window. He typed "Dear Nick" and then backspaced and wrote "Dear Brother." Shit, he probably wouldn't read past the "Dear" much less open the e-mail when he sees it is from me, Francis thought. Francis simply typed "Nick." The e-mail was brief, but in it he told him about his new job, and expressed their concern for him. He went on and told him about Marina and that she had gone back to Turkey. He didn't tell him he would be going to visit her, but he did mention where she was working. Finally, he said he was worried too and wanted to hear from him. Francis didn't have trouble expressing his feelings to his father or to Marina, but, with Nick, it was hard; there were too many bad feelings. He ended the message with "Take care, your twin, Francis." Before sending, he marked the message to receive a read receipt and clicked send.

Washington, D.C., Homeland Security Building

James Reynolds never particularly cared for public speaking assignments, but knew it was all part of the job. While not the most dynamic speaker, he was renowned for his attention to detail and his ability to respond to the toughest of questions without getting flustered. As part of his work investigating the activities of white supremacists, Reynolds often gave briefings to other agencies, especially lately in the newfound spirit of cooperation and sharing of information. Reynolds, unlike many of his cohorts at the FBI, was not reluctant to share data, thinking it could only help in the long run. The glory and recognition of catching the bad guys were secondary to actually catching them, at least in his opinion.

Today was the first in a series of joint sessions with new personnel at the Department of Homeland Security. Next to the new Electronic Command Center was a small auditorium that seated about fifty people. In attendance today were people representing the old customs agency, the Secret Service, airport security, and the bio-terror detection group represented by Francis D'Abruzzo.

Reynolds introduced himself and began with a brief history of the white supremacists' movement in the United States. Many of the people in attendance knew very little about the movement, Francis included. Francis was intrigued as Reynolds continued with a description of some of the known groups, including Olsen's and others. As Reynolds displayed tables of data, Francis was appalled at the numbers of people involved and the fact that many of the groups were not isolated to the mountainous states, as he had thought. There were groups in almost every state in the Union including his native Virginia. Reynolds continued describing how the groups funded themselves and described other criminal activities outside of their litany of hate crimes. Finally, Reynolds spoke of some disturbing developments.

"First of all, we've seen an increase in the number of more highly educated and wealthy people who are either directly involved or are providing material support for these groups. As stated earlier, originally many of the groups were mostly composed of what we would think of as blue collar, lower intelligence individuals. These newer associates cover a broad range of ethnic groups within the white population, and are not solely represented by what would normally be thought of as persons of Northern European descent. We have even seen some people of Mediterranean descent, mainly Italians.

Finally, and we can touch on this at some other sessions, I recently read a news feed from the Wiesenthal Institute that made mention of some contacts between these organizations and al Qaeda. I have included a summary of the report in the handout I gave to you and have provided a link to the complete report."

Francis, like many of the others present in the room, were struck by this last sentence. It seemed like such an unlikely pairing to Francis, and he could see that others in the room were trying to fathom this possibility as well. Reynolds opened the floor for questions and, not surprisingly, most regarded this last bit of information he had given to them. All Reynolds said was, for now, it was only a suspected link, based mainly on one confirmed meeting in Cyprus. He again directed them to the report, and, pulling out his copy, said, "All we have to work with right now is a description of the man that was suspected of being an American, and I don't want to get into too much detail. Actually, we don't have much; he is a man in his early- to mid-thirties with short dark hair and blue eyes. At this point, they are not sure he is an American. As we get further information on this, we will undoubtedly release to you all that we obtain. In the meantime, we are going to increase our surveillance efforts and covert operations to infiltrate these groups."

Mersin, Turkey

Nick had slept pretty well and woke around 7:30. He showered and ate some of the food he had taken from the cruise ship. The room still smelled like the Ukrainian prostitute's perfume and Nick took a deep breath, taking in the pleasant smell. He expected the ambient odors where he would be traveling in the near future would get progressively worse, so he should appreciate what he had now. Since he was anxious to get going, Nick decided to leave for the train station a little after eight. The weather was colder than the night before, and it was drizzling. He walked quickly to the station, avoiding the drug alley again.

The first thing he did was check to make sure his train was on schedule. It was. After verifying the train's itinerary, Nick fought his way through the crowded station to a newsstand to buy a copy of *International Herald Tribune*. There was a bench off to the side of the newsstand and Nick walked over, unfolding the paper at the same time. There were articles about the slow economy and rising unemployment. Reading further down the page, he saw an article about the new US Department of Homeland Security. The article mentioned the various agencies being merged and the expected effect on some of the employees' salaries and rankings within the structure.

Further, there were descriptions of the Homeland Security Advisory System and explanations of the different levels. A description of the Electronic Command Center told it was expected that, once up and running at full capacity, it was going to make it extremely difficult for terrorists to operate within the United States. Nick laughed; he thought the new office was a waste of time and that the government was fooling itself. There was just no way they could account for everyone and everything. There was just too much bureaucracy.

What made them think any of these groups would start working together? They never had in the past. Olsen had told him this was probably the best time to act since so much change was going on within the government, and Nick agreed. There were bound to be lapses in security, as one agency was transformed into another. Besides, Nick was well aware of the inept and lazy government types. He had seen plenty of them in his old neighborhood growing up and was sure the modern equivalent was no different, probably even worse since they let in all the fucking niggers, spics, and Jews to replace the whites.

Nick went back over to the stand, bought some bottled water and gum and headed over to the platform to board his train. The train was old with hard green seats and didn't look particularly safe. Thankfully, it seemed that not too many people were boarding. Nick found his seat, tossed his bag into the metal luggage rack and sat down next to the window. It would take about ten hours, and he had to change once in Narli.

Right before the train was about to leave, a family of four boarded the train—husband, wife, and two children (a girl and a boy). Nick really didn't care much for children and hoped they would not make too much noise, screaming or crying and babbling away incessantly in Turkish, which sounded really odd to him. The train left, about ten minutes behind schedule, and headed east toward the Turkish border with Iraq. He had called the telegraph office the night before and confirmed that his contact had received the message. Nick looked out the window, away from the family. It was raining harder now.

CHAPTER SIX

Olsen Compound, Outside Bozeman, Montana

Unexpected problems had occurred with the satellite uplink Olsen's technicians had established with the Internet provider. With Olsen standing over them, fuming and ranting, the techs kept trying to reestablish the link. "You fucking little pricks, I need to have twenty-four hour access to this," Olsen shouted, his face beet red and veins protruding from his neck. "You assured me this would not happen again. Motherfucker! Why haven't you got it up?"

The two techs had been working for nearly three hours, checking everything from the satellite dish outside, to all the cabling, power supplies, and routers; they even pulled apart one of the gateways and checked the motherboard. It really didn't help that Olsen followed them everywhere, ranting, pushing, and asking technical questions he really knew nothing about. They knew that part of the problem was that he was a cheap bastard, despite his enormous wealth, buying a lot of old crap they had to jury-rig. At least that's what they thought. Olsen knew secondhand stuff was harder to trace than brand new equipment.

"I need this up and running within ten minutes," Olsen screamed, gripping the Colt 45 he always had holstered to his right hip. The techs saw this, but continued working, thinking he would be hard pressed to find other equally skilled white supremacists. Not like he could advertise. "Wanted, White Supremacist Computer Nerd needed for interesting, challenging assignment in creating networks that will assist in taking down the federal government. Must be self-starter."

Finally, the problem was found and well within the ten-minute limit. It turned out to be a problem with the software they had created to access the network; it wasn't a hardware problem after all. A parameter that helped to continually modulate the IP address of the gateway was not correct. They had just installed a new version of the software and the parameters value had been changed, but they had neglected to update it. Feeling stupid, they told Olsen about the problem and that it had been resolved, promising not to make such a glaring mistake again. Olsen didn't respond, and, still fuming, he went to his command chair and called up the portal. Opening his access program, he saw a new message from Nick. His rage deepened as he read the message. "Ran into some heat in Athens, was able to elude, still on schedule to make it to the gate."

Who the fuck would know he was in Athens, and why would they try to kill him? Olsen wondered. At first he thought it was his new partners in terrorism, but he couldn't see why they would want to stop them. The way the bastards tried to kill him didn't fit either Mossad's or the CIA's modus operandi, but he wouldn't put it past the Jew bastards. Who could it be, and how much did they know?

John Whitaker, his second-in-command, entered the room and was bringing some papers over to Olsen. Olsen, with his hand on his chin, was thinking, trying to divine who could know of Nick's whereabouts. Olsen turned to face Whitaker. "We have a problem. Someone tried to kill Nick in Athens. He escaped and is still on track to get to the Gate, but I want to know who and why. It could severely compromise our mission. The way I see it, there are many possibilities. One, maybe someone has accessed our portal. Get the nerds to create some kind of snooping program to see if anyone who is not supposed to be accessing it is. Next, maybe we have a mole. We might need to make an example of the next person who shows any doubts or disloyalty. Thirdly, that Slavic bastard who told us about the bug, Andrei, maybe he sold us out."

Whitaker was writing notes and replied, "I'll put the nerds to work. I believe they already have some pirated software that they can use. As for the mole, I'll get a security detachment working on that. One more thing, I know a few skinheads in Spain. Maybe they can check out Andrei for us. They work cheap."

"Ok, but hold off on Spain for the time being. I'll let Nick know of our suspicions before he gets there. We may still need the doctor's help, at least for the time being."

"Yes, sir."

Habur Gate, Turkey

Nick had managed to sleep during much of the trip from Mersin and had also spent some time going over maps and some Arabic and Turkish. He had been studying vocabulary and sentences for awhile and had become fairly proficient, at least in Arabic. When he changed trains in Narli, few of the locals there spoke English. One local spoke French, thinking Nick was French perhaps, and tried to converse with Nick in that language, but Nick hadn't spoken French since high school and was never very good at it anyway. The guy was just looking for a handout anyway, and Nick, surprising himself, gave him some lira.

Eventually, he was able to get the information he needed for the transfer from one of the conductors, and was able to make his connection. The first conductor he spoke to wasn't very helpful and instead asked him why he was going to Habur and seemed to be implying he was going to buy drugs.

Habur, at a much higher altitude than Mersin, was chilly, and the cold greeted Nick as he disembarked from the train. The station was alive with activity, full of locals, and, more notably, police and the military. Nick looked very much like many of the locals. About forty minutes before the train was set to arrive in Habur, Nick had changed to another coach on the train and found the bathroom. Like most of the trains he had traveled in, it was nasty and cramped, barely big enough for him to stand in. The mirror, a piece of metal instead of glass, was dull and graffiti scrawled. He hooked his bag on the hook on the door and took out some clothes. "Goodbye, Sean Fallon. Hello, Ada Toprak," he said to himself. He looked in his bag and pulled out a Turkish passport. Nick glanced down at the hole in the floor that passed for a toilet and watched as the railroad ties sped by.

He took a leak and then disrobed, tossing his shirt and pants into the hole as he took them off. He turned and looked at the wound on his right shoulder. It had started to heal pretty well, and the scab was flaking off. He picked at it and drew some blood. "Damn," he said, looking for something to daub the wound with, only finding some half-used towels from someone else's bathroom trip. Can't use that, he thought, and looking into his bag, found some dirty socks, and applied one of them to the bleeding. Once it had started to coagulate, he withdrew a dark brown pair of woolen slacks, a white heavy cotton shirt and a brown tunic from the bag. He also took out a cap and some brown leather boots.

Inside his bag was another bag, a duffle bag of sorts, and a small leather briefcase. He put the briefcase inside the duffle, along with what remained of his clothes and food, and shoved the other bag into the toilet hole. It got stuck and Nick had to put a small portion of his arm in the hole to force the bag all the way through. This almost made him gag; there were some dried bits of feces stuck to the side of the toilet hole. He managed not to touch the sides, but he still made sure to wash his arm with as much soap as he could. He looked into the dull mirror and saw the five days' growth of beard. While patchy in parts, it had come in quite heavily in others. Nick figured he had to look as ratty as possible.

The woolen pants actually felt pretty good as he walked away from the train station. They were a bit too big, but, compared to the tight black jeans he had been wearing, they were quite liberating. Nick had memorized the town layout while on the train and walked determinedly toward the post office. He tried to look down and not make eye contact with any of the local police. The streets were full of vendors and merchants of all kinds, including vegetable and meat sellers, clothing and electronics dealers, and stalls with almost every brand of American cigarettes. There was even a stand where a guy was selling guns, pistols, revolvers, automatic handguns, and machine guns. Nick wished he had a gun, considering the people he was about to meet. The post office, a small square building made of brown stone, had a line leading out of the building's front door.

On the corner, a slight man, wearing sunglasses and sandals, was sitting on the ground with a blanket full of vials of essential oils, jars of honey, and tea laid out in front of him. As Nick approached, there were two women haggling with the man over a jar of honey. They went back and forth for a few minutes until the women finally paid, walking off with two jars. Nick, speaking a phrase of Arabic he had memorized said, "A man at the station told me that you have almond flower honey."

The man on the ground did not look up. "No, but I know where you can get some." The man motioned to two other men who were sitting at a café across the street drinking coffee. Both were carrying sidearms. They stood and walked over toward the merchant, who was still sitting on the ground. The merchant stood and said in English, "You must come with me. The salesperson I told you about is very close."

One of the men from the café gathered the merchandise, rolling it up in the blanket. The other stood behind Nick as he and the merchant walked away from the post office toward a side street. Nick said nothing; the man said nothing. The man walking behind Nick was breathing heavily and would periodically greet people coming in the other direction. Turning left down the second street to the right, the grade started to go slightly downhill. Halfway down the street, on the left-hand side, a black gate was loosely clinging to its mud-brick wall supports.

The man walking in the rear passed Nick and the merchant and unlocked the large black metal lock that held the gate doors together. The doors swung outward, and the escort waited as Nick and the merchant entered. The escort did not enter, and instead, closed the doors behind them. Nick did not hear him lock the gate, but heard his breathing and knew he was still waiting outside. Five other men were milling about the area inside the gate, and all turned with emotionless glares to Nick. Finally the merchant broke the silence and said in perfect English, "So, Ada... I guess that's what you'll be going by. I really don't care what your real name is. Do you speak any more Arabic; besides the one sentence you spoke to me earlier? How about Kurdish?"

Nick hesitated for a moment, and, almost feeling some shame, or maybe it was concern, said, "I memorized about fifty phrases. I can speak some French, Spanish, and English, of course."

"Well, Spanish will really help you in Iraq," the merchant laughed.

Nick was not amused and was angry. He didn't need some sand nigger making fun of him. He then confidently said, "You're the one we paid to do all the talking. I'm here to make sure you get the job done, understood?"

The merchant laughed again. "Ok, cowboy. Don't worry about that. We may have to improve your disguise though. I could tell you were an American from one hundred meters away."

Nick looked at his clothes and thought: The only thing I need to do is rub some goat shit on myself and then I'll look just fine. He smiled and the merchant returned a quizzical glance.

"You can call me Hassad, but I advise that you not talk much during the trip. There are men here that told me they wanted to slit your throat, but, lucky for you, I talked them out of it."

Nick replied, "I imagine the other seven million that my boss promised you may have something to do with that as well."

Hassad didn't respond to Nick's remark, simply instructing him to put his bag into the truck. The truck was a small oil tanker with the words "Turkish Petroleum" written on the side in Turkish and English. Hassad entered on the driver's side, and Nick got into the passenger's side. He was about to close the door when the man who had escorted them from the post office stopped him short and motioned him to move to the middle. Nick found himself sandwiched between the smallish Hassad and the much larger escort.

Hassad started the truck, and, as he put it into gear, his right hand brushed against Nick's left knee. Nick instinctively pulled back, as he would, had any man touched him. Hassad, laughing, said, "Don't worry, cowboy. We kill all the fags over here; you have nothing to worry about." They exited the compound as one of the other men inside opened the gate.

Washington, D.C.

The meeting had ended and most of the other people had left the room. James Reynolds was packing up his laptop and putting leftover handouts into his briefcase. "Mr. Reynolds?" Francis said, as he approached the FBI agent.

"Yes?" Reynolds replied.

"I wanted to introduce myself. My name is Francis D'Abruzzo. I'm heading up the Biohazard Defense Analysis branch. I thought your talk was interesting. Disturbing, but interesting," Francis said.

"Thank you. It's a crazy world we live in. Ten years ago, I never would have considered any of the possibilities that I talked about today." Reynolds paused. "The work you do must be fascinating."

"Yes, I imagine it will be once we get started. There are

many challenges ahead, but I'm confident that we can find some good solutions. Any of the people you talked about today have any bio-terror capabilities?"

"There's always that chance, but we have no specific evidence to indicate that they've tried anything to date. Maybe you could suggest a means for tracking this activity?" Reynolds asked.

"Well, my area of expertise is in the development of detection systems for actual releases, but there are things that would be required, and I imagine you guys are already looking into the purchases of lab equipment, reagents, etc." Francis said.

"Yes, yes, of course," Reynolds replied.

"You said you don't have much to go on concerning the American that met with al Qaeda in Cyprus. Have they created a composite?"

"We have some footage from a video surveillance system, but it's pretty hazy. Sound like someone you know?" Reynolds asked, noticing Francis had similar features, black hair and blue eyes.

"It sounds like a lot of guys. Who did you get the tape from?"

"The Cypriot National Police handed it over. It was from a resort bar where some of the people ate. The resort submitted it after seeing the report in the paper. We confirmed three of the guys as al Qaeda. With the American, as I said, it's hard to say," Reynolds said.

"Listen, can I get your e-mail address? I want to keep in touch, and maybe I can help out if you start seeing any bio-terror activity with the white supremacists' groups."

"Sure, but I think, at this point, it's unlikely. I think those boys enjoy a more hands-on approach. You know, drive-by shootings, bombings; it makes them feel like men, I suppose," Reynolds said as he handed Francis his business card.

"Men? Far from it. Again, I really enjoyed the talk. I'll be in touch if I hear anything," Francis said as he turned and left Reynolds to his packing.

As he left the auditorium, he thought it was odd when Reynolds had said, "Someone you know?" He had been thinking about Nick again, and when Reynolds gave the description of the American, he turned and looked at his reflection in the glass panel of the doors. Short dark hair and blue eyes, just like Nick and I, Francis thought. Hell, there are probably millions of guys with those characteristics. Again, he thought of what Reynolds had said—early- to mid-thirties. It couldn't be Nick, he wouldn't get messed up with people like that, Francis thought.

Francis went back to his office and called up the link to the report that Reynolds had given him. The report had been updated to include still frames from the surveillance video from the resort. He looked at the frames and at the police photos of the people they had already identified. The stills of the American were fuzzy as Reynolds had said, but Francis could make out his build and gauged his height relative to one of the men who had been identified. He looked about six feet tall. He couldn't make out any distinguishing marks. Nick had a keloid scar under his left ear that he had gotten when Francis had pushed him into a pool when they were kids. Francis didn't mean to hurt him, but Nick twisted as he tried to keep from going in, and, when he fell, he caught the side of his head against the rim of the pool.

Francis remembered the guilt he felt after his father came running over, first to attend to Nick, and then to whack Francis in the head. Nick hadn't been hurt really badly, just a cut, but enough for eight stitches. For a week, his father didn't stop talking about how he could have killed him or damaged his hearing. Nick basked in the attention. Francis could still see Nick's face as he rode in the front seat on the way home from the pool with their father laying into Francis.

He checked his e-mail and saw a message from Marina, one

of those electronic cards. As yet, there was still no read receipt from Nick. There was also a message from Jim, and Francis hoped he had found something. Anxiously, he opened the e-mail, but, unfortunately, all it said was that he hadn't had a chance to check up on Atlas, but would do so as soon as possible.

Francis opened the card from Marina. It wasn't his birthday, and he wondered why she had sent it. It turned out it was the anniversary of the day they had met at Johns Hopkins. It always amazed him the things women remembered. He clicked on the reply button and began to write her an e-mail, thinking back to the time they had spent together in Baltimore.

Habur Gate, Turkey

The line of oil tankers all looked pretty much the same. Nick and the two al Qaeda had been waiting for about twenty minutes at the border crossing. In his mind, Nick was going over some of the phrases he had remembered. "My name is Ada, I am from Narli," he said in Turkish. Nick glanced over at Hassad; he looked nervous. Jesus, these guys were willing to die for their cause; he wasn't expecting to see this side of Hassad. The other guy was asleep against the passenger-side door. Nick double-checked his papers and had them ready for when the Iraqi border guards asked for them. Hassad and his men had been making runs into Iraq for the past four months, buying diesel fuel, and illegally taking it back to Turkey in defiance of the United Nations' sanctions. They did this partially for the funds that it provided their cause and partially to evaluate the possibility of moving freely across the border with Iraq. They were not alone in the illegal fuel trade; hundreds of trucks crossed back and forth across the border every day. Hassad's superiors had recommended to Olsen that this was the best way into Iraq, blending in with all the other known and welcome traffickers in the illegal oil trade. Olsen had thought it would have been better to come

73

through Syria, or even Jordan, but he reluctantly deferred to al Qaeda. Some of Olsen's men didn't want to send anyone into Iraq, but Olsen insisted he needed one of his own men to guarantee the exchange was made.

The truck approached the border gate. The border guard, standing on the step of the truck, looked in. Hassad nodded hello and handed the man his papers. The guard glanced at the papers, and looked over at Nick and the sleeping escort. "Why are there three of you?" he asked.

Hassad was ready for this question. "One of our other trucks has broken down. These two guys are coming with me to fix it. We need to get it back as soon as possible." This was a lie, of course, but the guard nodded, looked at Nick again and asked him his name. Nick replied in Arabic and Hassad did as well, showing his obvious nervousness. The guard looked at both of them and returned the papers, as Hassad gave him some dollars. The guard pocketed the money and stepped off to the ground. Hassad exhaled and put the truck into gear, jolting the escort from his sleep. They crossed the border and were now heading south through Kurdish Iraq, following the long line of trucks in front of them.

"I guess I surprised you back there. You didn't expect me to know what he was saying." Nick laughed. Hassad didn't reply and glared at Nick. Nick spoke again, "I guess you thought a cowboy like me would blow it, thought all I knew how to speak was cowboy, eh?"

"Ok, how about I let you out here. I'll stop the truck; see how far you get, eh, cowboy? You think you will make it back to Turkey, back to the United States? You would be dead in a day," Hassad said.

Nick knew he was right and reluctantly acknowledged in his mind that he needed these people. The escort reached into a bag at his feet, pulled out some bread, and motioned to Nick to take some. Nick looked over. The man's hands were filthy; he refused, despite the gnawing hunger pains in his stomach. The escort began to eat noisily with his mouth open and his lips smacking together. Nick closed his eyes and tried to get some sleep, but he couldn't and began daydreaming about all the places he had been in the last couple of months and where he would be going in the near future.

He imagined the look on his father's face, the big CIA agent, if he knew he was in Iraq. Shit, I'd love to see that, he thought. I guess that would really make him proud.

The road led deeper into Iraq, as it followed the path of the Tigris River. All that could be heard was the deep moan of the diesel engine as the three partners in terror sat in silence.

CHAPTER SEVEN

Ash Sharqat, Iraq

Al-Jaffar was sitting in the room with three armed men. When they told him to come, he had thought they would be leaving Iraq soon after. He hadn't expected to wait for so long, in a small cramped house; he was not even allowed to go outside. Al-Jaffar had told them repeatedly that his boss would be looking for him, and, since he hadn't left Iraq yet, he was sure they would find him. The Republican Guard would learn where he was for sure. At times, Al-Jaffar thought maybe he had been sold out; maybe they weren't going to take him to Turkey as promised, but, if that were the case, they would have surely killed him by now and taken the canister. He still had the canister and was not dead, so he imagined they would fulfill their promise. The men rarely spoke and only talked to Al-Jaffar when it was time to pray. All they did was sit and wait and listen to his complaints.

"At least let me go into the courtyard behind the house. I need to feel the sun's rays and breathe some fresh air," he would ask, but they would just motion for him to remain seated or to lie on one of the two beds set up in the room. He had to sleep in the same bed as one of the al Qaeda men. When he first arrived, one of the men had taken his car and driven it to another part of the city. They had given him their reasons for not letting him go outside the very first day he arrived, saying they didn't want to risk the possibility of encountering police, Kurdish militias, or even elite Iraqi military units, including the Republican Guard. Besides, there were rumors that US Special Forces and possibly Israeli Special Ops were in the area. At the time, Al-Jaffar had agreed to be sequestered, but thought they would be leaving the next day for Turkey.

Needless to say he was restless. He lay down on the bed,

took out the book about Provence and began leafing through the pages. With the money he was going to get, he could live quite comfortably. Al-Jaffar had such great plans for his retirement in France. He could take cooking lessons and maybe even teach at a university. He could finally regain the respect he used to have before the problems in Iraq. I could have a garden, with figs and cherries and grapes. I could raise animals, he thought. One of the men that were guarding him came in the door and motioned for him to get up, even grabbing him by the arm. In the process, Al-Jaffar dropped the book on the bed. He was told to get his bag, with the canister, and follow them. Finally, he thought, we're leaving; we're going to Turkey. The man said, "Be silent and come along." As the two of them left the room via a side door, two Republican Guardsmen entered via the front.

Al-Jaffar said to the man, "I have left my book. My book, I want to get it, please." Angrily, the man grabbed his arm harder, and again said, "Silence," but in a more subdued and quiet manner. They had not gone very far, merely the short distance across a back alleyway to the courtyard of an adjoining house.

Crouching behind a wall, the man again said, "Be silent. There are two Republican Guardsmen that followed me into the house. I don't suspect that they are looking for you, but we couldn't risk them talking to you." Back in the house, a Republican Guard was speaking to the remaining three al Qaeda men. "There was another man, the one that we followed here. Where is he?"

"No, there are only three of us that live here. There is no other man," said the lead al Qaeda, noting that while the man's Arabic was good, it seemed rather odd.

"He was shorter than any of you and was wearing a white tunic," the Republican Guardsman said.

"I believe that you are mistaken," the lead al Qaeda man replied.

As the one Republican Guardsman continued to ask questions, the other man was looking around the room, picking up items and then throwing them to the ground, or pocketing anything he thought might be of value.

"I am not mistaken," the Republican Guardsman shouted back, drawing his pistol from its holster. "Tell me where the other man is. He is a suspect, and we need to talk to him. If you are protecting him, we will arrest you as well. Tell me where he is!" he shouted.

By this time, the other Republican Guardsman had seen the book on the bed and picked it up. He started flipping through the pages, turned to the three al Qaeda, and, with a quizzical look, held the book out to show the men and asked, "Planning a vacation somewhere?"

The lead al Qaeda, thinking quickly, said, "My girlfriend, she studied in France. It is hers from when she was there. I guess she left it here." The Republican Guardsman looked at the book again and slid it into his back pocket.

The other Republican Guardsman, still seething, stepped closer to the al Qaeda he was addressing his questions to, grabbing the man by his clothes on his right shoulder, his gun pointing at the man's temple. "You have one final chance to tell me," the Republican Guardsman said.

Calmly, the man answered. "Please, I must insist that you are mistaken and he—" The lead Republican Guardsman pulled the trigger and shot him in the head. The al Qaeda fell to the floor and blood spurted from the bullet hole. One of the others attempted to flee out the same door Al-Jaffar had used only minutes before and was immediately shot in the back by the other Republican Guardsman.

The remaining al Qaeda stared back and forth at his comrades lying on the floor with ever expanding pools of blood forming around their lifeless bodies. He raised his arms above his head and began to talk.

Outside, Al-Jaffar and the al Qaeda had heard the gunshots.

Al-Jaffar fell down closer to the ground and clutched the bag with the canister, feeling its hard metal form. The al Qaeda looked as if he wanted to run to the aid of his comrades, but held back as his face contorted in anger. "There were only two shots, so they're still talking to the other man. We have not seen him exit from the building. Get up. We must leave here now, while they are still talking," he said. Al-Jaffar was crippled with fear, and the al Qaeda looked at him again and said, "If you want to make it to your precious France, then get up!" Al-Jaffar rose and followed the man as he went through the house of the yard in which they had been waiting and out the front door, purposefully checking for any other Republican Guardsmen that might be in the area.

They went a few doors down, and, on the other side of the street, entered another house. This, like the other one they had been in, appeared to be empty. Exiting the back door, they crossed one more street and entered a small market, a butcher shop. The store was empty except for the proprietor and a small girl. The proprietor was sitting in a chair in front of the display case against the back wall of the shop. He didn't look surprised as the al Qaeda entered the store, pulling Al-Jaffar by his shoulder, who, in turn, clutched the bag in his arms against his chest. The man rose to his feet and said, "What is it?"

The al Qaeda said, "I will explain in the truck." The man turned to the little girl and told her to go home. He led Al-Jaffar and the al Qaeda out the back and to a small, refrigerated truck. Opening the back doors, he helped the al Qaeda push Al-Jaffar into the back. They slammed the doors and locked Al-Jaffar inside the dark space. The freezer smelled like spoiled meat and, fortunately for Al-Jaffar, the refrigeration unit was not working. Al-Jaffar, still clutching the bag, heard the engine start and was thrown to the back of the refrigerator as they sped off.

Iraq, on the road from Habur Gate

Nick was awakened by a beeping noise and looked to see Hassad fumbling around for his cell phone that had slid across the dashboard of the truck to the passenger side. Nick, not wanting to become a statistic in an Iraqi traffic accident, reached over, grabbed it, and handed the phone to Hassad. What followed was rapid, frantic Arabic with Hassad finally motioning for Nick to wake the escort. Nick nudged the man, and he slowly woke, stretching his arms and yawning. Hassad, not looking at the road, turned to the other man and spoke to him in Arabic. The man was awake now. Nick was feeling out of the loop and said in Arabic, "What's the problem?"

Without hesitation, Hassad started explaining to him in Arabic and gesticulating with his right hand. He said one or two sentences before realizing his mistake and then spoke, in a somewhat calmer tone, in English. "There was an incident. We need to change where we are meeting the others."

"Incident?" Nick questioned.

"Yes, yes. Not a problem. The man you want to see is ok; he was not harmed. There were some others, but it's not your concern," Hassad said.

"Well, I'd say it is my concern if there is someone that may know we're coming here," Nick said.

"I don't think that is the case. I am positive that no one knows of your presence here," Hassad replied.

"So what happened?"

"Three of our men who were with the doctor were killed by Republican Guardsmen. The fourth was able to get away because he saw that they were following him. It was strange, however, they—" Hassad said.

"Strange? Why would it be strange to see the Republican Guard?" Nick asked.

"We have dealt with them before, and they have never given us problems. It is not uncommon for them to kill people, but there was no reason. The Republican Guard doesn't know of our identity, and, if they did, they would not care if we were here, as long as they get their cut," Hassad said. "The man that escaped with the doctor, he has his suspicions. He thinks that they may have been just posing as Republican Guardsmen... quite possibly Mossad."

"Mossad, the Israelis, fuck! Do they know what's going on?" Nick asked.

"The fool didn't realize this until after he had left the building. He called someone he knows that has connections to the Republican Guard, and they didn't know of anyone fitting the description of the two men that entered the house. He said had he known he would have surely killed them in the street where he first saw them," Hassad said.

"I'm glad he's got the doctor, but can anyone tell me if they know about me or about the doctor?" Nick asked.

"I suspect that they don't. Why kill the men at the house? If they knew about you, they would surely wait and not have entered when they did. They were there for one thing—to kill the men in the house, including the one that escaped. They must not have known about the doctor," Hassad said.

Nick knew he was right. Why kill everyone if they knew? Feeling relieved, but still anxious, thinking there were people looking for the bunch that was helping him. For the first time since the cab ride in Athens, he was concerned. "What now?" Nick asked.

"There is another place. It is outside the city. They have taken the doctor there. The only problem is it's not near any industrial area, and the sight of this truck may draw some attention, but we have to risk it," Hassad said. "We are going to wait till it is darker." He pulled the truck off into a rest area. "They will call when the doctor is secure. Once we get there, we will have to turn around immediately and head to Turkey."

"Are you certain that whomever it was that killed your friends don't know about the other place?" Nick asked.

"Yes, don't worry. I am certain," Hassad said.

Ash Sharqat, Iraq

The two Republican Guardsmen left the house and the three dead men, but not before tearing through every drawer, cabinet, and mattress in the place. They found nothing. Nothing until they opened up a can of kerosene and found a hidden compartment in the bottom. There were maps, some fake passports for Syria and Turkey, and about three thousand American dollars. As they left the building, a small child in the doorway of a house two doors down looked over. The head Republican Guardsman looked his way, and the boy went back into the house. Yitzhak knew this sort of terrorizing was not uncommon in Iraq, and the neighbors would stay in their homes so as not to invoke the wrath of the Republican Guard. He also knew they would have to move fast; the man who had gotten away may have alerted his cohorts.

"Yitzhak, why the hell did you shoot the man? We needed to get all of them," his partner asked.

"He wasn't telling me the truth, besides, I think he knew. Knew I wasn't Iraqi. He was listening to my Arabic, and his eyes told me he knew. Better to kill him now so that he wouldn't tell everyone," Yitzhak said.

"Ok, I suppose, but you—" He stopped short. By now they were at their vehicle and had boarded. Aviv, his partner, pulling the travel book from his back pocket, turned to Yitzhak and said, "Why do you think they have a book about France?"

"Not sure, we'll have to go through it thoroughly. Maybe they used it for coded messages," Yitzhak said.

Confidently, Yitzhak drove the vehicle, an Iraqi military car, past some Republican Guard, giving a mocking salute as he recognized a high-ranking member. The officer returned the salute without a second thought. "We need to change vehicles. Look for a suitable car. We will ditch this one and confiscate someone else's. We are Republican Guard after all. We can do that sort of thing," Yitzhak laughed. They drove off toward the eastern part of town, away from the Guard barracks, in search of a car.

"There, ok, we will circle back, leave this car, and disable it. That pickup truck over there is perfect," Yitzhak said as he directed his partner's attention to a white pickup that was in a dirt parking lot next to an appliance store. They circled back and got out of the car. Yitzhak's partner, Aviv, opened the hood, removed the distributor cap, and threw it into a rock-strewn field. The plastic cap cracked and split as it hit the ground. They removed two large duffels from the car trunk and headed back toward the truck. As they approached the vehicle, which was not new, but in good condition, the owner was walking over to the driver's side.

Yitzhak spoke, making sure his accent was better this time. "Are you the owner of this truck?"

"Yes, yes, I am going home now. Have I done something wrong?" the owner said.

"No, of course not, but we need it. Our car has broken down, and we need to get someplace in a hurry," Yitzhak said.

"I can drive you there if you like," the man said.

"That will not be necessary. Give me the keys. You will get the truck back tomorrow morning."

"Please sir, I can drive you. It is no problem," the man insisted. He had reached into his pocket and withdrawn the keys. The man was holding them in his right hand, his elbow bent at an angle, pointing upward. Yitzhak looked around, and, before the man could react, he had his wrist in a lock, pinning the man's arm and elbow against his lower right arm. The man winced in pain and dropped the keys to the ground.

Yitzhak's partner bent down to pick them up. "Thank you. You will get the car back tomorrow morning. We will have someone bring it here." The man lowered his eyes and nodded. Yitzhak's partner tossed him the keys, and they got into the truck. The two drove to an isolated area outside of town, a small dried riverbed. Yitzhak drove the truck across an old rusted steel bridge. Once across, he pulled off the road to the right and slowly guided the truck into the riverbed until he had pulled it into the shade of the bridge. He turned off the engine and reached behind him into his bag, withdrawing a tunic and pants, typical of the Kurdish people of Northern Iraq.

"Let's look at the maps now," he said, reaching over and taking them from his partner. There were five maps, two of the city itself, one of Iraq, one of Turkey, and one of only Northern Iraq. There were no marks on the city maps. Yitzhak checked them for the location of the house they had just come from, and it was not marked. As he closed the map of the Kurdish regions, he noticed what looked like an impression from writing. It wasn't English or Arabic—that much he knew.

"Give me the vial," he said to Aviv. From the kit he withdrew a vial containing some carbon powder. Yitzhak folded the map so it formed a ten-inch square with the writing impression facing toward him. Applying the carbon, he could see the words appear. "It's in Turkish, I think," he said.

His partner withdrew a laptop from his bag and booted it up. "Ok, I've logged in. Read to me what you have," his partner said.

Yitzhak read the letters "m e z b a h a" as his partner typed them into the on-line dictionary. "Slaughterhouse."

"Ok, slaughterhouse. While we're still on-line, check for

information about butchers, abattoirs, and commercial slaughterhouses," Yitzhak said.

Accessing a GIS system, he located eight locations, six butcher shops, and two slaughterhouses. "You think that this may be one of their safe houses?" Aviv asked.

"Could be, or maybe they just had a cookout one night and needed a good butcher. Since it's in Turkish, it may even be a location in Turkey somewhere. I think it will be worth checking it out," Yitzhak said.

"Yitzhak, one of the butchers is in the same neighborhood we were in today."

"I doubt they are that close. Where are the slaughterhouses?" Yitzhak asked.

"There is one by the Central Market, and the other is on this side of town, a few miles out," his partner said.

"Good, I think the first area is too busy. Let's check the second location when it gets dark," Yitzhak said.

Aviv turned off the computer, and they both got out of the truck, changed into the Kurdish clothing and loaded the munitions they had hidden under the bridge into the pickup's bed.

CHAPTER EIGHT

Olsen Ranch, Montana

Not a day passed when Olsen didn't train himself and his men with armaments. Today was no exception. Over the last ten years, he had stockpiled bullets and other small arms, many having been bought from military quartermasters looking to make a quick buck. Olsen, an excellent shot, was using an old military Colt 45. He loved the feel of the steel in his hands, the recoil, and the smell of the ignited powder. Boom! He fired off a round at one of the three painted cardboard figures he had set up in front of him. The range was rather sophisticated and included devices that would not only raise and drop the figures, but moved them to any of fifteen different positions at varying distances. Boom! He released another round and watched as it pierced the cardboard figure of an African-American male, raising a small submachine gun. Boom! Another round hit the mid-section of a soldier clad in camouflage wearing a beret with the distinctive blue Israeli Star of David. A figure rose almost directly in front of him, and he hesitated at first, but then Boom! He released a round hitting the figure in the middle of the forehead.

He nodded to his associate who was operating the system and holstered his piece. He laughed because he had hesitated before firing at the last target. He looked again at the face staring back at him. "Sorry to have to kill you, my friend, Mr. Osama bin Laden, but I'm sure you knew that we would face each other one day," Olsen laughed. He looked again and spat on the cardboard figure.

Olsen listened to the muffled sound, the *phumph* mortars made when they were fired. Twenty of his men were in the adjoining range practicing with some of the thirty mortars he had acquired. Their target was an old car at the far end of the field. Olsen raised the binoculars he was wearing around his neck to observe the practice, and noticed that some of the men were not that accurate, that maybe they should be trained in other weapons' systems. They were also working with some low-tech homemade mortars, and it was possible they were the ones that were not as accurate. They were made from parts easily obtained from any Home Depot. Targeting them was a problem, and they relied more on experience to get it right. When the time comes, they will be ready, he thought.

Olsen's second-in-command approached him from behind. He cleared his throat, and Olsen turned to face him. "Any more information about Athens?" Olsen said.

"Not yet, sir. The nerds have been trying to tap into Interpol's database, but have not been successful. Nothing on the newswire. It's being treated there as an isolated incident among local crime syndicates," Whitaker replied.

"What about our friend in Spain, Andrei?"

"I contacted the skinhead group in Malaga, Spain. I didn't tell him specifically about the doctor, but he did tell me that they've had some run-ins with the Russian mob in Malaga, but he didn't mention any old, Russian doctors," Whitaker replied.

"I expect to hear from Nick in a few days. I will tell him to proceed with the plan, but he'll have to be cautious when he goes to see the doctor, obviously. We may have to send someone over to help him out, give him some cover when he pays the bastard," Olsen said.

"Yes, sir. May I suggest we call the skinheads instead?"

"Sure, contact your friend again, and see if his group wants to have another run-in with the Russians. I'm sure they'd like to kick some ass."

"Yes, sir, I will check, and, if they decline, I'm more than willing to make the trip if need be. I speak Spanish, and I was there when I was in the military. I know my way around," Whitaker said.

"Yes, I think it may be better to send you. I don't want to get too many others involved at this point. You have a passport?" Olsen asked.

"I have a genuine one from the US, and I have fakes from Ireland and Australia," Whitaker said.

"Good, when we give Nick the heads up, I'll let him know that you're coming. Can your friends hook you up with some firepower?"

"Undoubtedly, sir. They smuggled in a ton of surplus British and Dutch weaponry. They're pretty well stocked," Whitaker said.

"Check with them, tell them you're there to assassinate some Jew bastard businessman. Say nothing more about the Russians. See if the nerds can get you a ticket. Use the credit card from the import company. Travel with the Australian passport. Nick should be in Spain in two weeks. I want you to be in Denver in one week and be ready to leave," Olsen said.

"Yes, sir."

Washington, D.C.

Francis had finally gained access to the IRS records and was able to find that Atlas Genetics, while not making much money, had indeed been filing taxes on a regular basis. They were a Corporation registered in Delaware. The only address he could find was a P.O. box in Wilmington. The phone number, also out of Delaware, simply had a voice mailbox, and, every time he called, it picked up. He was not able to get hold of a real live person. The tax records listed the CEO's name, Dr. Pablo Zapiola. The name sounded familiar to Francis, but he couldn't place it. He was not able to find a phone number for Dr. Zapiola. He called Jim.

"Francis, what's up?"

"Anything more about Atlas Genetics?"

"Yeah, I did find that last year, there were two occasions where a representative of Atlas brought back samples, semen samples that is, once from Brazil and once from Argentina. The phone number listed on the permit is in Delaware. I didn't call it though," Jim said.

"Yeah, I have that number. I called it twice; it's just an answering machine. I haven't left a message, don't think I will."

"Oh, yeah, the CEO is a Dr. Zapiola. I've actually met him before at a conference, a USDA conference in Texas. He's Argentine, I think. About sixty-five, grey hair, distinguished looking. He told me he was a medical doctor, but had been working in agricultural biotech for about five years," Jim said.

"I saw the name on the tax records; it sounded familiar. Argentina, huh?"

"Yeah, Argentina. Beef cattle is big business down there. I'm not surprised," Jim replied. "Francis, you still there?"

"Yes," Francis said.

"Hey, I have to go, but I'll let you know if I find anything else. By the way, I heard you're taking some time off."

"Yes, did I tell you that?"

"No, I think I heard it from our boss. Not sure." Jim said.

"Yes, I'm going to Turkey. I'm visiting my... an old friend. I had the vacation planned long before coming here," Francis said.

"When do you leave?"

"End of this week. I'll be gone for two weeks, but you have my cell phone number, right? If you hear anything more, give me a call," Francis said.

"I have your work cell. You have a personal one?" Jim replied.

"Yes, I'll send you an e-mail with all my contact information, including my personal e-mail."

"You think your brother is up to no good? From what I can tell, it looks like a legitimate operation, no history of anything strange or unusual."

Francis didn't want to delve into family secrets or reveal anymore than he had to about his father's concern for his twin, so he replied, "I just haven't seen my brother for awhile. I need to talk to him, you know, family stuff."

"Sure, no problem. Hey, you want to get a beer after work?" asked Jim.

"Yeah, sure. There are some good places up on Capitol Hill; give me a call later."

CHAPTER NINE

Ash Sharqat, Iraq

Dusk was falling as the oil tanker with Nick and Hassad pulled up next to what looked like an abandoned building. The sky was clear, and the wind was still. Nick noticed the small refrigerator truck parked off to the left side of the building. The building itself was set up against a small ridge and at the end of a long, worn, pitted gravel road. There were no other buildings in sight, and the only other structure was a small carport-like structure that had another vehicle parked underneath. There were no lights on in the building, but Nick could make out the main doorway. He smelled smoke, the smoke of a wood fire and the odor of cooking meat.

"This is it. Looks secure," Hassad said. Hassad got out of the driver's door, and Nick and the escort exited the passenger's door. Nick's legs had stiffened up from the ride, and he felt his left calf tighten somewhat. Slowed by this, he fell behind Hassad and the other al Qaeda. The three approached the door, and Hassad called out in Arabic. The door opened to reveal a small room lit by a kerosene lamp. The al Qaeda who had rescued Al-Jaffar from the other house was standing in the doorway, and the man from the butcher shop was seated to his left. Hassad said, "My brother, you look tired. Please tell me of the events of the day."

Hassad and Al-Jaffar's rescuer embraced, hugging and kissing each other alternately on the cheeks. Hassad entered, as did the escort, followed shortly by Nick. Nick didn't hesitate; he had become impatient with the seemingly slow manner in which these people operated. Nick didn't greet the man in the building, nor extend a hand, but he asked, "The doctor? Where is he, and does he still have the canister?"

Al-Jaffar entered from a door to Nick's right, looking tired and scared. "So you're the American? The one to whom I am to give this?" He held out the silver canister containing the samples from his laboratory.

Nick nodded and said yes.

Hassad said, "Cowboy, there will be time for that later. You must be hungry. Please, let's wash up and eat. We will leave tomorrow morning early."

Nick, not wanting to spend another day in Iraq, wanted to take the canister and leave right then and there, but knew he would have to wait until the next morning. "I'm not hungry. Is there a bathroom I could use?"

Al-Jaffar's companion pointed to his left.

Since Nick had entered the room, the man who greeted Hassad had said nothing to him; he simply stared. His gaze followed Nick as he made his way to the bathroom. He looked back at Hassad. Hassad asked, "The Republican Guard? What did they look like? Can you recall? Did they look Iraqi?"

"Yes, they did. I had no reason to suspect that they weren't," the other al Qaeda replied.

"Had you seen them before?" Hassad asked.

"Before that day? No, I had not, but I had been stopped by other Republican Guard in the past."

"Your friend with connections to the Republican Guard, is he sure they were not who they said they were?" Hassad asked.

"Yes, he is positive. I am confident they have no idea where we are. Tell me, brother; this American, how could you travel with him? Did you not want to slit his throat?" the al Qaeda asked.

"Believe me, in any other circumstance, I would not have hesitated to do so, but he's just a pawn in a greater plan. Killing him would do no good," Hassad said.

Al-Jaffar, listening to the conversation, said, "You can't kill him, no—"

Hassad turned to him and told him to shut up. "Let's eat. Smells like you have some mutton cooking?"

Nick had finished in the bathroom and was four feet from entering the room where the other men were. Hassad had entered another room that was being used as a kitchen. Nick looked up as he was adjusting the belt on his pants. As he did so, he was thrown to the floor, his back against the wall behind him. He heard the explosion and saw the flash at the same time. Still conscious, he looked up through the settling dust. Al-Jaffar's rescuer and the butcher were both lying on the floor near the back of the room. The butcher's head was missing. The other lay bleeding from a wound to his chest. The escort he had ridden with from Turkey lay dead near the front door, the frame of which was still standing next to the gaping hole that had been the front wall.

Al-Jaffar, wounded but alive, lay five feet away from Nick, the silver canister still in his grasp. Nick looked across the room and could see the prone figure of Hassad holding an AK-47. He saw Nick and said, "Is there a weapon near you? There were some leaning against the wall in that hallway."

Nick replied, "No," and reached over and dragged Al-Jaffar into the same hallway as he.

A second explosion, and Nick was splattered with the flesh and blood of one of the al Qaeda. Hassad ran across the room, tucked into a roll, and landed right next to Nick and Al-Jaffar. Nick pried the canister out of Al-Jaffar's bloody hands and shoved it into his shirt. Hassad started to move into an adjoining room as Nick looked back at Al-Jaffar reaching up with his right hand as he lay dying. Grabbing Nick's shoulder and pulling him close, he said in English, "I was wrong; you must destroy Anzu. Destroy it, please for Allah's sake, I beg you."

Al-Jaffar's eyes glazed over, and he fell back onto the floor and began to say a prayer, the prayer he had learned as a child. Nick looked at his chest. He had a gaping hole under his right collarbone. Al-Jaffar's pants were also soaked with blood. Nick looked at him, and, as he chanted the prayer, bubbles of blood formed on his lips. Al-Jaffar's breathing was heavy and deliberate, and he shouted between prayers in Arabic, "I have released Anzu into the world. Anzu the destroyer is awakened."

Hassad was behind Nick, and he shouted, "We have to move now, leave him. You have what you came for."

Nick wasn't hanging around for Al-Jaffar's sake. He couldn't care less. He was waiting for the expected assault by whomever it was that was attacking them. He certainly didn't want to run out into the dark blindly. Nick turned and crawled along the floor with Hassad. Another explosion rocked the room they had just left, followed shortly after by small arms' fire. Hassad was knocked to the ground and lost hold of his gun. Nick fell back against the wall and was hit hard by some adobe brick that had been shattered by the explosion, slamming into his right side. He felt a sharp pain, and his right arm went numb. The dust hadn't yet settled, but Nick could make out two forms, wearing clothes typical of the Kurdish region, entering through the hole that used to be the front of the building. Hassad looked like he was knocked out, and, for all Nick knew, he was faking it; he didn't have any obvious wounds.

The wall to the hallway Nick had entered had fallen in front of him and it provided good cover. Nick picked up Hassad's gun with his left hand and supported it against a wooden beam lying about two and one half feet in front of him. Hassad had already engaged the action, and the gun was ready to fire. Nick fired a quick burst at the lead figure, and the man dropped to the floor. Nick swung the gun to his left and fired another quick burst, hitting the second man in his right leg, but he did not drop and tucked and rolled behind a pile of rubble.

The first man was either dead or dying; Nick heard no sounds from him. He did hear Hassad moan and try to lift himself, then he dropped back to the floor. Nick knew he had to move since he expected that the second man had grenades. Turning to Hassad, he saw his eyes were open, and he was taking deep breaths. He needed him for the trip back and said, "Hassad, move it! We have to get out of here!"

Hassad lifted himself onto his hands and knees, looking drunk. He surprised Nick by how fast he was able to crawl into the next room and toward a doorway that led to the carport. At that point he stood and leaned against the doorframe, breathing heavily. Nick, holding the gun in his left hand, tried to help move Hassad out of the doorway, wrapping his arms around his body and cupping his hand underneath Hassad's right shoulder.

There were no more sounds coming from the building, no gunfire or grenade explosions. Nick moved behind the vehicle in the carport as Hassad held himself up against it by holding the handles to the back doors of the truck.

"They must have someone with night vision waiting to pick us off, Hassad," Nick said.

"Yes. I feel like I have to vomit," Hassad replied.

"I want you to wait here, I need to check out front for anymore of these guys," Nick said. He slowly walked around the left side of the truck, and, crouching behind the side mirror, scanned the area in front of the building, but it was too dark, and he couldn't see anyone. He listened, but there was no sound, only the burning sound of what used to be their tanker truck. He walked back behind the vehicle and saw Hassad had recovered for the most part, but had a long stream of drool hanging out of his mouth to which he was oblivious. "Hassad, take the gun. I want you to get in the passenger's side. We need to leave now."

Hassad took the gun and walked around to the other side. Nick entered the driver's side and looked around for the keys. He first looked under the sun visor but finally found them in the ashtray. He sighed and started the truck, half expecting a rocket or rocket-propelled grenade to come through the windshield, but there was nothing. He pulled out and headed back down the dirt road that led to the building, having to drive off the road to avoid the burning truck. When he had gotten to the main road, he noticed the canister had become cold. He turned on the lights inside the truck, withdrew the silver canister from the inside of his shirt, and saw there was a small patch of ice forming around about one centimeter of the area where the lid was screwed on.

"Damn it! It was damaged by one of the explosions," Nick said.

"Hassad, look around in the truck. I need some material or cardboard." Hassad rummaged around on the floor in front and behind the seats, but found nothing.

"Ok, tear out some of the padding from the seat," Nick said. Hassad pulled a large knife from a sheath on his belt and cut the seat between them. He pulled out a piece about two-feet square. Nick handed him the canister and said, "Wrap that around this and tie it off with something and try not to knock off the ice that has formed. That's probably blocking the leak." Hassad took the canister and did as Nick said. By now they were a good five miles north of the compound and heading back along the Tigris to the Habur Gate.

Habur, Turkey

The ride back through Iraq had been rough. Nick never thought he would be glad to see the al Qaeda compound in Habur again, but he was. On the way, they had seen Kurdish militia, but they weren't stopped until the border. Nick had tucked his fake Turkish and Irish passports into his clothing before they had reached the slaughterhouse, which was fortunate, because everything else he had, including his American passport, had burned along with the truck. It was probably better, he thought, not to have an American passport at this point. Hassad, unlike Nick, did not have any passports, and Nick thought he should cross back into Turkey by himself through the Habur Gate. Hassad would just have to find another way over the border if he wanted. Fuck him, Nick thought. He almost got me killed. Obviously, someone knew about the slaughterhouse. They should have made plans to go someplace else. He was a jackass.

Against his wishes, Hassad insisted they would cross the border together. They had even stopped along the side of the road and fought over this issue for about an hour, attracting the attention of some Kurdish shepherds. Nick, finally, reluctantly agreed, and he slid over to the passenger's side as Hassad took over the driving.

"How the hell are you going to get across the border without a passport, and with so many Kurdish troops in the area?" Nick had asked him.

"Cowboy, things are different in this part of the world. Talk to the right person, and you can get anything you want," Hassad replied. Thinking back, the little hairy shit had been right. All he had to do was pay one of the Turkish border guards. He held out Nick's passport and enclosed about 400 dollars inside. Hassad smiled and said, "I hope to have a good trip to Turkey." The guard pocketed the money, handed back the passport, and waved them on through.

There were fewer men in the al Qaeda compound in Habur now, only one young man and an old man, quite possibly an assistant and not an actual al Qaeda member. Nick didn't really care one way or the other. Almost everything had been cleared out. Nick gathered they must have heard about what had happened in Iraq and figured they should move. One thing that was left was an old Pentium laptop.

"Hassad," Nick said. Hassad was sleeping in a chair and leaning back against the wall with his mouth open and his head dropped to his chest.

"Hassad!"

"What do you want, cowboy?" Hassad said.

"Do you still have an Internet connection here? I need to contact my people."

"You saw the dish on top of the building when we arrived this morning, didn't you?" Hassad replied.

"No, I didn't," Nick said.

"Yes, we still have a connection. Please give my regards to your boss."

"Do I need a password?" Nick asked angrily.

"Yes, yes, you do. It is Twin Towers." Hassad laughed.

Nick knew the things he and Olsen and the others had planned were equally or even more devastating then the attack on September 11th, but somehow hearing that Middle Eastern bastard say those words made him angry. Before he booted up the computer, he asked Hassad, "Did you check on securing some more liquid nitrogen and a new canister?"

Hassad shrugged and walked away, saying, "As you command, cowboy."

Nick logged onto the Internet and went to the portal site. There was a new image, which meant there was a new message from Olsen. "Received your message about the cab ride. We are looking into it. At this point, continue as planned. Will inform as to the nature of some additional help we will be sending you."

Nick typed a reply. He had to tell Olsen about the problems in Iraq although Hassad had told him they were only after his men, there was no way they could know about Nick. He might be right, but since he fucked up in bringing him to the slaughterhouse, Nick couldn't really be sure if he knew what he was talking about or not. First the good news, then the bad news: "I have the item in hand, ready to move on to the next phase. Have moved back over the border. Saw more heat in Iraq, serious heat. The doctor was killed. May have been CIA or Mossad after our contacts. They assure me that they can't possibly know about my presence or what I was doing here." Nick hoped Hassad was right.

He sent the message and was about to close down the computer, but he stopped and went to check his e-mail instead. There were two more messages from his father and an e-mail from his brother. "What the hell does he want?" Nick muttered. He clicked on the message and was prompted for a return receipt and clicked no. He didn't expect to be nervous, but he was. He read on. Homeland Security? I guess now that they have wonder boy, they'll save the world for sure. He read past the part about their concern about where he was and then saw the last part of the message about Marina and her new job. Istanbul?, he thought. That was where he was originally supposed to take Al-Jaffar and then take a flight to Africa. He was thinking when he felt Hassad standing behind him, trying to read his e-mail.

"Is that how you contact your boss, with e-mail? How fucking stupid," Hassad said.

It was the first time he had heard Hassad curse and thought it was funny. "No, it's my regular e-mail. So what's going on with the liquid nitrogen?"

"Can't get any here, but I did find another insulated canister. It's bigger; you can slip the one you have into it. There are a few labs in Ankara. We can give you the addresses, but you're on your own from here. If you want to try, break into one. That is up to you. Their supplier is in Istanbul. We have that address, too, but I think you need a permit to buy it. It's not like a gasoline station," Hassad said.

The hole in the seal was small, but big enough that Nick thought it might not last until he got to Africa. "I know where I can get some," he said to Hassad, "but I have to leave tonight. I want the truck."

Hassad said, "Take it, please. I don't need it. I'm leaving

here as soon as you're finished with that computer."

Nick shut down the computer and got the bag Hassad had given him. He went into the courtyard, and the old man gave him the newer bigger canister. Nick took the bundle of seat insulation that contained the canister. He ripped off the binding that Hassad had tied on it, opened the bigger canister and slipped the smaller one inside. He turned and Hassad tossed him the keys to the truck. Nick caught them, and, before he could say anything, Hassad said, "So, put that shit to good use and good luck."

The last part caught him off guard, but Nick replied, "Thanks for your help. Good luck to you, too." He got into the driver's side of the truck, and put the bag down gently onto the floor of the passenger side, started the truck, and headed off toward Istanbul.

Ash Sharqat, Iraq

When Yitzhak awoke, it was early morning, the sun not having risen very far above the horizon. He could smell burning gasoline and coagulated blood. He had been in battle many times before, but he had only sustained minor wounds. He looked down at his leg and saw a large red spot on the cotton clothing he was wearing. Since he was still conscious, he knew that even though he had lost some blood, the wound wasn't very bad. The shot hadn't hit an artery, or he would have been dead by now. He propped himself up onto some of the fallen building and looked around. He saw the head of one of the dead al Qaeda. He looked over and saw the body of a man lying on his back with his hand extending upward. He wasn't dressed like the others and had street clothes on. He couldn't remember seeing the man before. He looked to his left and saw the body of his partner lying face down, a large pool of blood surrounding him. He didn't bother calling his name, knowing he was dead.

As he reached into his pocket to get his phone, he heard

some muffled talking coming from the other side of his partner's body. With some effort, he stood and withdrew his sidearm from its holster. He walked over, hopped over, favoring the leg that was not wounded. He looked past his partner's body to one of the al Qaeda. It was the one they had followed to the other house, the one they said they were looking for when they were the Republican Guard. The man's face was covered in blood and it looked like he had suffered a wound to his eyes, or at least one eye.

Yitzhak stopped in front of him and holstered his gun. This man was no longer a threat. He again reached for his phone and pressed a code to dial the number for his commander. "Yitzhak here. We took out the rest. Aviv is dead. We need someone to come get us. I have a leg wound, so I am not sure I can drive. There is one still alive. I will interrogate him until your arrival. I sent you the coordinates last night."

He turned off the phone, put it in his pocket, and bent down to address the man on the ground. He didn't know how lucid the man was. He began speaking in Arabic. "What is your name, and how many men were in this building?" he said. The man didn't answer and was still murmuring. Yitzhak couldn't make out what he was saying. "How many men? I see three bodies including yours. How many other men were here?"

The man was not altogether. He began feeling his face for his eyes and muttered in Arabic; this time Yitzhak understood him. "My eyes are not working."

"You have wounds to your face and your eyes. Someone is on the way to look at you," Yitzhak said. This was a lie, but Yitzhak thought it might get him to speak. The man would probably be dead shortly, and they needed to try to get some information. "How many others were in the building?"

The man finally stopped groping at his face and said, "There were five altogether, including the American."

"What American?" Yitzhak replied.

The man was still in shock and said, "The American that was here to meet the doctor. Didn't you see him when he came in?"

Yitzhak began to think that maybe the man was delusional because of his injuries, but asked, "Tell me more about the American."

"He was here to help the doctor. To bring him to Habur and then France in exchange for the sickness," the al Qaeda said.

"The sickness? What do you mean sickness?"

"The doctor had made something that the American wanted to give to his people, a disease," the man said.

Yitzhak stopped and didn't ask any more questions. They had simply been sent here to wipe out the cell that was running diesel fuel between Iraq and Turkey and find some former Hamas members. There was nothing about any doctor and an American. "Who was the doctor?"

"He was Iraqi," the al Qaeda replied.

Yitzhak looked over at the body on the floor in civilian clothes, thinking that must be the doctor; he didn't look American. "Tell me about the American. What did he look like?"

"He was tall, thin, dark hair, and blue eyes," the al Qaeda said.

"Anything else? Anything else?" Yitzhak said as he poked at the man on the ground with his hand. Then he noticed the man had stopped breathing and was no longer fidgeting or trying to find his eyes. He was dead.

Yitzhak stood up and began looking around for anything that may be of use. He found nothing. He pulled the phone out of his pocket again and hit the code to call his commander.

CHAPTER TEN

Washington, D.C., FBI Building

Reynolds had just returned from another seminar, this time at CIA headquarters in Langley. He had had to return to the office. It seemed like he was working late a lot lately, and it was taking its toll. It was Tuesday night, and he normally would head to the gym after work, but he hadn't worked out for at least two months. The talk had gone pretty well at the CIA, with none of the usual inter-agency grandstanding. It was around 8 p.m., and Reynolds was searching for some papers and reports he had left on his desk. He stuffed them into his briefcase and was heading out the door when the phone rang. He was about to let his voice mail pick it up, but thinking it might be his wife, he thought it was better to answer. "Hey, honey, I'm leaving now. Is there anything you want?"

"Well, I guess I didn't tell you that I like pistachio ice cream. Do you think you could pick some up for me?" the distinctly male voice said.

Reynolds, taken aback by the comment, asked, "Who is this?"

"Sorry, Mr. Reynolds. This is Francis D'Abruzzo, from the Department of Homeland Security."

"Mr. D'Abruzzo, I thought you were my wife. I figured she would be the only one calling me this late at the office. What can I do for you?"

"I was thinking of the talk you gave the other day, and I kept thinking about the description of the American that was at the meeting in Cyprus," Francis said.

"Yes, what about him? Did you download the study?" Reynolds replied.

"Yes, yes, I did, but I wanted to see if you had any more information," Francis said.

Reynolds had just given the talk a few days ago and was somewhat annoyed Francis was calling him so soon, but thought maybe he knew something. "No, nothing further, but, again, I'll let you know. I've been pretty busy. You really seem to have a strong interest in this guy," Reynolds said.

"Well, it's sort of coincidental, but the way you described him, well, he sort of sounds like me."

"To be honest with you, I noticed that," Reynolds replied. "You have a relative that may be messed up with those people?"

"Not that I'm aware of. I only have one brother, a twin, and I haven't seen him in a year or more. He did say some things once about a woman I dated that were somewhat racist. She's Jewish, and he questioned why I would want to date a Jew bitch, but never anything beyond that," Francis said.

"Well, that doesn't make him a terrorist. It's probably just a coincidence," Reynolds said.

"Exactly. Lately, I've been trying to track him down. He's working for a company that breeds farm animals, Atlas Genetics. I haven't been able to get much more than a phone number and that had only an answering machine."

"I'm pretty busy these days, but in the spirit of the new inter-agency cooperation, I can see if I can find anything for you. We may have some databases that you haven't looked into yet," Reynolds offered.

"That would be good. I'm going out of the country for awhile, but I can give you my cell phone number, or you can just send me an e-mail."

"Ok, what is it?" Reynolds asked. Francis gave him his cell phone number, and Reynolds scribbled it onto a pad on his desk. "May I ask where you're going?"

"Sure, I'm going to Turkey. I have a friend that lives there, and I promised to visit her. Istanbul, to be exact. Have you been?" Francis asked.

"No, I've been to Greece and to Egypt, but never to Turkey. I've heard it's beautiful. My wife wants to go on a cruise there, maybe when things cool down," Reynolds replied. There was a pause on the phone as Reynolds waited for a reply from Francis. "Mr. D'Abruzzo, are you still there?"

"Yes, yes, I just thought of something else about my brother. I'm not sure why I didn't think of it before." Francis said.

"What is it?"

"I found a few books and magazines my brother was reading once. One was the magazine *Soldier of Fortune* and then he had a book, *The Turner Diaries,* and another called *Tel Aviv Stranglehold* by..." Francis hesitated.

"By Michael Olsen!" Reynolds finished his sentence.

"Yes, that was it. Have you seen it?" Francis asked. "It was pretty twisted. All about Israel's control of the United States."

"I've read it alright, and I've even met the author."

Olsen Ranch, Montana

Normally Olsen didn't display any signs of worry. Instead, he would lash out at his subordinates, and they could tell something was troubling him. Today, however, he kept re-reading the police report he had received from San Francisco. He was incredulous that one of his men had been so careless. "The fucking little prick!" he yelled, which made the nerds stop and turn to look at him. "Get back to work, you little shits! I told him to be careful; I told him not to fuck up, and what does he do?" The nerds didn't look up this time or respond to his question. "The fucking loser gets stopped for running a red light. RUNNING A FUCKING RED

105

LIGHT!" he screamed, his voice echoing through the cavernous bunker.

The nerds decided to go outside to check on the satellite dish. They had seen Olsen become very violent and strike some of his subordinates, and this being a particularly bad episode, they thought it was a wise move. Olsen saw them leaving and said, "Go ahead, you wussy little nerds; I can always find out where you are and shove my fist down your throats then!" One of the nerds broke into a run and left the cavern as quickly as possible.

What had angered him even more was that he was packing heat, two shotguns, and an H and K sub-machine gun. Word had gotten back to Olsen that the man had taken them from the safe house out in Gilroy to go into the city because he felt he needed some protection. "As if the cocksucking fags in San Francisco could take him on," Olsen said in a more mellow, though still angry, voice. His audience had left.

Olsen could only sit and ponder whether or not the police had found anything else that wasn't listed in the report. All three of the men he had sent to San Francisco were in the car. He knew they wouldn't talk, but if the police went to the house and found anything—the manila envelope he had given them or a link on their hard drives to the portal—for instance, he knew it could ruin all the plans he had been making. "RUINED by some shit who runs a red light!" he screamed once more. By this time, one of his higher-ranking members had entered the room, and the nerds had returned as well.

"We're pretty certain that the police haven't located the safe house," the man said as he cautiously approached Olsen. "As you had suggested, they set up a Web cam and motion detectors that would send a signal back to us, and we haven't received any such indications. Might I add, it was a good idea to do so? Did you want me to go sanitize the house and set up an auxiliary team in their place?"

Olsen looked over at him and said nothing. He demanded perfection and sending in an auxiliary team to him meant they had failed. "If you could, while you're out there, can you break into the jail and put a bullet in the fucker's head?" Olsen said with a twisted laugh.

"Sir, I think that it would be prudent, at a minimum, to sanitize the house. I can be out there by tomorrow morning," the man said.

"Yes, go out there. Get everything and bring it back," Olsen said as he rubbed his forehead.

Somewhat hesitantly, the man replied, "Yes, that will be no problem, but while we're talking about this, I wanted to suggest something."

Olsen stopped rubbing but kept his hands on his forehead. "Yes?" The nerds stopped what they were doing and began looking at each other with furtive glances, back and forth, and toward the door.

"Sir, I mean this with the utmost respect, but I think this incident has demonstrated something, and, believe me, I mean no disrespect, but I think..." the man said, hesitating. By this time the nerds had moved closer to the door and were fidgeting with some cabling.

"Please, feel free to speak your mind," Olsen said.

"I think that we may be stretched thin. Maybe we should pull back some of the teams and concentrate on Washington, Los Angeles, and New York," the man said. Olsen sat up in his chair and did not reply, waiting for more from his subordinate. "I also think that we can accomplish our objective with the stocks of anthrax that we have on hand, especially since Nick seems to be attracting attention overseas. Maybe we should bring him back home and forget about the virus, at least for the time being," the man said. By this time, one of the nerds, the one who had run from the room before, had left and the other remained, and transfixed on the events of the room. Olsen stood and sighed. He didn't yell, he didn't rant, but he did have a look on his face that was unlike anything the tech had seen before. His jaw was clenched, his eyes were big, and his face twice as red as he had ever seen.

"Sir, as much as anyone else I want to accomplish our goals, but I—" The man fell forward and slumped to the ground, blood spurting from his neck; Olsen's second-in-command had come up from behind and slit his throat.

"We will have no more of your treasonous talk here," Whitaker said as he looked over at Olsen who had already withdrawn his Colt 45 from its holster. The remaining nerd stared in stunned silence, even though he had seen this countless times before. He watched, as the man, whose throat had been slit, lay on the floor, gurgling, gasping for air, and clutching at his throat. He made a vain attempt to grab his sidearm, but Olsen had moved forward and stepped on his hand, holding it in place on the floor.

The man looked up at Olsen once, slumped to the floor, and was still. Olsen turned to the nerd and said, "Get someone in here to clean this shit up." He went over to Whitaker and slapped him on the shoulder with a closed fist, not exchanging any words.

Road to Istanbul

Nick had been driving for more than twelve hours. The truck didn't run very well, and he had to stop and add oil at one point. He followed the road along the Syrian border until he came to the town of Tarsus, near Mersin. There he turned northwest and took the road to the next biggest town, Konya. He hadn't eaten since the afternoon before, and his stomach was growling and aching. Since he needed to buy gas, he decided to stop and look for some food that he might want to eat. He turned off the highway and headed into town and found a gas station. The owner could tell he wasn't Turkish and tried to rip him off, but Nick was beginning to feel surprisingly comfortable dealing with all these foreigners and was able to catch the scam.

Parking the truck off to the side of the gas station, he walked across the street to a small grocery store. Nick looked around for about five minutes and finally found some decent-looking bread and some sucuk, Turkish sausage. As he was paying for the food, he saw the proprietor was also selling disposable cell phones. He asked the merchant whether it was good only in Turkey. "No sir, it will work in almost all of Europe," the man replied.

"Ok, I'll take one," Nick replied.

He tossed the food onto the passenger seat and headed back out to the highway. The weather had gotten worse, with rain and wind, which made driving difficult because only one of the wiper blades on the truck worked well. The good blade was, fortunately, on the driver's side. Nick ate as he drove and began making better time as the weather began to clear. All the drivers on the road were driving fast, including Nick, but he made sure to drive more carefully when he spotted police cars or military vehicles. He was driving without his license, which had burned in the truck with most of his other possessions.

By late afternoon, he had finally made it to the city of Izmit and had to stop once more to get gas. Close to Istanbul, the town was much more cosmopolitan than the other towns he had stopped in since leaving Habur. As he was pumping gas, he noticed a few people were looking at him. He was filthy, and he hadn't showered in three days. He was sure he smelled, and, as he inspected his clothing, he noticed there were spots of blood from the al Qaeda members who had been slaughtered. He was so concerned about getting some more liquid nitrogen for the canister he had neglected to change out of his disguise. Nick didn't think he would be able to explain this, if anyone approached him. Fortunately nobody did, they only glared, probably thinking he was a farmer; the truck he was driving looked like a rural vehicle. Even a few policemen had passed by and simply stared at the odd-looking character. Nick wasn't normally so careless, but, considering the urgency with the canister, he had let things slip. Nick didn't want to fail Olsen, and that was his primary concern for the time being.

He definitely needed to clean up and get some new clothes. He drove further into town and found a clothing store. Hassad had given him some cash, enough for him to get to Spain, but he would have to let Olsen know he needed some more when he got there. After purchasing a pair of pants, a nice white shirt, a leather belt, a small hard-sided suitcase, a travel bag, and some loafers, he left the store and went to a small shop and bought some soap.

Nick left Izmit and continued to drive along the coast toward Istanbul. Finally, he found what he was looking for. There was a public beach with a bathhouse. Nick turned off the road and onto the beach into a gravel parking lot, at the end of which was the bathhouse. The beach was empty except for a few men fishing, but they were about one hundred meters away and didn't even turn to look as Nick parked the truck. The surf was a little rough, and the wind was blowing sand and trash around. The bathhouse didn't have a shower, but it did have a sink and Nick quickly bathed, using the pants he had been wearing as a towel. Nick looked into the mirror as he fiddled with the buttons on his shirt. His beard was almost completely grown in, not as patchy as when he had taken the train to Habur. He liked it, and thought it would help him remain anonymous. He was pretty sure the attackers in Iraq had been killed and was confident they hadn't seen him in any case. Looking at his beard again, he saw some flecks of grey near his chin and close to his sideburns. He had just turned thirty-four, and thought he was young to be going grey; his old man hadn't turned grey until his late sixties. He hadn't really lived a very stress-free existence and was not surprised to see the grey as he pulled at it with his fingers. He tossed the dirty clothing into the trash can and headed out the door.

As soon as he was out of the building, he saw there were two teenagers, one leaning against his truck, the other trying to open the passenger side door with a slim jim. Shit, I should have brought the suitcase with me, Nick thought. He covered the distance to the truck rapidly. The teenager leaning against the door jumped up, brandishing a six-inch blade. The other continued to work, and Nick heard the door latch open. As Nick moved toward the teen with the knife, the boy began waving his extended right arm out in front of himself at shoulder level. Nick goaded the boy into taking a stab at him. As he did, Nick slid to the youth's right, stepping back with the thrust. He extended his right arm under the boy's. As the teen pulled back to make another thrust, Nick crossed his left arm over the boy's forearm and grabbed his wrist.

Nick pulled his right arm over, back toward himself, and applied pressure with his left forearm. As he secured the lock, he extended downwards, drawing the teen's face toward his rising knee. Nick's knee met the boy's chin, and Nick heard the boy's bottom teeth slam against his upper teeth as his knee made contact. The boy fell to the ground and did not move or make any attempt to get up; he was out cold.

This all happened in a few seconds, and, as it was progressing, the other youth had opened the door and grabbed the suitcase with the canister. As he turned to pull it out of the truck, Nick had already disposed of his friend. He had not yet turned around completely, and, as he tried to, he felt a horrendous pain as Nick drove the heel of his right foot into the side of his right leg. He screamed in pain and tried to reach into his pocket for a knife, but felt the palm of Nick's hand slam into his chin. Like his friend, he dropped to the ground, but his head caught the door hard on the way down. Nick, breathing heavy, looked down and saw blood coming from the teen's nose. Nick pushed him away from the door and looked over toward the fishermen. It didn't look like they had noticed or heard the boy's yelling, but Nick knew he had to get out of there fast. Fortunately, the wind had picked up and that was probably why the men hadn't noticed.

As he drove away, leaving one dead teen and another knocked cold, he felt no guilt; he actually felt charged up. Nick had never killed anyone before, not without a gun at least, and now that he had, it didn't make any difference to him. He saw there was a small amount of blood on his right knee, and, grabbing a paper bag he gotten when he had stopped to buy some food, he tore off a small bit and used it to blot the blood and clean his pants.

Habur Gate, Turkey

Hassad and the remaining al Qaeda had moved from the house where they had taken Nick to a larger house in a more affluent area right off the Central Market. Since it was near the market, it was always bustling and crowded. These neighborhoods made it difficult for US intelligence or the Israelis to track them, since they were not able to use infrared technology, and it was easy for someone familiar with the streets and alleyways to blend into the crowd if spotted. Hassad had decided, along with the others, that they needed to lay low for awhile. They had made quite a lot of money in the last three years in the illegal oil business and could now live quite comfortably.

The day after Nick had left with the truck, Hassad had disassembled the satellite dish and destroyed the laptop. In about a month, he would head back to Pakistan. Some of his men had even talked about possibly lending assistance to the Palestinian cause. The recent run-in with Mossad had enraged them. Hassad had no interest in fighting the Israelis himself, preferring operations like the one he had just completed. It's not that he shied away from combat, quite the contrary. He had even fought for awhile against the Northern Alliance in Afghanistan with the Taliban, long before the American troops had arrived.

He felt himself to be quite a skilled soldier, despite his smallish size, but he also felt he was highly intelligent and could serve the jihad against the United States and the Israelis better by using his brain. He had devised the fuel-smuggling program and had been the one who arranged for the sale of the virus to Olsen. Both operations had added greatly to the wealth of his commanders, and he was confident he would soon be rewarded for his efforts, despite the plan's violent end at the hands of Mossad. They were close to ending the fuel smuggling anyway; competition was increasing and tensions in Northern Iraq made it difficult to move about at times. Besides, the money they had gotten from Olsen was almost double what they had made from the fuel operation.

Thinking back, Hassad was happy he had studied for a brief time in the former Soviet Union; despite the fact, his time there was one of the most miserable periods in his life. If he hadn't, he never would have met Dr. Statnekov. He never really cared for the doctor, but the information Andrei had given him made his life a lot better.

It was almost noon. Hassad, thinking he deserved some rest after the problems at the slaughterhouse, had slept in. He went to the nearby market area and began walking slowly from stall to stall, picking up the fresh fruit being sold, drawing it to his nose and smelling it. The watermelons were especially nice, and he purchased a small one and put it into his shopping satchel. As he took in the smells and sounds of the market, he soon began to forget the events of the last few days. Yes, he thought, life will be very good soon. I'll be able to return to my family and see my wives and children.

He continued walking around the market area for about an hour and a half. By the time he was finished, it was well after 1:30 in the afternoon. The safe house was not too far away, and he left the market to return home. The house had a large living area and three bedrooms upstairs. There was also a family room and a large garden area in the back. Hassad decided to go into the garden, via the back gate, and enjoy the watermelon he had purchased. Entering the gate, he found the garden unoccupied and the house quiet. The others had all risen earlier than he, and he assumed they were still out in town, shopping or otherwise enjoying the time off.

Hassad set the bag with the melon on a table next to an outdoor grill. The night before, he and his men had grilled some meat, and the fire was still smoking. He collected a few pieces of wood from a pile. He thought a fire would be nice; it had gotten colder since he had left the market. He sat down next to the grill, took one of the smaller pieces of wood and began to poke at the still red embers in the bottom of the grill. He began blowing and poking some more, the smoke turning into small yellow flames.

He heard the back door to the house open. It was a man he had never seen before. Hassad dropped the glowing stick and began to reach under his tunic for his pistol. The man was quicker than he, and, as he stepped closer, he pinned Hassad's right hand against his left side. The next thing Hassad felt was the jolt of a taser, as the man, using his left hand, jammed the device and its prongs against Hassad's right side just under his rib cage. Hassad dropped and shook, hitting the grill, and sending a cloud of ash and sparks into the air and onto the ground. He then fell in the other direction, hitting the table, and sending the bag with the watermelon smashing against the ground next to his head. He blacked out as the man gave him another jolt as he lay on the ground. This one was under his chin. The last thing he felt before blacking out was the clenching of his jaw and the tightening of the muscles in his neck.

Hassad awoke and found himself in one of the upstairs bedrooms in the safe house. Three of the other five men who were staying there were bound and gagged, one bleeding from his nose and the other looking dazed. The man who had attacked him in the garden was alternately pacing back and forth in the room and going to the window to look out onto the street. In his hand, he had an Uzi submachine gun, and on his belt, the taser he had used to subdue Hassad and a large military knife. Looking at the knife Hassad would have preferred the man had used that on him; he could have died with honor rather than be tied up like a goat waiting to be sacrificed.

He tried to talk, but the gag in his mouth prevented that. It was also very tight and made breathing difficult. He struggled against his bindings, but was not able to affect any change to them. As he did, he slipped down from the position he had been in, leaning against the wall, and lay in a fetal position with his hands bound to his feet.

The man pacing across the room noticed the movement and came over. He spoke in Arabic, but with a slight accent Hassad immediately recognized as Israeli. "Ok, now that you are awake, I have some things I need from you before I slaughter your Arab ass!" he yelled. Hassad said nothing and simply glared up at the man. The man threatened him with the taser and still Hassad simply looked at him, not trying to speak. The man reached over and took the gag out of Hassad's mouth. He picked him up by his bindings with both hands and threw him against the wall.

Hassad was impressed with the man's strength, but only said, "There are ten men that will be coming back here soon. You think you can do that to all of them, you worthless Jew?"

Yitzhak approached him and said, "I have already killed them. They are hanging on meat hooks in the basement like the pigs they are." Hassad tried to spit on him, but his jaw was slammed shut by Yitzhak's fist. Hassad reeled back in pain and said nothing. Yitzhak said, "You were there, you were the one with the American. I know because your friend at the slaughterhouse told me before I drove my knife into his gut. Your friend was a coward and died selling out you and the others in this room."

Hassad replied, "Why would I want to hang out with an

American? I kill those Jew-loving bastards for a living."

Yitzhak walked across the room and kicked a man with a bleeding nose in the face. He came back to face Hassad again. "Tell me now what his name is, and I will spare your life. If you don't tell me, I will kill you."

Hassad smiled a toothy bloody smile. "Your friend over there already told me that he is going to Istanbul. All I want from you is a name and what it was that the Iraqi doctor gave to him," Yitzhak said.

Hassad replied, "I don't know any Americans." Yitzhak had known it would be difficult to get this man to talk. He pushed him to the ground again and pulled down his pants. He then pulled down his undergarments, and, without hesitation, took the end of an electric cord he had pulled from a lamp and applied the two live ends to Hassad's genitals. Hassad wailed and tried to kick at Yitzhak, but had no control over his limbs. Yitzhak looked directly at Hassad and applied another jolt. This time Hassad lost control of his bowels and messed the floor on which he lay. He could also smell burning flesh. He was sweating and in great pain, but he did not speak.

Yitzhak grabbed him by his head and pulled him through his own excrement. Hassad was still defiant and spat out the bits that had gotten into his mouth. He was unable to wipe away the stuff that clung to his beard. He had been through some rigorous training and had even been tortured by his superiors to prepare him for this, but they had not done anything as foul as this. Yitzhak once more held the electric wires to his genitals. This time he did not retract them and held them there for almost two full minutes. Even if Hassad had wanted to talk he was unable; he had passed out again. He came to in about twenty minutes and was not completely coherent, but could hear himself talking, slowly and deliberately. He heard himself describing Nick in great detail and that he was going to try to get some more liquid nitrogen from a woman at the Forensic Institute in Istanbul. He made no mention of Olsen, not that he knew, but he mentioned Cadiz, Spain.

As he lay still, he heard Yitzhak's voice. "I believe I said I wouldn't kill you if you gave me what I needed, and, normally, I am a man of my word, but since you people so like to be martyrs, I have changed my mind." Hassad felt the blade against his neck.

CHAPTER ELEVEN

Gilroy, California

Sitting in his rental car, Whitaker could see there was one police car sitting in front of the house where his compatriots had set up the West Coast operations. The nerds at the ranch had given the heads-up about the police; the surveillance system had picked them up. One officer had gone through some of the rooms and had picked up one of the laptops, but he had not tried to log on or use it according to the nerds. One policeman was standing on the front porch; the other must have been inside or out back. Olsen's man had been there for about an hour and did not see them leave with anything. They seemed only to be securing the house until someone else came. He could only assume they were waiting for the Feds from San Francisco to make their way down and take over the scene. He had to act fast and get in and out before the Feds arrived.

He had been paying attention to the neighborhood traffic and had seen only the occasional pedestrian walk by. The house was not on a busy street, but there were cars that came by, one every half hour or so. He had promised Olsen he would take care of sanitizing the house and wanted to be as good as his word. If the men who had been caught had let on about the house, he didn't know what else they may have revealed, but, no matter what the police already knew, if they found the laptop and broke into the programs it contained, they would know what was going on.

It was about three in the afternoon, and traffic had become less frequent on the street. Whitaker noticed the man on the front porch had been periodically checking in about every half hour. He had just checked in, and Whitaker knew it was time to make his move. He started the car and drove past the house to a curve in the road, bordered on one side by some tall trees. The next house was about a half block away, and, on its border with the house, had the same tall trees. He exited the driver's door and went around and opened the trunk, pulling out a sniper rifle. Leaving the trunk open, he knelt down behind the car near the back left taillight and sighted the officer on the front porch. From this angle, the officer's back was facing him as he leaned against the metal railing of the small porch. Whitaker didn't hesitate and quickly fired a shot. He knew it would have to be a headshot since the cop could be wearing body armor. Looking through the scope he could see the officer's head explode; the man fell forward onto the porch.

Whitaker had to act fast. The other cop had undoubtedly heard the shot and was most likely heading toward his partner.

He laid the gun in the open trunk and swiftly moved toward the house, using its side as cover. Whitaker had been there before, when they were looking for a house, and he knew the layout well. He intended to enter the house through the side door and sneak up on the remaining officer from behind. He was close enough to hear the officer yelling into his radio and made out only a few words of the frantic talking. Filled with adrenaline, he forced open the side door and entered the laundry room. He deliberately walked toward the front of the house and rounded the corner from the laundry room as it met up with the kitchen. He could hear the remaining officer and the sound he expected, the dragging of his partner's lifeless body into the foyer.

Gun drawn and extended out in front of him, Olsen's man took the left turn from the kitchen into the living area and could see, about ten feet directly in front of him, the remaining officer, a gun drawn in his right hand. With his left, he was checking for a pulse on the neck of his dead partner. Whitaker didn't say a word and let off two shots, the first catching the left side of the officer's head, the second hitting right in the middle above the cerebellum. The officer jerked around as he fell and managed to get off a few shots, but they were wild and hit the ceiling. Now that he was closer, Whitaker could see they weren't wearing body armor. He stepped closer with the gun still drawn and put two shots into the chest of the second officer and two into the back of the one he had shot earlier.

With the two policemen out of the way, he went back into the kitchen and headed to the smaller of two bedrooms on the floor. He needed two things, and, per instructions, they were always supposed to be kept together. The room had a small bed and two desks. One desk had a police scanner, and Whitaker could hear the chatter and activity that had been provoked by the killing of the first officer. Next to it, he saw what he was looking for—the laptop and its bag. He looked inside the bag and found the second item he was looking for, the manila envelope, still sealed. There was a large computer monitor in the room, but he did not see another CPU. He knew he had only a few minutes left.

He left by the same door through which he had entered, and, as he made his way to his car, which still had the trunk open, he saw a young teen on his bike looking into the trunk at the rifle. Without hesitation, he raised his gun, and, as the boy stared in terror while trying to get his bike turned around to get the hell out of there, Olsen's man put two bullets into the boy's back. "Wrong place at the wrong time, kid," he muttered as he threw the laptop and envelope into the trunk, closed it, and got into the car to leave.

Washington, D.C.

Francis was not getting any work done. The network was having trouble, and, when he was able to get onto his computer, he found he had a virus. He reluctantly admitted, at least to himself, that he had probably gotten it while surfing the Web trying to find information about Atlas Genetics. He was sitting in a chair away from his desk, reading over some technical reports about bio-terror defense research projects at the University of Massachusetts sponsored by the National Science Foundation. Routine stuff and not particularly interesting, but he had to get into the habit of keeping up-to-date with the literature. There was a technician working on his computer, trying to isolate and remove the virus. Francis couldn't help but think of the irony of having a virus on his machine and its relation to the nature of his work in protecting the US from biological attacks, including viruses.

The tech was not speaking, and Francis continued his reading, stopping only to ponder what e-mails he may have received; he was the type who constantly checked them. Maybe Jim had more information, or maybe Nick had replied. The latter was not very likely, he thought, but he found himself thinking increasingly about Nick, especially since his phone call to Reynolds. Francis looked at his watch. It was around two in the afternoon. As he went back to his reading, his office phone rang. "D'Abruzzo, Homeland Security."

"Frank, it's Marina. How are you doing?" the soft voice on the phone replied.

Lying, Francis said, "Hey, I was just thinking about you. You ready to see me?"

"Of course, I can't wait, but you sound nervous. What's wrong? Are you sure you want to come?"

Francis was not nervous, but pensive; perhaps Marina misinterpreted this for anxiety. "No, no, I'm not nervous. I just have a ton of work before I leave, and I'm preoccupied with some things. Nothing special."

"Are you sure? What is it? Or can't you tell me? Is it some work secret I can't know about?" Marina said.

Growing up, Francis had seen what the secret nature of his father's work had done to his relationship with his mother, and he started to think about that. He said, "No, nothing secret. It's not something I really want to talk about right now. Ok?"

Marina, disappointed, replied, "Ok. It's not your father, is it?"

"No, no, it's not my father. Listen, I really prefer not to talk about it right now, but we can when I get there. Really, it's not that important," Francis said, annoyed, remembering how persistent Marina could be sometimes.

"Did I tell you I'll be coming to the States for a conference the week before the 4th of July? Maybe we could spend the fourth together? The conference is in Baltimore." Marina said.

"Sure, that would be good," Francis said, even though he wasn't thinking much past the end of the month.

"Frank, can you send me your father's e-mail address? I wanted to send him a message. Maybe he could come up to see us. I'd really like to see him again."

"Sure. Hey, listen, I have to go. I have to get some work done before I get over there. I'll see you soon."

"Ok, Frank... I love you, see you soon," Marina said, hoping for a reply.

Francis hesitated, but then said, "Love you too, take care."

As he hung up the phone, he thought with everything that was going on, maybe he should cancel, but he put that thought aside and went back to reading the journals. He would go to class tonight, wanting to get in as many workouts as he could before heading over.

"Sir," the tech said, "I have the virus isolated. It should only be a few more minutes, and the hard drive will be clean and you can get back to work. Sorry it took so long. This was a particularly nasty version of a virus some hacker in Russia wrote. I haven't seen this one before. I'm surprised it made it through the firewall."

"Hey, that's my fault. I used my personal e-mail. It probably came through that. You get a lot of viruses from Russia?" Francis asked.

"Yeah, but they come from all over the place. I've had some recently from Japan, Brazil, and Argentina. I wish I could travel to all the places these viruses have been to," the young tech said.

Francis laughed. "Yes, and get there as fast, too."

The tech left the office and Francis sat down and went right to his e-mail account. He saw a message from Jim and a delivery receipt from Nick's e-mail account, but no read receipt. He opened the e-mail from Jim.

> "I found something pretty interesting about Atlas Genetics. It's not uncommon for many companies, but for such a small outfit, I don't really see the point. They have an offshore bank account in Bermuda with a large sum of money in it. More than you would expect for what appears to be, at most, a two-man operation. There has been some recent activity with money going to accounts in Spain and Switzerland. With a little more digging, we were able to find out that the accounts in Spain are for someone named Dr. Andrei Statnekov. We couldn't get anything on the Swiss accounts, but I'll let you know if I find anything else. I have your cell phone number. Does it work in Turkey? Send me the number of the person you'll be staying with. Have a good trip."

Istanbul, Turkey, Turkish Forensic Institute

Marina was busy reading journal articles about large-scale DNA fingerprinting methodologies. Like many other forensic agencies around the world, they had a backlog and needed to investigate better and faster ways to reduce that backlog. Her new job was very different from the job she had had at the NIH. The job could get very routine, simply analyzing DNA evidence from crime scenes and not designing, running, and analyzing experiments. She was, however, fascinated by the details of the crimes and was impressed with the attention to detail and care the investigators used in examining the evidence. She was brought on board to help increase the use of robotics and automation in the analysis of DNA evidence. It was for that reason she would be going back to the United States to a conference in Baltimore sponsored by the Oak Ridge National Laboratory. She continued with her reading until the phone rang. "Hello, this is Dr. Aryan."

"Dr. Aryan, this is the front desk. You have a visitor. I just wanted to let you know before we send him up," the guard at the front desk said.

Marina said, "Ok, send him up to my office. The door is open." She was expecting a new post-doctoral student, although looking at her watch she saw he was about half an hour early. Marina returned to her reading until the guard came to the door and knocked, motioning for the man he was escorting to come into the room. She set the paper down, stood, and turned saying, "You're a bit early—" She stopped short. The man standing in front of her was Francis's double; except he was a little heavier and he had a beard.

She stood with her hand extended, and the man reached out and grabbed her hand, saying, "Nick D'Abruzzo, you remember me, right? I think we met once before, but it was very brief."

"Of course, I remember you. I thought you were Frank. Oh, I just talked to him recently. What are you doing in Istanbul?" she said. "Oh, I'm sorry, please sit down."

Nick took the chair next to her desk. In his hand was a travel bag. Nick was nervous, still shaken by the murder. He wanted to get out of Turkey as soon as he could. He thought to himself again that maybe he should have tried to buy some liquid nitrogen somewhere, especially since she said she had just talked to Francis. What if he calls right now while I'm in the office, he thought. He said, "I really don't want to take up too much of your time, and I'm in kind of a hurry myself, but I ran into a problem with the work I was doing here, and, well, my brother sent me an e-mail saying that you were working here." Nick hadn't remembered how pretty she was—big dark eyes, full lips, and full lush breasts. She was also quite tall. Francis always did attract better-looking women than he did, even though the two of them looked exactly alike. He could never understand why. He looked at her name on her lab coat, Marina Aryan. The name struck Nick. Aryan? How could she have a name like that? She didn't look particularly Aryan. Marina smiled and asked, "What kind of work is it you do? Frank didn't tell me."

Nick was about to reply and caught himself looking at her breasts that were slightly exposed through the top of her lab coat. She leaned back in her chair when she noticed his eyes and crossed her arms across her chest, looking a little bit annoyed. "I work for an animal breeding company, Atlas Genetics. I was here collecting some samples, and the container I have was damaged. It has a leak, and I need some more liquid nitrogen. By the time I noticed that there was a problem, I was already well on my way here, and I couldn't get in touch with the people I had worked with in collecting the samples. So, I called here," Nick said.

Marina, still sitting back in her chair with her arms crossed, looked over at Nick and was stunned by how similarly he and Francis spoke. "I'm surprised your company didn't make arrangements for you to obtain some here in Istanbul."

"We're a pretty small company. Actually there are only five people, and I wasn't able to get in touch with them either. I don't speak Turkish, and I just thought... I can pay you for it.

That's not the issue."

Marina stood and said, "How much do you need, and do you also need a new container?" Nick pulled the weathered beat-up canister, the larger one into which he had slipped the smaller one, out of the travel bag. Marina was taken aback by the condition of the container and was going to ask him about it, but he made her uncomfortable, despite the fact he was Frank's twin, and she wanted to get him out of her office.

Nick said, "I guess the container looks odd to you. I have the good one inside of this. The other one had a leak."

"Sure," Marina said. "Follow me. I can let you have some, and you don't need to pay for it." Nick stood and followed her down the hallway to a room that contained freezers and a pipe that led to the large tank on the outside of the building used to store the liquid nitrogen. She used an insulated bucket to dispense about two liters of liquid nitrogen. As she did so, mist flowed over the sides of the bucket and danced along the floor until it evaporated. Nick had unscrewed the top of the canister and set it on the floor next to where he was standing. They stood in silence as he transferred the liquid nitrogen from the insulated bucket to the canister. Again the liquid nitrogen smoke flowed over the sides of the canister and settled to the floor surrounding their feet with fog.

Marina was standing with her arms crossed, and, as he handed her the bucket, said, "So have you talked to Frank lately?"

"No, I haven't," Nick replied curtly.

"How is your father?"

Nick abruptly said, "He's fine, fine." Wanting to change the subject, he said "Are you sure you don't need some money for this?"

"No, it's not much. By the way, Frank is coming here to

visit. I'll tell him you stopped by," Marina said.

Nick didn't say anything as she escorted him from the building, and, at the door, thanked her again. As he left the building, she watched him as he got into the vehicle he was driving. It was a small beaten-up pickup truck. Like the canister, this struck her as odd. Marina headed back to her lab and immediately picked up her phone. She needed to call Francis since something about Nick just didn't seem right, not just the canister and the truck. His clothes, while somewhat rumpled, looked brand new and were not a style she would expect to see an American wearing.

Since coming to work at the Forensic Institute, she had learned to look at and notice the smallest details in a person's appearance. She must have picked this up from the criminal investigators at the Institute; she had never paid particularly close attention to these things before. There was also his reluctance and hesitation to talk about his family; the idea seemed to make him nervous. While physically the same as Francis, socially he was so different it made her feel uncomfortable.

She dialed Francis's home phone since she figured he was probably at home and asleep. The phone rang four times, and she was about to hang up when a groggy voice answered.

"Hello?"

"Frank, I am really sorry to call and wake you, but something just happened that I have to tell you." One thing about Marina, unlike some of the other women he had dated, was that when she had to tell him something she would never hesitate to call, no matter what time it was. It was one thing that particularly bothered him. There were some nights he would awaken having dreamed she had called and then the phone would ring. He should have guessed it was her, but she hadn't done it as much since leaving.

"What happened?" he said, looking over at the clock.

"Your brother Nick was here. He stopped by to get some

127

liquid nitrogen. He said he was working for a breeding company."

Francis sat up in bed, fully awake. "Did he call? He just showed up?" Francis asked, realizing it meant he must have at least read his e-mail. How else would he know where she was?

"He didn't call me directly. He just came by. He was well dressed, but the clothes were obviously of Turkish design. He wasn't very talkative, at least about you and your father, and he's just so completely different from you. He really made me feel uncomfortable."

"I know he works for a company called Atlas Genetics, and I've actually been trying to get some information about the company so I could get in touch with him. I sent him one e-mail, to which he hasn't replied," Francis said.

"Yes, that's the name of the company he said he was with. One strange thing is he had a beaten-up container. He said the other one had a leak. The other thing was he was driving an old pickup truck, not something you would expect to see a businessman visiting Istanbul driving."

Francis didn't reply; thoughts of his conversation with Reynolds were flashing through his head. He had to find out more information about Atlas, but had hit a wall and didn't know where else to go.

"Frank?"

"Yes. Marina, did he say anything about where he was going?"

"I assumed he was going back to the United States. I should have asked," she said, sounding disappointed in herself.

"There was really no reason for you to ask such a thing," Francis reassured her.

"Are you still coming to see me?"

"Yes, yes, I'll be leaving this Saturday morning. Can you try to find out some more information about where my brother might have stayed or possibly where he may be going? Anyone you work with have good contacts within the police?" Francis asked.

"Of course. I know someone that I can call. I'll see if they have anything, maybe about the truck or about plane tickets and such," Marina said, getting a charge from her newfound role as a criminal investigator. "The guard at the front desk probably has the number that he called from. I guess you'll want that?"

"Sure, give it to me," Francis replied.

Marina put Francis on hold and called the guard to get the number. "It looks like it's a cell phone," she said as she read the number to him

"Ok. Thanks, I'll see you Sunday morning," Francis said. They said their goodbyes, and Francis got up, showered, and headed into work early.

Ataturk International Airport

Nick didn't feel good about the meeting with Francis's girlfriend. He thought he should have tried to find another source of liquid nitrogen, but the problems at the beach made it even more urgent that he get it fast and get the hell out of Turkey. The last thing he wanted was to have any encounters with the Turkish police or spend any time in a Turkish prison.

He had gotten what he needed, but at what price? Maybe she had seen the truck. He couldn't say for sure. He knew she would undoubtedly tell Francis, but what the hell could he do about it? He hadn't told her where he was going. She most likely thought he was returning to the United States. It never came up in conversation. The sooner he was out of the country the better. To cover his tracks, and since he wasn't able to get rid of the truck before meeting with Marina, he left it about five kilometers from the airport and caught a cab the rest of the way. The area where he left it was semi-industrial, and there were many similar vehicles.

For the first time, Nick actually had some apprehension about where he was going next. It was the one continent he had never been to, and he knew little about it. While he had concerns about Iraq, being with Hassad had made him feel more at ease, despite the trouble they had encountered. Maybe it was because he was traveling alone now and most things he had heard about the Sudan made him uncomfortable. Since Nick still had his Irish passport, he would once again be Sean Fallon. He laughed, thinking that everyone, except maybe the English, loved the Irish, and he felt a little less apprehensive.

Nick looked up at the monitor listing the departing flights. He still had about half an hour before his flight to Cairo and thought about sending another message to Olsen, having found an Internet terminal. The airport, however, was too busy, and the message would have to wait. Nick thought it might even have to wait until he got back to Europe, not knowing whether they even had Internet access in the Sudan. Maybe he could try in Cairo, and laughed, thinking someone might see the big Star of David on the website he would open. Wouldn't that be interesting?

Nick got up from his seat and moved closer to the gate. After everything that had happened, he was going to fly first class. Most of the other passengers waiting to board the plane seemed to be Egyptian or Turkish. There were two people, a man and a woman, who looked European, but Nick wanted to try and avoid them, so he pulled out a paper he had purchased and began reading. Originally, Nick was supposed to be traveling as a representative of Atlas Genetics, but the forged export papers he had made were destroyed in the truck fire in Iraq. He didn't have time to have any others made and had to risk transporting the canister in some luggage he had checked. He made sure he didn't have to change planes in Cairo; since he didn't want to have to go through customs there, thinking security in the Sudan would be more slack. He had to disembark from the plane in Cairo and had a two-hour wait in the terminal, but he would be taking the same plane to Khartoum. He thought Khartoum sounded miserable.

Nick heard the call for the first-class passengers to board, and, as he gathered his belongings, he saw the two Europeans moving toward the boarding gate as well. Fuck, I'll have to try to speak with a better Irish accent, he thought.

As he stood in line behind the others, he saw they had Canadian passports. The woman looked back at Nick, and he tried not to let on that he had noticed, instead fumbling with his passport and boarding pass. The plane was a Boeing 757, with the first three rows of seats for the first-class passengers. Nick followed the Canadians onto the plane and was glad to see they were two rows further back in the plane then he.

As Nick went to sit, he realized he had the cell phone he had purchased in his back pocket. He had meant to throw it away before boarding the plane, but had neglected to, since he was thinking about his impending trip to Africa. He took the phone out of his pocket and saw it was displaying a missed call. Nick checked out the number, didn't recognize it, and thought it must have been a mistake. The only time he had used the phone was to call Marina's office when he had gotten to Istanbul. He turned the phone off and put it into his carry-on bag. As the plane pulled away from the terminal, Nick noted only about half of the first-class seats were occupied. No one had sat next to him and that was fine with him.

Nick looked out the window at the tarmac. As he turned back to assume his normal position for takeoff, feet on the floor, head back, staring at the seat in front of him, he noticed the Canadians had moved up to the two empty seats across from him, undoubtedly because of the greater leg room they afforded. Nick thought he would have to feign sleep the entire way. They looked much too happy, which made him even less interested in talking to them then before. Fortunately, the flight would not take too long, and he hoped they weren't continuing on to Sudan. As they reached level flight, he heard the woman say, "Are you from the United States?" when she caught him opening his eyes.

Nick sighed, hesitated, and said to himself, Ok, Sean, time to use some of your Irish charm.

He started to speak and his voice cracked. He cleared his throat, and, in an accent that sounded, at least to him, like a mix of Jamaican and Indian, but not at all Irish replied, "No, actually I'm from Ireland." Now don't ask me any more questions, you fucking bitch, he thought with a smile.

"Oh, cool, I want to go there sometime. I've been to Scotland, but I heard Ireland is so much better," the woman replied. Nick didn't answer and hoped she would get the message. "My boyfriend and I are going to Egypt to see the pyramids."

Nick could only think: Why else does anyone go to Egypt? He nodded, not wanting to try the accent again, although she didn't seem to have noticed. Fortunately, their conversation was interrupted by the stewardess as she came by asking them what they wanted to drink. Nick ordered a whiskey and water and a beer. He had been smoking a lot since coming to Europe and craved a cigarette as well.

As soon as the stewardess had passed, the woman once again tried to engage Nick in conversation. "What are you going to Egypt for? I mean, is it for business or a vacation?"

Nick took a long slow sip of his whiskey, and, without looking at her said, "Business."

"You look sort of like a doctor. Are you a doctor?"

Nick took a sip of his beer, set it down on his tray, and turned to look at her. He found it kind of amusing that she

132

thought he looked like a doctor, considering his background. "I work for the World Health Organization. I'm going to Egypt to investigate a minor outbreak of," he paused, trying to think of an appropriate disease, finally remembering something from his parasitology class that sounded bad, "schistosomiasis."

"That sounds really serious. Is it something we should worry about?" she asked, sounding somewhat concerned.

"I'm sure you'll be alright. It's usually associated with much more rural areas," Nick said, not really knowing much about the disease, but knowing the woman knew nothing at all about it.

"Well, I think it's really wonderful that we have people like you in this world who are willing to risk their lives to help others. It must be very rewarding work," she said.

Nick mentally caught a glimpse of the blood from the kid he had killed in Turkey. "Yes, I love what I do."

The woman smiled, pulled out a book, and began reading; Nick kicked back the whiskey and took a long swig of beer.

CHAPTER TWELVE

Washington, D.C.

Francis was late getting to the airport. There had been a lot of traffic on Route 123 in Oakton, and then, when he tried to get to the toll road via Hunter Mill Road, the bridge right past the horse farm after Lawyers was closed. It had rained a lot during the day, and the rain only got worse, so he had to fight his way through the back roads of Reston behind nitwits moving in a slow methodical crawl. He was partially to blame. He had spent some more time trying to dig up anything he could find about Atlas Genetics. He didn't know why he bothered; he had exhausted almost all public records. It just really bothered him not knowing. He had tried the cell number Marina had given him, but had not gotten an answer and there was no voice mail.

As he made his way onto the Dulles access road, he got a call on his cell phone. "Mr. D'Abruzzo? This is Agent Reynolds. Are you still in the US?"

"I just turned onto the Dulles access road, and I'm heading to the airport now. What is it?"

"I have more information about the mystery man from Cyprus, and we have confirmation that he is an American. Seems he's been busy. We have confirmation that he was seen in Iraq."

Trying to talk on his cell phone, Francis moved into the left lane so he could leave the toll road and get on the access road, but the rain was heavier now, and his car was fogging up. As he moved into the left lane, the car directly in front of him pulled over without signaling. He managed to avoid hitting the car by pulling back into the lane in which he had been driving, but in the process, dropped his cell phone into the space in front of the passenger seat. The phone shut off.

"Fuck!" he yelled. He managed to get into the left lane just in time to make the exit to the access road. When he had made it over, he fumbled for his phone, finding many things except his cell. He decided to be safe. He would have to wait until he had parked his car.

After about fifteen minutes, he made it to the satellite parking area and turned on the overhead light. The cell had slipped behind the floor mat that was curling up around its edges. He called Reynolds. "Mr. Reynolds, I had a little trouble back there. Tell me what you've found."

"Sure. We have some intelligence that the Israelis were working on breaking up a fuel smuggling operation run by al Qaeda between Iraq and Turkey. We gave them the green light, apparently because there was one man they were interested in that had ties to Hamas, and it wasn't a big operation," Reynolds said.

Francis had finally caught the bus and had only about an hour to get through check-in and security. Reynolds continued. "They had eliminated a part of the group, and they attacked another stronghold that same evening. Needless to say, some people got away, including the American. Same description as the guy in Cyprus, but here's the kicker. Before the al Qaeda that disclosed all of this information kicked off, he said the American was in Iraq for a disturbing reason." The bus had made it to the terminal, and, as Francis was exiting, Reynolds finished what he was saying. "The guy said that the American was there to pick up a disease that some Iraqi doctor had created."

Francis continued walking into the terminal, stunned by Reynolds's last sentence. "What kind of disease are we talking about?"

"We have no idea. We know the Iraqis have anthrax and botulin toxin, among other things, but everything they have is readily available elsewhere in the world."

"How good is the intelligence? I mean has it been

confirmed? Maybe the al Qaeda was trying the frighten the guys that killed him?"

"We're pretty sure the source is valid. How long are you going to be out of the country? I may be needing your expertise," Reynolds said.

"Two weeks, but I can always cut it short. You have my cell, and I sent you the number of where I'll be staying," Francis said.

"Ok. Let's hope they get the guy before he gets to wherever he intends to use this stuff, whatever it is."

Francis didn't reply. He had walked to the first-class desk of the airline and showed them his Homeland Security badge. He normally didn't like flexing his muscle, but the conversation he had with Reynolds had changed his mind, and he decided to start taking advantage of the perks afforded him.

Beyoglu District, Istanbul, Turkey

The week had seemed inordinately long to Marina. She was glad the weekend had arrived and was really looking forward to seeing Francis. Her boss, suspicious that she was not happy and was thinking of returning to the United States, had loaded her with work. He constantly told her how he had gone out of his way to get her the position and felt she was ungrateful. She thought he had actually hired her because he had some interest in her and was taken by her looks.

A new case had arrived at the Institute, and it was given higher priority than the others because it involved the death of the son of a high-ranking general in the Turkish military. She promised her boss she would come in on Sunday and start the analysis, but she really needed to take a day off and get some shopping done before Francis came. He reluctantly agreed to let her take the day, knowing that, despite her seeming unhappiness, she was a much more efficient worker than some of the others.

Normally, Saturday was her day to sleep in, but she awoke early and headed out to the local market and then to a clothing store close to her Beyoglu neighborhood apartment. As she made her way to the front door of her building, she flashed a smile at the doorman, who commented she was up early. "I'm having a visitor this weekend, and I haven't had time to do any shopping this week," she replied.

"Very well," he said. "I'll see you later."

On the street were a few people enjoying the fresh early morning air, exercising, and going to local shops. Marina began walking the few blocks to the market. As she was waiting at the intersection on the next block up, a car pulled up with the engine still running. Inside a man fumbling with a map, rolled down the passenger window and asked, in heavily accented English, "Excuse me, miss, could you please help me? I am trying to find Kaba Sakal Cad that leads to the Hagia Sophia."

Marina replied, pointing, "Sure you need to go—" but was interrupted by the man as he opened the passenger door and moved into the passenger seat.

"Please, my English is poor. Could you please show me on the map." As he spoke, he sat on the seat with his feet resting on the street.

Marina could see that the passenger seat appeared to be broken, with the back resting on the rear seat of the car. Marina moved closer and positioned herself so she could get a better look at the map the man was still fumbling with. "Ok, it's really easy, but I'm in a hurry, so let me have the map," Marina replied as she moved forward to take the map with her right hand.

The man's next movement was so swift and unexpected Marina had little time to react. He stood, dropping the map to the ground, and, in an instance, had his right arm around her neck. She was about his height, but was not able to stop him

137

as he pulled her into the back seat. Marina let out a scream, but, as swiftly as he had pulled her into the car, he had shut the passenger door and driven off, without saying a word. Marina tried to remember some of the things Francis had told her to do in such a situation, but she was petrified with fear and could only stare out the window as the man drove off. Finally, he neared the Mosque of Suleiman and stopped the car. He turned around to face her, holding a gun. Marina returned the man's intense stare and said, "If it's money you want, I have 500 dollars in my purse and—"

"Don't talk," Yitzhak said, "I will do the talking. Who was the man that came to see you? I want his name, and I want to know what the two of you are up to. Tell me now, and I won't hurt you."

Marina had had many visitors that week, including a number of post-graduate students. "I'm not sure who you're talking about, and why don't you tell me who you're while you are at it?" she said, surprised by her own self-confidence.

"The American, you bitch, and stop fucking with me. Who is he? What are you doing, and where is he now?"

"Nick. His name is Nick. Nick D'Abruzzo. He needed some liquid nitrogen for the semen samples he was transporting. I have not seen him in years," she said.

"You're lying. I know what he had was not semen, and I know you are a molecular biologist. Tell me what you're doing, and you will live to see tomorrow."

"Please, you must believe me. I had no idea he was in Turkey, and he stopped by without any notice. I only helped him because—" She stopped short, not wanting to mention Francis, thinking that would only enrage him more. "What does he have?"

"Where is he now?" Yitzhak barked.

"I don't know. I assumed he was going back to the United States. I didn't ask because he made me nervous. Honestly, you could have asked me this without kidnapping me," she said as tears began to well up in her eyes.

A group of people was walking toward the car, and Yitzhak motioned with the gun and told her not to say or do anything. Reluctantly, Yitzhak began to believe she didn't know any more than she was saying. He put the gun in the holster inside his suit. "Ok, Miss Aryan, I believe you, for now, but tell me what he was wearing. Did you take him to the airport?"

"No, I walked him out of the building after he filled the canister with liquid nitrogen." She paused. "He was driving a really old beat-up pickup truck, white, missing a hub cap on the driver's side front tire." She described the details as best she could. "I didn't see the license plate, but it certainly wasn't a rental car."

"Is that all? His clothing? His hair? Did he have a beard?"

"Yes, he had a beard with some grey in it, and his suit was a Turkish design, definitely not American," she said.

"Ok, Miss Aryan, you may go, but tell no one about me, and remember, I will be keeping tabs on you," Yitzhak said, motioning that she could exit out the passenger door. Marina quickly got out and, as she was shutting the door, Yitzhak quickly drove away, his license plate obscured by the glare of the early morning sun. Marina collected herself and headed back toward the market. She still had shopping to do and was even happier she would soon be in Francis's strong loving arms.

CHAPTER THIRTEEN

Khartoum, Sudan

The wait in Cairo had been longer than Nick had anticipated. The airline was about to cancel the flight because it was less than half full. That meant off-loading the luggage and staying overnight in Cairo. Eventually some more passengers showed up and the flight took off, late but still on the same plane. It was late in the evening, and the airport was empty except for a janitor and a security guard who were talking near the front exit. Nick had tried to call his contact in Khartoum, but was not able to get in touch with him. He was the only light-skinned person in the airport, and, for some reason, he felt even more ill at ease than when he had been in Iraq. Everyone looked like a criminal to him. Despite the fact that his flight was the last one to land, the luggage took a good forty minutes before it started appearing on the luggage carousel. Nick began to think the handlers were outside rummaging through every piece of luggage on the plane. Hell, they would be in for quite a surprise if they opened mine.

Grabbing his suitcase off the carousel, Nick immediately went to the first row of seats and opened it. The canister was still there, just where he had put it. Perhaps the long flight and lack of sleep were making him more paranoid than usual. Realizing this, he took the canister and put it in the travel bag he had used for his carry-on, zipped it shut, and headed for the door.

Despite the inactivity in the airport, there were still a large number of taxis waiting along the street out front. In the taxi line was a black Mercedes, against which leaned a tall light-skinned Arabic-looking man. He was dressed well in a dark pair of slacks and a well-pressed collared shirt. Dropping the cigarette he was smoking, he stepped on it and walked toward Nick.

"Mr. Fallon, I assume you still need a ride," the man said in deliberate, well-enunciated English. He had a slight hint of an English accent. Nick was trying to get away from an aggressive taxi driver looking for a fare and hesitated, not being accustomed to being called by his Irish alias.

He looked over at the man who was smiling broadly and said, "Dr... Dr. Salih Al-Fardi. Yes, my flight was delayed. I guess I didn't expect you would still be here."

"Of course. We have important work together. I called and they told me it would be delayed. My car is right over here. Please, let me take your bag," Al-Fardi said.

Nick quickly replied, "That's ok. I can carry it," not wanting to lose control of it.

The man, still smiling, replied, "Very well." He put his left arm around the back of Nick, without touching him, and led him toward the car. "If there is anything else you need, please let me know. I have some water and some food in the car. We have a long drive ahead." Dr. Al-Fardi motioned for Nick to sit in the back seat of the Mercedes. Dr. Al-Fardi entered the front passenger seat. There was a driver waiting to drive them to the lab. "Would you like something to eat or drink, or maybe a cigarette?"

The car sped off around the taxi stand and out onto the road leading away from the Khartoum International Airport. Nick was feeling hungry and asked, "What do you have to eat? I am hungry."

"I have some bread, and I thought you might like some chocolate. It's Swiss. Toblerone, I believe," Dr. Al-Fardi said.

"Chocolate sounds good, and some water, please."

Dr. Al-Fardi reached into a bag at his feet and withdrew a large Toblerone and a liter of water and passed it back to Nick. Nick opened the package and began to break off a few pieces. Since the doctor had made him feel at ease, he offered him a section. The doctor declined and said, "Mr. Fallon, you have had a long trip, and, if you like, please take your rest. There is a blanket on the floor behind the driver's seat and a pillow." Nick was tired and began to reach over for the blanket as the doctor spoke again. "Mr. Fallon, I guess you have the luck of the Irish, as they say, considering that you survived the unpleasantness in Iraq and in Turkey."

Nick stopped and turned to face the doctor, who couldn't know about the murder on the beach. "What unpleasantness in Turkey?"

"Your friend Hassad and the others. They were killed by an unknown assailant. We knew that you had escaped. You were not aware of this?" Dr. Al-Fardi asked.

Nick was stunned by the news of Hassad's death. He didn't expect he would be and swallowed hard. He took a breath and said, "What do you mean unknown? It must have been Mossad. They were the ones that hit us in Iraq."

"Some people here thought it may have been you and that you actually are not who you say you are. That you work for the CIA. Your father, he was CIA, wasn't he?" Dr. Al-Fardi asked with a grin.

Nick didn't know how much these people knew about him, but he wasn't surprised they would have access to such information. Olsen knew about his father, as did other members of the Aryan Front. He never concealed the fact and was quite proud he was working against the establishment for which his father had toiled. "Yes, yes, he was, but you have nothing to worry about."

"No, of course not. Olsen has assured us of that, but how do we know you are not Francis?"

Nick was angry that this man he had just met knew so much about him, including the existence of his brother. He paused, trying to think of a good reply, and said, "Francis? Shit, your boys in Turkey would have killed him. He would have given himself away a long time ago."

"Mr. Fallon, I know you are who you say you are. We have our sources. I am just playing with you. I guess you're surprised at how much I know," Dr. Al-Fardi said.

Nick was, but he didn't reply. The doctor said, "Very well. Get some sleep. We have a lot of work to do and will start as soon as we arrive in Al Fashir."

Istanbul, Turkey

It had been a long flight. The plane had been delayed at Dulles because of the weather, and there was an unexpected maintenance issue in Frankfurt. Francis had slept as much as he could, but the last conversation he had with Reynolds and the stresses of his job were starting to get to him and had kept him from sleeping well. Regardless, he was happy to finally have landed and was hoping he and Marina could just spend a day at her house and relax. Customs was not too bad, and, since he didn't check any luggage, Francis made good time getting to the terminal. He was felling quite groggy and didn't like being so out of it.

He stopped along the hallway leading to the exit and took off his jacket. As he was bending over to shove it into his carry-on, he was awkwardly pulled into a strong hard embrace. Of course, it could only be one person, and, as he straightened his back and stood, he looked down to see the back of Marina's head as she buried her face into his chest. "Marina?"

She did not look up and held him even closer, not replying. He could hear she was sobbing, and, despite the fact she could be emotional at times, he realized this was somewhat unusual for her. In a soft voice, he asked, "Marina, you can't really have missed me that much. Why are you crying?"

She raised her head, and he saw the tears and redness in her eyes. She pushed away and hit him on the chest. "Of course, I missed you, but something happened, and I'm really upset.

Don't be such a jerk!"

"You know I'm just teasing you. What happened?" Francis said.

She looked up again and put her right hand behind the back of his neck and leaned forward and kissed him. "I don't want to talk about it here. Do you have all your bags? Let's go back to my apartment. I really need to talk to you."

"Sure, I need some rest. I brought you a present. I think you'll like it," he said, not wanting to upset her further.

They walked hand in hand toward the exit where Marina had a cab waiting for them so they didn't have to wait with the others.

Marina only spoke about the city and the sights as they headed from the airport toward her downtown apartment. She didn't let go of Francis's hand once and looked at him longingly with her large soft brown eyes. Marina paid the fare and tipped the driver after he took Francis's bag from the trunk. The doorman had seen the cab approach and had the door open for the two of them. Marina smiled and nodded hello to the man who was checking out her tall handsome friend.

Marina's apartment was on the eighth floor, and, as soon as she had opened the door and Francis had set down his luggage, she put both hands around his neck and drew him close to her. She kissed him deeply, stroked his back, and began pulling his shirt from out of the back of his pants. Francis wanted to tell her to stop. Things were still somewhat cloudy between the two of them, and he was agonizingly tired, but he felt one of her hands on his buttock and the other starting to probe the front of his pants. Francis had only been with one woman since Marina had left, an old girlfriend who called him when she found out things were not going well with Marina, but he never cared for her the way he cared for Marina.

She had his shirt off, and his belt was partially undone. She didn't speak, but smiled and was no longer crying, which made Francis happy. He picked her up and carried her to the couch a few steps away. He remembered how she had always liked to be on top of him, and he sat down and positioned her on his lap with her legs opened across his. He kissed her neck and smelled the fragrance she always wore, a combination of cinnamon and cardamon. Damn, she smells good, Francis thought, and was soon awake and giving his full attention to her body and her smell. Francis took a deep breath, and his penis hardened even more. Marina could sense she had awakened her groggy lover and stood and finished taking off his pants.

She stood in front of him and removed her shirt, revealing the light pink bra she was wearing. He remembered how he had loved her soft white skin. He reached up and cupped her right breast in his left hand. She sighed and kicked her head back as he put his right hand up under her skirt and played with the band of her panties. He moved his hand to the front latch of her bra and undid it with one quick motion. Marina sighed and laughed. She was always impressed with Francis's ability to remove a bra with such speed. Her breasts burst from the bra and Francis took the left one in his hand and began to kiss the nipple and areola of the right. He had her panties down around her ankles and his right hand was caressing the inside of her thighs, close to but not touching her genital area. Marina stood and pulled his boxers off, almost shredding them in the process.

She stood over him with her bra and a skirt still on and looked down at him. "I am so glad to see you." Francis stood, and picked her up. She wrapped her legs around him, and, using his right hand, he grabbed his penis and put it inside of her. He felt the walls of her vagina tightened around his penis, and he held her for a moment before he began to thrust in and out while holding her up with his arms, his hands under her buttocks.

She began to talk to him in Turkish and that only added to

his arousal. He knew she was going to have an orgasm when she talked Turkish, and, shortly thereafter, she did. He felt the contractions of her lower torso and the walls of her vagina clamp around his penis. When she came, she sighed and said "Oh God" in Turkish. It was one Turkish phrase Francis knew well. Francis carried her back to the couch and sat down with her sitting on top of him, his penis still inside of her. He continued to thrust and listened to the ever growing litany of Turkish Marina spewed as he thrust into her again and again. Marina came once more and, then, finally Francis did. He stopped, leaving himself inside of her. She leaned forward and put her head on his left shoulder. She caressed his head and kissed him on his neck and the side of his face.

Francis could only think of one thing to say, and, while she continued kissing him, he said, "I guess I missed you more than I thought."

Marina looked up and smiled. "I guess you did. I have to admit, that was pretty good. Maybe now you can get that nap you wanted. Maybe not," she laughed. "Tell you what, honey. Go into the bedroom. I'll bring us some coffee. Are you hungry?"

Francis loved the way Marina always looked after him after sex. No matter what time of day it was, she knew exactly how to treat a man afterward, whether it was morning and time for coffee or evening and time for a good scotch or beer. It was so unlike many of the American women he had dated, who didn't seem to know all the subtleties and warm things to do for a guy afterward. She stood and started to walk away, pausing only once to brush his penis and say, "I have big plans for you today!"

Francis rose and went into the bedroom. Marina came in shortly after with the coffee and some pastries. She sat on the side of the bed with her back to Francis, wearing only the soft silk robe she had put on after removing her skirt. Francis sipped the coffee and was about to speak when he heard her crying again. She had never cried after sex before. He took another sip and said, "You never did tell me what was wrong. I guess we forgot to talk about it. What happened? Is it a problem with your parents? Your brother?"

She turned around to face him. "You remember I told you that I saw your brother?"

Francis's first thought was that perhaps something had happened between the two of them, and he asked angrily, "What did he do? Did he hurt you?"

Marina shook her head, drew a breath in through her nose, and wiped away a tear. "No, not him, but someone else, someone who was looking for him." Francis didn't speak and reached out and touched her on her cheek. Marina continued. "He pulled me into his car. He had a gun, and I thought he was going to kill me. He said that he knew that Nick and I were up to something and wanted to know what we were doing." By now Marina had composed herself; Francis had drawn her closer to him. "What do you think he was talking about? I gave him liquid nitrogen, nothing more, Frank."

Francis remembered the conversations he had had recently with Jim and Reynolds. The mystery man came to mind as he began to think of his brother. The man Reynolds had said had been to Iraq. The money transfers to banks overseas by Atlas Genetics.

"Frank, what do you think?" Marina persisted.

"What did the man look like? I mean did he look American?" Francis asked.

Marina knew what Francis meant, despite the fact that American could mean anything these days. "No, he was definitely not American. He had an accent, but I couldn't place it. He wasn't Turkish, of that I am sure. I told him that all I knew was that I had supposed that Nick was returning to the States. What upset me was that he said he was going to keep tabs on me. I was really afraid that he was going to hurt me."

Francis didn't reply, but gave her that confident look that said nobody would be hurting her while he was around. "Frank, I'm sorry, but I have to do some work today. I promised my boss. Do you mind? I have cable and some videos," Marina said.

Francis said, "How about I come with you? I'd like to see where you work and, besides, I don't want to scare you, but, if that guy knows where you live, he undoubtedly knows where you work as well."

Marina smiled and said, "Sure you don't mind?"

"Hey, we have two weeks together, and one day is no big deal," Francis replied.

Marina rolled over Francis's body and lay down beside him on the bed. She began rubbing his legs and leaned over to start kissing him on his chest. They made love one more time, showered, dressed, and headed off to Marina's office.

Al Fashir, Sudan

Nick and Dr. Al-Fardi traveled most of the night in the Mercedes, stopping only once at a military checkpoint. Nick couldn't sleep and remained in the car as Al-Fardi spoke with the military men in a jovial manner, even offering them cigarettes, which they gladly accepted. As morning approached, Nick had drifted off to sleep and was awakened by the sound of the car horn. The car was traveling along a rutted, dusty roadbed and was approaching a walled compound. The walls were mud, about eight feet tall. The structure was the only one within sight as the barren landscape stretched off into the horizon. The driver of the car leaned on the horn again and a gate opened, revealing the interior and a group of about five or six armed men wearing long white robes and dark head covers. All of the men wore sunglasses. He thought back to the night before and remembered that even though it was late and dark, Dr. Al-

Fardi had been wearing sunglasses as well. Rather conspicuous, he thought.

The driver rolled the car slowly through the gate and exchanged greetings with some of the men, reaching out of the window to touch their hands as he passed. These men, while still Arabic-looking to Nick, were more dark-skinned and weathered than the doctor.

The doctor looked back and saw Nick had awoken, smiled the big gold-filled smile he always seemed to have available and asked, "Did you get a good night's sleep?" Nick nodded that he had, still yawning. Al-Fardi spoke again. "I imagine you have never been anywhere on earth like this, have you? I personally think it is amazingly beautiful. There are so many colors in the sand, and it is, I would have to say, very peaceful. Some people don't like the isolation, but, at times, I quite enjoy the solitude."

Nick didn't speak, but he could relate to what Al-Fardi was talking about. There were parts of Olsen's ranch where he could camp and hike and live off the land for days and not see or hear another person. It was so quiet, the only man-made noises were the occasional faint sounds of distant passenger jets, but that was it.

Inside the walls were two buildings, one made of the same adobe mud material as the walls. The other was a more modern structure with a corrugated tin roof constructed out of some type of block. Nick could see a large generator outside of the modern building, and there were small metal tubes on the roof for ventilation. The building also had a large air conditioner in one of the windows, running full blast, dripping a pool of condensation onto the ground below.

As the driver pulled around to the right side of the modern building, Nick saw a large green tent about thirty-feet long and ten-feet high about fifty meters away. Next to the tent were some crates and pallets. "Mr. Fallon, did you need any more rest or shall we get to work?" Al-Fardi asked as they exited the vehicle.

Nick now understood why everyone was wearing sunglasses: the sun, even in the early morning, was oppressive. Nick shielded his eyes and turned toward Al-Fardi, who was standing with his back to the sun. "I think we should get started. Where are the animals? Are they inside the tent?"

Al-Fardi looked at Nick, with the big grin on his face, and said, "The animals, they have not come yet, but they will be here soon. I thought we might go over some safety procedures and look at some of the equipment to make sure it meets your standards. Please let us get out of the heat." They went back around in the direction from which they had come; Al-Fardi opened the door to the modern building and let Nick enter, carrying the bag with the canister. "The driver will take your suitcase to the other building where we will be staying. Don't let the outside condition discourage you. It is actually quite comfortable, particularly if there is a sand storm."

Nick entered the building and saw a rather well-stocked mini-laboratory. The building had two rows of lab benches that stretched along the walls almost to the other end. There were centrifuges, a Metler balance, a lyophilizer, a fume hood, two refrigerators, incubators, a freezer, and a number of large storage containers on small wheels. Nick smiled. He was impressed that such a lab could exist in the middle of nowhere.

"I am very proud of this lab. I have better equipment than many of the hospitals in the Sudan. Though, I must admit, that much of this was supposed to end up in many of the hospitals. I thought it was more suited to my purposes," Al-Fardi said with a laugh. Nick walked further into the laboratory and set the travel bag with the canister down on one of the benches. He unzipped it and withdrew the canister. Unscrewing the top, he looked in and saw that about one third of the canister was still filled with the nitrogen he had taken from Marina's lab.

"Do you have some insulated gloves?" he asked Al-Fardi, who, had become silent as he watched Nick open the canister.

"Certainly, yes, I will get them." Al-Fardi went over to the other side of the small building and took out a pair of white insulated gloves from a drawer. He handed them to Nick and grabbed one of the small wheeled storage containers and pushed it toward Nick, saying, "We can put the canister in here until the animals arrive."

As they were putting the canister into the storage container, a man entered the building and spoke Arabic to Al-Fardi. Nick had heard a truck engine and asked Al-Fardi, "Are they here?" meaning the animals he had expected to use in their work.

Al-Fardi said, "Once you have that closed up, let's go outside and take a look." Nick could feel the heat of the outside entering the lab, and the man stood in the doorway with the door still open. He looked out past the man and saw another man was leading five children past the entrance of the lab and toward the tent. The children did not look like Al-Fardi or the other men. They were obviously black Africans. Nick looked over at Al-Fardi, but he was already leaving the lab and heading out the door, talking to one of the men who had driven the truck into the compound.

Nick followed him outside and saw Al-Fardi examining one of the children. She was small so Nick wasn't sure how old she was. Her eyes were wide open, and she looked very frightened. There were two other girls and two boys. All of them were dressed in tattered clothing and were not wearing shoes. Al-Fardi continued his examination of the girl, feeling her lymph nodes under her jaw and poking at her abdomen as if checking her liver. When he finished with her, he looked at the other children in turn and then motioned for the men to take the children into the tent. One of the boys spoke up. Nick recognized it was not Arabic, and Al-Fardi replied to the boy. The boy nodded and followed the others into the tent. Al-Fardi turned toward Nick and said, "They are Dinka, from the South of Sudan. They are all orphans. Their parents were killed in some recent fighting in that area."

Nick said, "You didn't have to keep this from me. Are these the animals that you kept referring to? I couldn't care less about what or who we use to get the job done."

"Yes, yes, they are," Al-Fardi said. "In this country, these poor children are worth less than animals. For the price we paid for them, we could probably have bought only one cow."

"What did you tell the boy by the way?" Nick asked curiously.

"I told them we were starting a school, and they were the first students to come."

CHAPTER FOURTEEN

Washington, D.C.

Reynolds was reading over the details of an incident in California. The ATF had been called in to investigate a house in Gilroy after the police in San Francisco had arrested three men carrying a large number of firearms. "Three killed, two police officers and one teenager," he read. "The assailants were not seen by anyone in the area. Both officers had been shot in the head. One with a thirty caliber-rifle, the other with a nine mm pistol." The ATF had sent the report to him because they had found a computer in a downstairs room that had links to white supremacist Internet sites. The report contained a list of the sites; Reynolds was familiar with most of them. There were also a number of Internet pornography sites with which Reynolds was not familiar. One was www.whitesupremacistspussy.com. Another link stood out and caught his attention. It didn't fit with all the other links: www.jewishdefensecouncil.com. Reynolds could only surmise they were keeping tabs on the enemy.

The men that were still sitting in a prison cell in San Francisco had records, but none of them had been involved in any incidents or acts of violence relating to white supremacist movements, or at least they had not been caught. They linked the men to the house in Gilroy through a receipt they had found in their car. The attendant at the convenience store had recognized the car and had seen it coming and going from one particular neighborhood, and, from there, the police were able to track them to the house.

Reynolds looked again at the www.jewishdefensecouncil.com link. He typed it into his URL locator in the browser of his computer. The site came up and it looked to be exactly what the link indicated it was. He clicked around and saw pictures of survivors of the Holocaust and stories of people who had been helped by the council. Nothing in particular stood out. He continued clicking around and opened a link to a report about recent problems with white supremacists. He laughed because it was a report he had authored in conjunction with the Wiesenthal Institute. He looked around for an address or a contact number, but found only a page for submitting information requests.

Picking up the phone, he called the chief of the Computer Analysis and Response Team. The group consisted of the top FBI computer experts, specifically trained in forensic science. He got his voice mail and left a message, "Hey, this is Reynolds. I need you to check out a few sites for me. I can send you an e-mail or call me back in about hour or so, if you can. Thanks." He hung up.

Something about the site just didn't make sense. Maybe they didn't want any unwanted people coming by their office or sending unwanted mail, but not having at least a P.O. box or a contact number didn't seem right. Reynolds picked up the phone and dialed the contact number on the report he had received from the ATF. He needed to take a look at the hard drive of the computer they had found.

Al Fashir, Sudan

It wasn't until after Nick had been outside in the tent for about half an hour that he realized Dr. Al-Fardi was right. He had repeatedly emphasized it was better to work through the night and avoid the exhausting heat of the day. Nick looked through the visor of the biohazard suit he was wearing and over at Dr. Al-Fardi. The doctor had purchased them from an ex-Soviet general. Nick was concerned since they weren't from a laboratory, but were, in fact, military chemical/biological warfare suits. Al-Fardi assured him they were new and that they had plenty more. They would only need to be in the tent three times and would not work with the virus every day, so Nick felt better in that regard.

The tent was unrecognizable as such from the inside. Before Nick had arrived, Dr. Al-Fardi and his men had lined the inside of the tent with thick plastic sheeting. There were two layers separated by about two feet. Half the tent was separated from the other by two more layers of plastic that formed a wall. One layer was attached to one side and the other to the other side. This was used as a door from the entrance to the interior where the subjects were kept. The interior of the tent was kept cool by running air conditioning over the outside layer of plastic, between the tent covering. An exhaust fan with a HEPA filter was attached to the side, creating negative pressure inside the double-lined interior. Still, condensation collected in the plastic and dripped on the floor, though not quite as much as before the AC unit was running at max.

Through the slightly opaque and condensation-covered plastic layers dividing the tent in half, Nick could see the cots. All five children had been drugged and were bound to cots inside the bubble that was formed by the plastic cocoon. Al-Fardi had taken care of that and had stripped the children naked as well. They had been secured at both the feet and the hands, with straps around their chests, stomachs, and just above the knees.

As Nick entered the children's area he met up with Dr. Al-Fardi, who had just finished securing the last of them. "Most, if not all, of these children would be dead in a year. That one over there is slightly malnourished as it is—," Al-Fardi was saying, when Nick interrupted.

"Like I said before, I could not care less just as long as we get what we need and get it done on time."

Al-Fardi nodded and said, "You have the walkie-talkie. Let me know if you need anything or run into any problems."

Nick had already removed the vials from the wheeled container and had them in a rack in his hand. Looking at the doctor, he said, "I think I have all that I need right now. It really shouldn't take that long." The doctor left, and Nick went over to a small wooden bench that had a number of plastic bottles of solution and a nebulizer. Nick was familiar with the nebulizer. He had suffered from asthma as a child and had had to use one just about every day to treat the condition.

Nick removed three of the vials from the storage container and lifted them, one at a time, from the rack and gave each one a little rap with his fingers to agitate the contents. He repeated this a few times and then took one of the plastic jars of solution and poured about twenty-five milliliters of the clear solution into a small plastic beaker. Removing the lids from the vials he poured one after the other into the beaker with the clear liquid. He then placed the empty vials into a plastic container on the bench.

The children had not been completely knocked out so their breathing was still regular and steady. The nebulizer was attached to an extension cord and was a small handheld unit that Nick could easily carry between the children. He poured the solution into the metal tank that sat on top of the unit and moved close to the first child. It was one of the girls. Her head had not been secured, and she had it tilted away from Nick. He thought he had remembered saying their heads should be secured, but it was too late. He set the unit on the edge of the cot, and, with his left hand, he pulled the child's head toward him. The unit had a two-pronged nasal attachment on a length of tubing, and Nick had secured it earlier before mixing the virus in the beaker. He shoved the prongs into the child's nose and flicked the unit on with his right hand. As the power came on, he could see the tubing leading to the nasal attachment had stiffened slightly, indicating the liquid was being aerosolized and forced out the other end. He held the attachment in her nose for about sixty seconds.

He moved to the next child, who was also a girl, but slightly smaller. Her head had not fallen to the side, and it was easier to insert the nasal attachment. He gave her only about thirty seconds because of her smaller size.

The next child in line was one of the boys. The boy's nasal openings were huge, and, despite the fact that his head had slumped to his left, Nick's right side, it was necessary to tilt him upright. As Nick withdrew the attachment, the boy coughed and choked a little, most likely irritated by the blast of aerosolized air. One thing Al-Fardi had remembered to do was gag each of the children, so, when the boy coughed, some mucus was forced out of his nose. Nick thought about treating him again, but thought the next treatment would do the trick if the first did not. He did the other boy and then came to the last girl. Her nostrils were smaller, and her head, like the first child's, was tilted away from Nick.

He reached over to move her head into a better position, and, as he did so, she yawned and moved it back. He did it again, and, as she yawned, she opened her eyes and stared groggily into space. Nick was able to keep her looking up even though she was only slightly sedated. He had asked for curare to keep the children still. The girl's body began to shake. At first, Nick thought she was conscious and was trying to get out of her bindings, but then realized she was most likely having a reaction to the sedative. Nick had seen plenty of laboratory animals react that way when he was a lab technician. Because of the shaking, he was not able to insert the attachment into her nose completely. He gave her the thirty-second treatment and removed the attachment. If she died from the reaction to the medication, not to worry, he thought. He was sure he had successfully infected the others.

He returned to the bench and set the nebulizer aside. Turning off the light he exited through the double-walled plastic barrier and headed toward the makeshift shower they had built. He showered in the heavily chlorinated water for about twenty minutes, fully clothed in the biohazard suit. The next level of decontamination involved a thorough scrubbing followed by another chlorinated shower.

Finally, he left the double-layered plastic tent structure and entered the area that had been made into an airlock of sorts. The entrance to the tent had been extended and attached to another small tent. It was here that he was finally able to remove the suit and exit into the warm Sudanese evening. As he walked out, he saw a group of men standing around, including Dr. Al-Fardi. Most of the men stepped back and looked at Nick cautiously. Al-Fardi stood his ground and said, "I've been talking with the men, and I'm afraid that I understand their concerns. We have set up a cot in the lab. You can sleep there tonight and for the rest of your time here. Believe me, I am not so concerned, but these men, they are not trained scientists like you and I. I hope you understand."

Nick didn't say a word. He wasn't particularly anxious to share a room with them anyway. He nodded, and, as he started walking toward the lab to get some sleep, the men parted and gave him plenty of room. One of the men had a scarf pulled up around his mouth, and another held his hand over his mouth and nose.

CHAPTER FIFTEEN

Istanbul, Turkey

Marina was working at her lab bench while Francis was in her office reading over some travel guides and maps. She had promised they would spend some time together after a few days of her processing the evidence from the murder of the general's son. The investigators at the scene had collected some hair and fiber evidence from both the dead teenager and from the one who had survived. The second teen, who had been knocked out, had a broken jaw and was still in the hospital because of the severity of the break. He would need corrective surgery to completely recover its use. He was, as yet, unable to give a decent description of the killer and was still apparently quite upset about the death of his lifelong friend.

Before Francis had arrived in town, Marina had already isolated the DNA from the hair evidence and was working on a new rapid DNA fingerprinting analysis that took only two days. She stood and walked over to the door that led to her office. Poking her head in the door, she said in a slightly teasing voice, "Hey, Francis, have I told you I'm sorry for dragging you here today?"

Francis was sitting in her chair and had his feet on her desk. In front of him were a number of travel guides and an empty cup of coffee. He looked up and smiled at her appearance in a lab coat, surgical gloves, and a pair of glasses that doubled as lab goggles. He set down a map he was reading. "I'm not sure if you did. In fact, I'm almost certain that you didn't."

She stepped closer to him. "Oh, well, I guess I'll have to say it again, but first maybe an apologetic kiss to make up for the trouble I have caused." Marina leaned forward and down to meet his mouth; he closed his eyes and opened his mouth slightly. Instead of her lips, he was greeted by the end of the cotton swab Marina had jammed into his mouth. He jerked back. Marina laughed. "I needed a sample as a control for the forensic evidence. I hope you don't mind doing your part for the Institute?"

Francis rubbed his jaw and said nothing. Marina leaned forward, kissed him on his forehead, and walked out of the office. Another hour passed, Marina working in the lab and Francis alternately reading the travel guides and looking at the Internet. Francis had his back to the door and had logged into his personal e-mail and was reading over some messages. "I hope you find our Internet connection to be satisfactory."

The voice startled Francis, and he swiveled the chair around and to face its owner. He stood and said, "I'm a friend of Marina's. She said she had to work, so I came along. I wanted to see where she worked." He extended a hand. "My name is Francis D'Abruzzo."

The man introduced himself as Marina's boss, Dr. Demirci. He was very curt and looked Francis over, paying particularly close attention to his face. He left to go check on Marina.

Francis went back to reading his e-mail and heard the two of them conversing in Turkish in the laboratory. Francis replied to an e-mail from his father, telling him he had arrived in Turkey safely. There was nothing from his brother, Jim, or Reynolds, and that made him anxious. He thought again that maybe he should have stayed home, too much was going on at work, and he was idling away his time in Marina's office. He closed down his e-mail file and the Internet browser.

"Frank," he heard Marina say as she and her boss walked back from the lab into her office. "I guess you two met. The other kid at the scene was finally able to give a decent description of the man who killed his friend and smashed up his jaw."

She spoke Turkish, and her boss extended his hand and held

out a piece of paper to Francis as he said, "We have the composite, maybe you would like to take a look at it." Francis grabbed the composite and took a good look at it. He looked at the composite and then at Marina and her boss. He looked back down at the paper again and said, "It can't be... Nick!" The face of the man on the paper, while bearded, looked astonishingly like his twin.

Marina spoke again. "The kid also gave a description of the vehicle they were trying to break into. It was a lot like the truck Nick was driving when I saw him."

Dr. Demirci said, "They have not recovered the truck as yet, but, from what I can tell, it looks like your brother may have had something to do with the death of this boy." Francis looked at Marina again and was silent.

Al Fashir, Sudan

Nick had slept through most of the morning. He was happy to be sleeping in the lab. It was air-conditioned and really quite comfortable. The noise of the air-conditioner and the laboratory equipment provided plenty of white noise and covered the sound of the wind that had picked up during the night. Nick could feel the force of the wind against the sides of the building, but it didn't do any damage. He wondered whether or not the tent was holding up. Nick got up and went over to the computer that was on the lab bench directly across from where he was sleeping. He touched the mouse and the screen came on. Checking the time in the lower right corner he saw it was 10:30. Al-Fardi had written the name and password for the Internet account on a slip of paper next to the computer. He had also left some bread and butter and a thermos with tea. Nick hadn't heard him come in. He must have been sleeping more deeply than he thought. It sort of bothered him that Al-Fardi had been able to come in without him knowing, thinking maybe he should have put a chair against the door, as well as locking it, before he went to sleep.

Nick poured a cup of tea and took a piece of bread to eat. One thing Al-Fardi hadn't done was change the default language of the Windows program. Nick hadn't noticed that when he had looked before. Bringing up the control panel, he finally was able to find the setting to change the language to English. He hadn't checked the portal since Habur and needed to let Olsen know where he was. The connection was very slow and disconnected a few times, but he was finally able to get to the site. Nick noticed there were no new postings for him, which he took as a good sign.

He finished off the heavily sugared cup of tea, savoring the sweetness and warmth, and poured himself another cup. He held down the "n" with his right index finger, the "a" and "z" keys with his left pinky, and the "i" with his right ring finger. Then while holding down the shift key with his right pinky, he hit the space bar four times in succession. A new message window appeared and Nick began to type. "Five animals are infected and will be providing treatment as needed," he wrote. He sent the message and the screen was refreshed.

He was about to close the site down when he noticed a new picture had appeared, indicating there was a new message for him. Clicking on the picture, he hit the keystroke combination again and the message appeared: "For the next round, we will be providing you with some assistance with security issues. The vice president of security will be on hand." Nick read the message, and thought maybe something else had happened regarding the Israelis and the attack in Iraq. Maybe the incident in Athens had been connected. Regardless, he got along well with Olsen's second and was actually looking forward to seeing a like-minded American. He had had enough of these foreigners.

There was a knock at the door, and, before he had time to respond, Al-Fardi walked into the lab. Nick closed down the browser and disconnected from the Internet. "I see you found the tea and bread. Is there anything else that you would like?

Some fruit, perhaps? We may even be able to get you some eggs if you like," Al-Fardi said.

Nick replied, "Not right now, thanks. The tea is really good. Did the wind this morning cause any problems with the tent?"

"Actually, two of the support-guy wires did come loose and one side of the tent has collapsed, but only slightly. It is not where the animals are, so you may not have to fix it right away."

"I was going to check them tonight and dose any of them that have not been infected. I can fix it then."

"Very well," Al-Fardi said. "Until then, perhaps you would like to join me and take in a little shooting practice. What do you think?"

Nick thought about it for a second and said, "Sure, sounds like fun. Let me clean up. Give me about fifteen minutes."

Nick could hear the shooting while he took a brief shower. He knew the sound from training on the ranch: a twenty-gauge shotgun. Walking out of the lab, he followed the sound, passing the tent with the children. In another ten yards, he saw Al-Fardi and two other men. One was manning the portable trap launcher, the other was standing behind Al-Fardi, holding another shot gun in his right hand. Neither of the men was from the group that had insisted Nick sleep in the lab. Only Al-Fardi was shooting, and, as Nick approached, he saw him shoot two clay pigeons in succession, dusting them as they say. "Nice shots," Nick said as he approached from behind. The man holding the gun looked at Nick and handed it to him, along with a bag filled with shells he could hang from his belt. Nick replied in Arabic. "Thank you."

By now, the sun had risen high above the horizon and was beating down on the group of men from behind. Nick felt his neck and realized he probably should have brought some sunscreen with him.

"Is the sun bothering you?" Al-Fardi asked.

"Yes, a little, I suppose. I normally tan pretty easily, but this sun, it's pretty harsh," Nick said.

Al-Fardi spoke to the man who had been holding the gun and the man dashed off in the direction of the house where Al-Fardi and the Sudanese men slept. "I went to medical school in England. That is where I took an interest in trap and skeet shooting," Al-Fardi said. "I used to shoot with a hunt club outside of London quite often, until I began beating them regularly. They didn't much appreciate it, I must say. In my experience, the British seem to be very open to other cultures, until we start beating them at their own game."

Nick said, "I wouldn't know. To me, it really doesn't matter much. I just try to do the best I can." Nick pulled four shells from the bag he had put on his belt and loaded the gun. As he finished, the man who had run back to the sleep area had returned and presented Nick with a traditional Arabic head covering. He extended it and said something in Arabic with a big smile on his face. Nick looked at Al-Fardi with a puzzled look; the man's accent was thick and he spoke fast. Nick didn't know much Arabic, and he certainly didn't know what the man had said.

Al-Fardi laughed and took the head cover from the man. He reached out to Nick, holding the covering, and said, "He said: Here, put this on, and you will be al Qaeda."

Nick took the covering, but didn't return the laugh. Even though it had been only a few minutes, he was glad to have it despite the ribbing he was taking; his neck already felt burned. When he had the covering secure and draped over his neck, he nodded to the man with the launcher who responded by launching two traps in succession. Nick had the gun under his right armpit while he secured the head covering. As quickly as the man had launched the trap, Nick had moved the gun into position and dusted both in order. Al-Fardi said, "I don't think my old hunt club would care for you much either, but not because you are Irish, Mr. Fallon."

Nick finally smiled, and they both laughed. Despite his earlier concerns about traveling to the Sudan and the dangerous nature of the work he was doing, there was something about Dr. Al-Fardi that made him feel at ease.

They shot for well over an hour and matched shot for shot for the most part, but Al-Fardi got the better of Nick in the end. Nick admitted to himself it was probably home turf advantage. When they finished, they walked past the tent and toward the main area of the compound. There were no sounds coming from within. Once it got dark, he would have to check on the children.

CHAPTER SIXTEEN

Olsen Ranch, Montana

Some of Olsen's men at the Bear's Den were getting bored. He could tell, even though none of them would dare complain to him. He had kept the news of the problems in Gilroy from them, not wanting to add to their anxiety levels. Whitaker had filled him in on the clean-up operation and the killing of the boy outside the house. He was certain that nothing had been left in the house that could point to Olsen. His men had trained and trained and were in desperate need of something to help them blow off some steam. Olsen considered the possible rewards he could give his men to help them through this tough period of boredom until the big day.

He could bring in a group of whores. He had heard about a particular group that provided some nice young Korean women, virgins all. What he liked most about them was that, for a price, they would provide women for snuffing. Olsen had killed plenty of men in his time. He had never killed a woman, but had severely beaten one or two for disloyal behavior.

Sitting in his command center, he pondered the possibilities. "That would be something they might enjoy," he said aloud, attracting the attention of his nerds who were busy working on upgrading some of the systems. "Not you, you fucking nerds! Real men like those soon-to-be heroes that have been training day in and day out," Olsen ranted. Thinking again, he realized maybe the whores would be too much of a distraction; maybe the men needed something to test their skills. After all, target practice and knifing dummies had gotten very mundane. He weighed the risks, though. It was very close to the day of judgment. "Should we risk it?" he asked himself again. This time the nerds did not turn around.

"Nothing that would garner too much attention, but, yet,

something that would give them the adrenaline rush they need to keep their skills honed." Olsen spoke aloud again as he rose from his chair and walked toward the exit. "Yes!"

"Nerds, gather the men and have them meet here immediately."

One of the nerds pushed a button on his console next to his PC and a siren went off. Within minutes, the room was filled with thirty men—all dressed in fatigues, some with shaved heads, others with crew cuts. None had facial hair; Olsen despised beards and goatees considering them suitable for fags and liberals.

Olsen stood next to his chair; it was raised above the surrounding floor. "'Men, I want you to know that I am very proud of how hard you have been training and the effort you have put forth. You are, by far, the best bunch of men that I have ever been associated with. The time is near for beginning the next and most important phase of our mission. I have no doubt that we will succeed." A cheer went up from the men. Olsen relished the moment.

He continued, "Sometimes training is not sufficient. We need to engage the enemy. Real life scenarios that will fill your body with adrenaline." The men cheered again, excited by the prospect of real-life engagement. "We will break into two teams, drawing lots so that the selection will be fair. I want nothing more than for all of you to experience a real battle, but, reluctantly, I have to ask that some of you remain behind. You will be rewarded in the future, you can be assured of that," Olsen said.

"We have plenty of ammunition, but we can always use more. The more we take from the enemy, the better," Olsen said. "There is a munitions depot run by the USDA. That would be the United States Department of Agriculture for those of you who couldn't care less about those government bastards. Not many people are aware of it, but the Forest Service maintains depots with munitions and explosives to help clear away snow at ski resorts and for clearing fallen lumber. There is one site that also contains a small cache of guns, mainly small caliber handguns and rifles. It is located in the Bitterroot National Forest and is not heavily guarded. I believe that there are only five employees at the site. That will be your mission. It will involve planning, reconnaissance and, ultimately, the take over and collection of the material they have stored." The men cheered again and began to draw the lots that the nerds had been preparing as Olsen was speaking.

Istanbul, Turkey

Though at first in denial, Francis had to admit the composite picture was his twin brother. It couldn't be anyone else. "What is he up to?" he wondered while Marina and her boss looked at him. Still staring at the photo, he spoke again. "Marina, I need to use your phone."

"Yes, of course," Marina said, sensing he wanted to be alone. She tugged on her boss's arm, and he left the office with her and shut the door behind him. Francis looked at the picture again and picked up the phone.

"Hello."

"Dad. This is Francis. I have to talk to you. I don't want to upset you, but I have some news about Nick."

"Son, what is it? Did you hear from him? Is he ok? Did he get my e-mail?"

"No, I haven't heard from him directly, but I have some news about him, and I want you to know that I will find out what's going on..." Francis said, as he felt himself getting choked up.

His father interjected, "Going on? Francis, listen, I can tell you're upset, but tell me, what has happened? Is he in some kind of trouble?"

Francis took a breath and composed himself, reining in the

feelings he had for his brother that he had suppressed but were now coming to the surface. "Dad, I'm not sure who he's working with, but Nick is involved in something very wrong. For starters, he... he killed a boy in Turkey and left another one hospitalized. Before I arrived, someone, she's not sure who or where he was from, someone pulled Marina into his car and began to ask her about Nick and what the two of them were up to."

His father did not reply immediately as if waiting to hear more details, and then asked, "She's alright, I hope. Did he hurt her?"

"No, she was pretty shaken up and... Dad, I have to find him. No one else knows him like I do. I need to track him down and stop him before he hurts someone else," Francis said with some difficulty; his feelings began to impede his speech, and he felt tears begin to form in his eyes.

"Francis, you do what you have to do. Is there anything I can do? I can call some of the people I still know at the agency, maybe they have some information, maybe they can help. The guy looking for him, was he CIA?" his father asked.

Francis smiled. He had never heard his dad string off so many words one after the other. Perhaps the emotion of the situation was getting the better of him too. "Dad, I don't want to upset you anymore than I have, but if you do find anything, maybe you could pass it on to someone I've been dealing with at the FBI, Frank Reynolds. I can give you his number. I'm not sure that I'll be able to keep in touch with you, but I'll try," Francis replied.

"Do you know where he might be?" his dad asked.

"No, I'm not sure where to start, but I have some information about some of the people at Atlas. I can start there."

"Ok, son, be careful. I'm afraid that I've already lost one son and your mother; I don't want to lose you. I love you, boy. Take care."

Francis, with the phone to his ear and his head in his hand, wiped away a few tears and said, "I love you too, Dad. I'll see you back home. Goodbye."

Marina had been waiting outside the office, and, when she realized Francis had hung up the phone, she came back in. She stood above him, brushed his hair back with her hands, and kissed him on the forehead. Francis had never cried around Marina, and he quickly pulled himself together.

He stood up and gave her a hug, and returning her kiss. Still holding her in his arms, he looked at her and said, "You know I really wanted to spend some time with you, but I have to leave."

She smiled. "I know. I knew it as soon as I saw the composite. I'm still going to the United States for the Fourth, and I will see you then. If you've found Nick by then. I don't imagine you'll have time to call me, but, if you need to talk, don't hesitate."

"Yes, of course. One more thing, I think I already know the answer, but when the DNA analysis results are in, let me know what you find," Francis said.

"I should have them in less than forty-eight hours."

Francis looked at her and then asked, "Are we—"

Marina finished his sentence, "Alone? Yes, my boss has gone home. What did you have in mind?"

Francis hadn't taken his hands from around her waist. He removed his right hand from her left hip, and, putting it inside her lab jacket, began to caress her body. She responded by placing her hands around his neck and burying her head in his chest. She felt her heart race and her breathing quicken. She wanted to make love to him right there, but she found herself grabbing his hand.

"We still have one more night together. Perhaps we should wait until we get back to my apartment. I know you're upset about your brother, but maybe we should go get something to eat. We can talk about it, and then spend a nice evening at home."

Francis smiled. It had been a long day, and, after she'd spoken to him, her lab didn't really seem like the place to make love after all. "Sure, you're right. Let's go get something to eat."

Istiklal Caddesi, Istanbul

The restaurant was not particularly crowded, which suited Francis just fine. They had talked about a lot of things and decided on their last night together they would not talk about Nick or the stranger who had assaulted Marina. Work was definitely off limits, too. At first their conversation was labored as they struggled to find something to discuss, but then it clicked, just like back at Johns Hopkins when they had first met.

Francis looked over at Marina, remembering their first date and how he had fallen in love with her right away. They started talking about Baltimore and the places they had gone and the things they had seen: The Charles Theater, Fells Point, blue crabs, the Inner Harbor, Haussner's Restaurant, Little Italy, the brew pubs, all the unique culture that was Baltimore. Even though neither one of them was a big baseball fan, there was something special about going to an Orioles game at Camden Yard. They had friends that were big fans and frequently insisted they go along. Marina particularly liked the Baltimore Museum of Art, and Francis agreed with her, it was one of his favorites.

They continued to reminisce about the early years of their relationship, agreeing Little Italy was one of their favorite places, especially Sabatino's. "After all this talk, I'm really looking forward to going to the conference," Marina said. "Is there anyone you want me to drop in on at the school?"

Francis shook his head no; he really didn't keep in touch

with anyone in Baltimore anymore, despite his fondness for the city. The waiter had cleared away their meals and began to serve them coffee. When finished, he walked back into the kitchen, and they were alone in the restaurant; all the other patrons had left.

"That's what I like about this place. Sometimes they leave it all to me, and I can just relax and not think about anything," Marina said. The booth they had been sitting in was hidden in the far rear corner, away from the door leading to the kitchen and the stairs that led to the upstairs bathrooms.

Francis, sipping his coffee and lost in conversation, did not notice the man as he slowly came out of the shadows formed by the light fixtures that hung down between the kitchen area and the restaurant booths. He spoke as he approached them. "It looks like you've had some time to clean yourself up."

Marina turned. It was the man who had pulled her into the car and held her at gunpoint. Yitzhak approached with his gun drawn. He had them cornered. He was standing with his back to the front exit and the hallway near the kitchen that led to a back door.

"This is not the man you're looking for," Marina said with a firm voice. "This is my fiancée. His brother is the man I told you about!"

Yitzhak laughed and said, "I told you not to lie to me once before. I can tell when people lie. Now I want you to stay here, Ms. Aryan. You, Nick, or whatever you are calling yourself, stand up and come with me."

"The name is Francis. Nick, my twin brother, has left the country. And don't talk to my fiancé like that again," Francis said, sizing the man up and looking for any weakness. The man in front of him carried himself with tremendous confidence, and Francis knew he would have to look hard to find a crack.

"I don't think, Francis," Yitzhak said with emphasis, "that you are really in any position to tell me how I might treat her. She is guilty as well. I know that you're working together on the virus and—"

Francis interrupted, "What virus? What the hell are you talking about? What is Nick up to?" Then it came together, the man in Cyprus, the man in Iraq, and Nick. They were one in the same. Nick had not simply murdered some innocent teen in Turkey; he was involved in something much bigger and more sinister. Francis stood, and Yitzhak stepped back, but, still holding the gun out, pointed it at Francis's forehead.

Francis glared at the man. "You shoot me, and you won't find my brother. Now I want you to get out of my way. I have to go and find him."

Yitzhak was not having any part of it, and, with the same confident look he had on his face when he had first approached them, he said, "I've already found Nick. Turn around and put your hands on your head."

Francis hesitated and looked at the barrel of the gun again. He looked over at Marina. "Frank," she said, "I don't want you to get hurt. Do what he says."

Francis turned slowly to his right and put his hands on his head. Yitzhak approached, and Francis felt him jam the gun into the back of his neck and begin to search him with his left hand. Francis found his opening.

Yitzhak had his left hand in Francis's pocket. Instead of just patting him down he had mistakenly put his hand in. Francis had only a second to react. He turned to his left, pivoting on his left foot, and extended his left hand down and around Yitzhak's left arm, locking it in place. In the same instant, he had pivoted completely around and extended his right arm across Yitzhak's neck, moving toward Yitzhak's rear. Francis had hoped to turn the other way and control the arm that held the gun, but there were chairs, and the end of a table prevented him from moving that way. He had Yitzhak pinned with his left arm and had broken his balance and extended his right arm completely around his neck, locking his head as well. He dropped his weight and fell into a kneeling position, smashing Yitzhak's lower back against his knee. Francis's body was positioned parallel with Yitzhak's, and, as Yitzhak tried to bring his right arm and hand across his chest to shoot, Francis released the lock he had on Yitzhak's left arm, and, blocking and grabbing at the same time, ended up grabbing Yitzhak's right wrist and applying a Sankyo lock. With this lock, he was able to turn Yitzhak's wrist up and away from him and lock his elbow in place. Yitzhak still fired, unloading the clip into the ceiling above Marina's head.

Marina screamed as the waiter and a cook came running out of the kitchen, the cook carrying a large heavy knife. Marina noticed their approach, and, speaking in Turkish, begged them off of Francis, explaining he was the good guy. The waiter cautiously approached Yitzhak from his right side, not knowing Yitzhak had spent all his rounds, and grabbed the gun, yanking it out of his hand.

Francis said to Marina, "Tell him to look for handcuffs or whatever he might have to restrain me. This guy is pretty strong." Marina did so, and the waiter said he could not see any, as he nervously looked Yitzhak over. The chef had left and returned carrying a small spool of some heavy rope.

Marina saw it, and said, "Frank, he has some rope. I will ask them to start tying him up."

Francis said, "Yes, tell them to start with his right hand and pull it down and around his back." The men began to tie Yitzhak up as he protested and began to give away his identity as he started to curse and use Hebrew words, which Francis immediately recognized.

CHAPTER SEVENTEEN

Al Fashir, Sudan

Condensation was dripping off the plastic that lined the tent. Nick, in the protective suit, could feel himself begin to sweat almost immediately after he had put it on. The children, while restrained, were no longer sedated, but Nick could tell the inoculations had been successful, at least on four of the five. The boy who had coughed when Nick had given him the germ was not infected, but Nick decided that four would be sufficient. The boy was awake and alert, but obviously terrified. He did not speak, but continued to look at Nick in anticipation of what would happen. Nick could see he had been crying, and he decided not to bother with him for now. The boy would be taken care of later, along with the others.

The other four children had fevers; Nick had verified this by taking their temperatures with the digital thermometer. Most had fevers well above forty degrees centigrade, one of the girls, the smallest, had a fever closer to forty-two degrees centigrade. The conscious boy began to speak in the Dinka tongue of his tribe; his gag had worked itself loose.

He spoke again, and this time it was in English which made Nick more anxious. "Mister? Mister? Please, the girl next to you, she is my sister, please do not hurt her," the boy said in amazingly clear English. Nick did not address the boy and continued his work. "Please, mister," the boy said again, this time louder. "My name is Awan, and my sister is Amiol. What is your name, and why are we here?"

It was more than Nick could take. Setting down the scalpel, he went over to the bench and found a container of potassium chloride and one of sodium pentobarbital. Filling two large syringes, one with the potassium chloride and one with the pentobarbital he went over to where the boy was. Without hesitation, he restrained the boy's head with his left

175

arm, pushing it away from him, exposing the veins in his neck. He stuck the one loaded with pentobarbital into the boy's left jugular vein and waited for it to take hold. The boy jerked back as Nick let go of his head. He looked directly at Nick and said one last time, "Please, mister," the last part slurring as the drug took hold. Nick waited for only a second and then followed the barbital with the potassium chloride. The boy's breathing remained steady for a few seconds, and then he took one last deep breath and was dead.

Nick returned to the bench and picked up the scalpel again, and, this time, a bottle of ether and a rag. He didn't want any of the children squirming around as he proceeded with his tasks. Moving to the first child he had treated, he opened the bottle of ether and soaked the rag, but not completely. He held it over the girl's mouth and nose until he was certain she was unconscious. When he removed the rag, he could see some green blood-speckled mucus running out of her nose and down the side of her face. Holding the scalpel in his right hand he cut the chest strap so that he could get to her chest. The girl's breathing was very shallow, and he could hear that her lungs were filled with fluid. He made an incision just below her solar plexus, cutting across her body from her right side to her left.

Next, he made an incision starting at the solar plexus and going just down to her navel. The blood that started oozing from the incision was not the bright red that one normally saw, but had more of a blackish tone to it. Nick spread open the t-incision he had made, and, reaching down with his left hand, he pulled aside her liver, pushing it over to her right side. Next, with a large pair of cutters that looked more like garden shears than a surgical instrument, he cut along the sternum toward the girl's neck. He was glad they were children; it was not as difficult as adults would have been. With his right hand, careful not to cut himself, he reached into the opening and sliced away with the scalpel at the diaphragm that was still attached to the underpart of the rib cage, so he could get to what he was after.

Once the way was clear, he set the scalpel aside and reached in with his right hand again. The lungs, now partially exposed, but still covered with the pleural membrane, were now accessible. He looked at the lungs and could see that fluid had begun to build up inside the pleural sac and chest cavity. The fluid was black as well, but blacker than the blood had been. According to the instructions that had been passed on to him from Dr. Statnekov, that was all he would need. The fluid, once dried and reduced, would contain the active virus. Nick knew he didn't have to cut the girl open, and probably could have drawn the fluid out through a much smaller incision, but he wanted to be certain it had the right color and was at the right stage. And he did sort of enjoy the more gruesome approach.

Nick went back to the bench and found another syringe, this one much larger and with a larger gauge needle. He stuck it into the pleural sac and began withdrawing fluid. The black viscous liquid was speckled with pus and coagulated blood, but it didn't contain many loose chunks of flesh. Nick drew out almost a liter of liquid in two hundred and fifty milliliter increments, squirting it into a large flask. He could hear the sound of the needle as it made a sound like sucking spit when it caught some of the larger pieces of coagulated blood. The girl had bled out a large volume of blood at this point, and her breathing was much more shallow and staggered.

He moved on to the next child, another girl, and, using the same mucus-coated rag, which now also had blood from the first victim, he gave her a dose of ether. This girl was sweating much more profusely, and her eyes, while open, were bloodshot and cloudy. Nick thought her infection may have progressed more rapidly, and, when he had cut her open, he found he was right. The fluid inside the pleural cavity had many more disintegrated pieces of her lung, making it more difficult to suck up the fluid. He noticed the infection had spread to her liver as well. Because of the state of disintegration of her tissue, he was not able to withdraw as much fluid as from the first child, only getting about five hundred and fifty milliliters. He put this in the flask along with that from the first child.

The infections in the remaining children were closer to that of the first child, and Nick quickly withdrew the fluid, finally ending up with about three liters altogether. Leaving the children to bleed, he distributed the liquid into four seven-hundred-fifty-milliliter centrifuge bottles. He would have to spin the containers for about thirty minutes to extract the virus-containing material from the liquid.

While the material was spinning away, he went from child to child and applied a lethal dose of potassium chloride directly into the heart of each. Nick stepped back, looking over the children who lay in front of him. His only thought was that he had completed the entire process in a little over an hour. One hour and fifteen minutes, he thought with a smile of pride.

When the samples were ready, he placed the containers in a liquid nitrogen bath to prepare them for the next step. They would have to dry overnight, so Nick left them and went through the crude decontamination procedure, first cleaning himself thoroughly with straight chorine bleach inside the area where he had dissected the children. As he left the tent, there were no men watching him from a distance; there were no men in sight, not even Dr. Al-Fardi. He heard no sounds, except for the sound of the AC unit of the tent and the lab. He went back to the lab, showered once more, and went to sleep.

Istiklal Caddesi, Istanbul

Yitzhak struggled against his bindings, and when Francis removed the gag, he yelled obscenities and spat. Marina knew the staff well, and one of the waiters had remained to lock up when they were finished. She and Francis had finally been able to convince the chef not to call the local police, at least not right then. They needed time to interrogate Yitzhak.

Francis said nothing, waiting for the man to calm down. He seemed to have boundless energy and was not at all willing to cooperate. After tying him up, they had bound Yitzhak to a chair. Francis was straddling a chair that was turned around with the back facing Yitzhak. Marina was pacing the room, and, to Francis's surprise, had shared a cigarette with the waiter. He had never known her to smoke before, but considering the run-ins she had had with Yitzhak, he didn't say anything. He was beginning to tire and his thinking seemed cloudy, perhaps from the time change, perhaps from the events of the past two days.

Yitzhak did nothing but stare back at him. He had finally stopped fighting against the bindings, but had drawn blood on one of his wrists in the struggle. The waiter had made some fresh coffee and poured a cup for Francis and one for Marina. Francis again held up his red passport and his Homeland Security ID together in his left hand and showed them to Yitzhak. "Ok," Francis said after taking a sip of coffee, "like I said two hours ago, this is who I am. We have the same goal in mind: stopping my brother. I know you're Israeli since I understood the Hebrew when you told me to kiss your ass. Do you think you're ready to tell me what you know? If not, I've had it. I'm thinking of turning you over to the police, but I just might leave you here with the waiter. I heard he use to box, and he's obviously pissed off that he has to stay here so late. I'm sure he had better things to do."

Yitzhak's eyes were still intense, but Francis could see the man was getting fatigued. Setting the passport and ID down on the table, he reached over to undo the knot of the gag. This time Yitzhak did not draw back or protest, so Francis knew he was ready to talk. The first thing he said was, "Let me have some of that coffee."

Francis looked over at Marina, and she went to find the waiter, who had gone into the back to get some sleep. "She will bring you a cup," Francis said, "but I'm not untying you just yet, so she will have to help you drink. Now, tell me why you want my brother and where you think he may be."

"It's personal," Yitzhak said.

"Well it's even more personal for me," Francis replied. "Let me guess, you ran into my brother in Iraq, and he kicked your ass." Francis joked. He was still angry, but felt some pride knowing that the D'Abruzzo twins had bested this guy.

Yitzhak didn't reply at first, and then said, "I didn't see him, but I did kill ten of his close al Qaeda friends." Marina had arrived with the coffee and set it down next to Francis's. She lit another cigarette and went back to the booth where they had been sitting earlier. Francis nodded a thank-you. In responding to Yitzhak's remark, Francis hesitated; he couldn't understand why his brother would be associated with al Qaeda. The only philosophy he had ever exposed was that crap he had read about in the Turner diaries. He had never had any association with Islam or al Qaeda.

Then he remembered the link he had seen on the screen in the Electronic Command Center back at his office, the link about the suspected ties between al Qaeda and white supremacists. He knew Nick was intelligent and had traveled outside the country before. He was obviously the right choice for whatever evil deed they had assigned him.

Returning his attention to Yitzhak, he said, "Tell what you know about my brother. Where did his friends say he would be going?"

"If I knew, do you think I would have come here? I would already be on the way out of this country," Yitzhak said.

"My guess is you know something, but not enough, and you still think Marina is involved somehow," Francis said.

Yitzhak looked back, as if to say, well, that's obvious and asked, "How about some coffee?"

Francis looked at the cup that Marina had set down and back at Yitzhak, "Not just yet. Besides, it's still too hot. I wouldn't want you to burn yourself after all you've been through tonight."

Yitzhak sighed and finally seemed to give in. "Ok, one of your brother's friends told me that he was going to Spain. I'm not exactly sure where or who he'll be meeting with there. He never gave me a name and place, just Spain. That is all I know."

Francis could tell he was lying, that he knew more, but he also knew he wasn't going to get anything else out of him. "Spain. Ok. That's it, huh?" Francis asked one more time.

Yitzhak nodded yes. At least Yitzhak had corroborated some of the information he had from Jim—the money transfer to bank accounts in Spain from Atlas Genetics.

Francis stood and said, "Ok, I think we're finished." Marina stood up and came over to where Francis was standing. He whispered in her ear, "Tell the waiter to call the police and give him this for his troubles," and handed her a roll of twenties. He looked down at Yitzhak. "I'm going to leave. The waiter will set you loose in three hours. That will give me plenty of time to catch my flight."

CHAPTER EIGHTEEN

Madrid, Spain, Barajas Airport

Nick had gotten pretty accustomed to the long and arduous traveling he had been doing, but this trip was especially difficult. The flight from Khartoum to Cairo had been delayed, and when they arrived in Cairo, they had to circle for nearly an hour and a half. The flight from Cairo was supposed to be direct to Madrid, but was diverted to Barcelona. The crew of the Iberia airline jet never said why, and the people at the airport in Barcelona were even less forthcoming. To make matters even worse, Nick would have to go to Madrid to get a flight to Cadiz. He had already missed the connecting flight since the plane had been diverted, so he had to first make arrangements to fly from Barcelona to Madrid and then from Madrid to Cadiz. Thinking back, he should have taken the flight to Gibraltar from Cairo, but it wasn't until the following day, and Nick was anxious to get out of Africa and thought Gibraltar would have tighter security. There he would have to go through the British and Spanish security checks.

The only thing that made the trip bearable was that he was able to move quite freely through customs with his Irish passport. As a bonus, Al-Fardi had acquired some exceptionally exquisite export papers for the samples, and he had no problems getting onto the plane with the metal briefcase full of "medical samples." He was supposedly bringing back material and samples for tsetse-fly research. He had to hand it to Al-Fardi; he had covered all his bases and had made the experience both productive and quick.

Nick exited the plane and had a two-hour wait in the air terminal for the short flight to Cadiz. He was traveling fairly light with only the metal suitcase and a small overnight bag with a few clothes. The terminal was crowded and busy. It seemed to Nick that just about every Spaniard who walked by him bumped into him or cut across his path. It was not at all what he had expected, and they all seemed to be quite pushy and rude. He thought it would be more like Buenos Aires. While the pace of the city in Buenos Aires was, at times, quite fast, the people were somewhat more polite.

Nick sat down on a bench next to his check-in area. There weren't too many people waiting for his flight. He didn't have anything to read and looked around at the Spanish people making their way to terminals or exits. He never thought he would appreciate Europe as much as the United States, but at least they didn't all look like they wanted to kill him. Admittedly, he was pissed off that he had to make his way through Spain, and would have preferred to head to Argentina in a more direct manner, but Olsen had made some arrangements with Dr. Statnekov that required Nick to spend about four days there. He was to arrange for the final payment and provide some of the viral samples he had collected. Maybe Dr. Statnekov had some sort of weird personal attachment to the bug. Nick didn't know, and he didn't care. He would make the payment, hand off the sample, and head to Buenos Aires. He figured he might be able to complete the tasks in fewer than the four days Olsen had agreed to. Statnekov didn't sound like someone he wanted to hang out with. For Christ's sake, he was older than his fucking dad.

Nick went back to staring at the people who passed. As he was looking at the crowd, he saw a school group walking his way—about ten children, boys and girls. He didn't know how old they were, maybe five or six. They were split into pairs, holding hands and walking one pair behind the other. Nick was impressed with how well dressed the children were in pressed pants and small cardigan sweaters. They all seemed very well groomed. He glanced over his shoulder as they passed, and the woman with the group gave Nick a pleasant smile.

Nick realized he was gripping the handle of the metal suitcase with his right hand as it lay on his lap. His grip was very firm and strong, too strong, so he loosened it up, but didn't dare let go. He looked at the suitcase and back at the line of children who had faded off into the terminal, and thought back to the final day in Al Fashir, after the samples had been dried and packed into the metal suitcase. The suitcase was thoroughly cleaned with bleach, and Nick made sure to again clean himself very well.

He went outside the tent and was greeted by Al-Fardi and one of the two men who had been at the improvised trap range. Al-Fardi said, "I guess we're finished with this now. Let's go back to the lab and have a drink." By the time he had finished, it was just getting dark, and, as he walked away with Al-Fardi, he could see that the other man had started to dismantle the tent. He stopped and looked as the man removed one support after the other and pushed the billowed tent material toward the center. The man doused the area with more than ten five-gallon drums of gasoline. Al-Fardi tried repeatedly to get him to continue on to the lab, but Nick insisted on watching. The man finally came toward the two of them, and, standing next to them and about twenty feet from the collapsed gasoline-soaked tent, he withdrew a flare from a bag he had slung over his shoulder. Striking the top of the flare with the inverted cap, he lit it, held it for a brief moment to make sure it was completely lit, and tossed it directly into the center of the tent material. Instantly, the gasoline ignited and shot flames about fifteen feet into the air. As Nick and Al-Fardi drove off into the darkness toward Khartoum, Nick looked back to see the glow of the fire as the men that remained continued to feed it with whatever combustible material they had, making sure nothing would remain that could infect them.

Nick heard the call for his flight, and, grabbing his bag, and the case, headed toward the gate.

Madrid, Spain, Barajas Airport

Francis hated leaving Marina alone after what had happened and after only being with her for a few days, but she assured him she understood. His feelings for her had only grown stronger in the time they had spent together, and he told her that before leaving the restaurant. He hadn't called his boss since he still had two weeks off, but figured he would have to call him soon if he were about to venture into territory outside his duties at the Department of Homeland Security. Nor had he called his father again, who was already upset by the news he had given him the last time they spoke. The one person he had called was Reynolds, only to get his voice mail. Francis had left quite a lengthy message including the details about the composite drawing of the murder suspect, the details of the encounter with Yitzhak, and the confirmation from Yitzhak that Nick had been in Iraq.

The only thing he had to go with now was an address, the address for Dr. Andrei Statnekov, and that was incomplete. He didn't have a street number, just the name of the street and the city, Malaga. He didn't have a phone number. At first, he thought he could check with the US Embassy in Madrid, maybe they could get an address and phone number, but he didn't want them to keep him from finding Nick. Something inside him said maybe he should turn all of it over to the pros, that he was stepping well beyond his training, experience, and abilities, but he felt if he gave in and went to the embassy, it would get bogged down and Nick would have moved on to the next part of his trip. Francis knew he couldn't risk that.

The flight attendants had assured him he would make his flight to Malaga; he did with plenty of time to spare. The plane was loaded with British and German tourists heading to the beaches on the Costa del Sol; he looked out of place in his wrinkled pants and shirt. After leaving the restaurant in Istanbul, he didn't return to Marina's apartment to get his bag and clothes, but went straight to the airport and got the first flight to Spain.

Fortunately, Francis had spent some time in Spain, having studied Spanish for one summer as an undergraduate in Salamanca. He had never been to Malaga, but had been to a small town nearby, just east of the city. He and a few friends from the language school had also spent a night in Gibraltar, just for the heck of it. So this part of Spain was not an unknown entity to him, and, while he hadn't studied Spanish for quite some time, he did frequently read in Spanish and was fairly competent.

The flight was short and getting through the busy airport was not a problem since he had no luggage. The first thing Francis did when he got out into the lobby was to find a copy of a city map. He sat down on a bench outside the front entrance of the airport and opened it up. He found the street, Calle Ayala, and, unfortunately, it was longer than a few blocks. Francis had thought if the street were one of those little streets one typically finds in Europe, he could just go there and start asking around the neighborhood. Instead, he would have to get some help. He thought the police or Guardia Civil would be suspicious, so he went to what he figured was the second best source of information in the city after the police. Walking over to the taxi stand, he found a taxi driver, a stocky older man, sun beaten, wearing a beret, sitting on a bench reading a newspaper and smoking a cigarette. While most of the other drivers were younger and Moroccan, this man had a look that said he was in charge.

Francis knew he couldn't flash his passport or Homeland Security ID; they would really mean nothing to the man and might cause him to be suspicious. As he walked toward the man, he looked up over his paper, with the cigarette dangling from his mouth, and motioned with his head that Francis should go to the taxi that was waiting at the stand; he was on break. Francis continued to approach, ignoring the man's gesture and sat down next to him. In Spanish, he said, "I need some information, and you look like someone who would be able to tell me what I need to know."

The man hesitated, set down the paper, and replied, with a mild Cockney accent, "And what kind of information would a Yank like you be needing besides where's the best place to get a bleedin hamburger and French fries with keetchup?" drawing out the last word. "I'm on break, you can talk to the pretty lass at the kiosk." He picked up the paper and took a draw on his cigarette.

Francis didn't quite know what to say next, but decided it was best to be straightforward with the man, without giving away too many details. "I'm looking for a Russian. I have a street name, but no number. Perhaps you can tell me what part of the street, or what part of town, I would find Russians. I mean, is there a club or a particular restaurant?"

The man set down his paper again, and turned to face Francis. "There are many clubs in town. Looking for some Russian tail, are we?"

Francis had forgotten that the word "club" in Spain had the same connotations as "massage parlor" does in the United States. Francis didn't respond to the man's remark, and said, "I can give you 100 Euros for the information, but I need the name of a restaurant and maybe a person, if you know one."

The taxi driver was about to make another smart-ass remark, but instead said, "I'll take 250, but honestly, lad, I don't think you want to have anything to do with the Med-vedkovskaya. I mean it, lad, they make those wop bastards in the *Godfather* films look like lady cricket players."

Francis was astonished the man would display such concern for his well-being and ignored the racial remark, but said, "200 and let me worry about the Russians."

The man took a draw on his cigarette. "Ok, lad, there's a pub at the intersection of Calle Ayala and Calle Orflia. You can go there, but only talk to the owner, Leonid. He's not Medvedkovskaya, but he is Russian. He's a good bloke, and can give you information, but he may be more expensive than I am. Ta." He stood and threw the cigarette on the ground. "On second thought, I'm off my break now. How about I give you a lift there? You seem like you'd be a good tipper."

Cadiz, Spain

Like his twin, Nick had not called Andrei in advance, but he knew Andrei was expecting him sometime that week. Nick had the address, but was not sure exactly where the doctor's house was located, but he knew it wasn't far from the beach. Maybe it was the one they flew over on the way into La Parra Airport in Jerez De La Frontera, but he wasn't sure.

The ride over to Cadiz from the airport, while not as fun-filled as the ride in Athens, had its share of thrills. The driver, a small energetic Moroccan man who spoke little English, drove quickly, swerved in and out of traffic constantly, and made liberal use of his horn. Nick had learned, from similar rides in cabs in Buenos Aires, to sit in the middle of the backseat when inside the city limits, just in case the driver ran a light and was hit from the side. The driver would periodically ask, in what little English he knew, "You American sailor? You from Rota?" Nick would shake his head as the man looked back, still accelerating and executing daredevil turns through traffic. Nick thought the man was an idiot. If the man knew anything about the Navy, he would know Nick's longish hair and scraggly beard were hardly Navy issue. Nick pulled at the beard and decided he should shave it off before heading to Buenos Aires. Perhaps another change of hair color was in order as well.

As the man pulled up to a two-story bungalow on Calle Honduras, he turned and said, "No Navy. You CIA?"

This time Nick found himself laughing as the man had a strange contorted face when he said "C I A." He laughed. "You're goddamned right I am. Now let's just keep that between you and me." As Nick got out of the backseat, the man, who had already run around the back and removed Nick's bag from the trunk, came to the side and extended a hand to take the silver briefcase. Nick drew the hand with the briefcase back and said, "I can take both."

As the cab drove away, Nick looked up and saw a grey-haired, robust-looking gentleman wearing a beach robe and a bathing suit approach him from the front door of the bungalow.

"Mr. D'Abruzzo, hello. I am Dr. Statnekov. Let me take your bag. Please come inside."

Nick had recognized him from the pictures he had seen back at the Olsen ranch, even though he was probably ten, or maybe even twenty, years older then in the pictures.

"I received a message from someone else in your company. He said you knew he was coming, and he would be here tomorrow afternoon. He said not to call him. I assume you know who it is?" Nick had received the message from Olsen and knew Whitaker would come to meet him. He didn't really see any need; he was still able to operate and complete the task despite the problems in Athens, Iraq, and Izmit.

Nick walked into the house and was impressed by the furnishings and decorations. It seemed the doctor was well-traveled as he had many exotic items on the walls and on the many bookshelves. The doctor motioned for him to follow and headed into a large professional-looking kitchen. "How about a drink?" Dr. Statnekov asked.

Nick set the briefcase down. "Sure, do you have any bourbon? Or maybe I'll just have a beer."

The doctor went to the refrigerator and took out two bottles of beer, opened them, and poured them into two pint glasses. "Ok, tell me about the trip. Tell me about your experiments. How did they go?" Dr. Statnekov asked after taking a long sip from the glass.

Nick never really cared for small talk. He just wanted to

finish his business with this man and get on with it, but he took a sip and said, "I don't really care to talk about Iraq or Turkey, but, as far as the Sudan is concerned, the experiments went fine. Only one of the subjects did not get infected, but, from the examinations of the others, I'd say that everything went really well."

"Good," the doctor said. "Did you know I am the one that discovered it? I am the one that re-engineered it." Nick had known he was the man who had made a ton of money selling the virus to Iraq and Iran after the fall of the wall. He wasn't aware he was the one, who had found it, and he really didn't care, but he could see the look of pride in his face. "If I had been in America, they would have named it after me," Statnekov continued, "but in the Soviet Union it was simply known as K-7, for the region where it was found, Kuznetsky, and for the level of modification. At first we thought it was a variant of the Crimean-Congo Hemorrhagic fever."

"We first found it in a coal mine. It seems the dust in the mine worked as a carrier for the virus. The miners breathed in the dust, and it made it easier for them to be infected. We didn't realize this until later and tried to use similar compounds in a dispersal system. However, despite all the genetic modifications we made, it is still difficult to culture. That is why it was never weaponized in the Soviet Union. We couldn't use humans like you and your associates." Nick thought back to the children and took a swig of the beer. He couldn't believe he still thought about them.

Statnekov said, "It was really very surprising, you know, that we couldn't infect sheep or goats or pigs, or even chickens. We could infect monkeys, but they only developed mild symptoms. We rarely used cattle, but then someone from the agricultural bio-weapons department suggested that we try it on cattle, with the idea that it could be used against the American beef and dairy industries. It was really quite astonishing. Those cattle looked just like the people I first saw suffering from it when we found it. It was carried by rats

190

that were living in and around the coal mine."

Nick didn't interject and simply nodded, sipping his beer periodically. "We later found other strains of the virus in the coal mine where we first saw the outbreak, but we couldn't infect cattle with it, even though it seemed to be perfectly viable and not much different from the original strain."

"Then it happened that a colleague of mine, a rather careless fellow, accidentally infected himself while trying to isolate some of the coat proteins from the virus. It was really quite sad; we didn't even let him leave the level-four laboratory. We just turned off the lights in the lab, so that we wouldn't have to see his death. Well, anyway, his mistake was a boon to my research. After isolating the virus from him, we could then infect cattle. It seemed that once it had passed through the body of a human and then through cattle, it became even more virulent then before. We never did infect any other humans, either by accident or on purpose, but I could tell that with every successive pass through the cattle, it became even more terrible."

"Is that it? In the case you have at your feet?"

Nick replied, "Yes, yes. I hear that I'm supposed to leave some with you. I guess you've found some more buyers?"

The doctor did not reply, but instead stepped forward, finished his beer, and said, "I have a container. We can transfer some of K-7 to it, once you have settled into your room. Please let me show you to your room, and we can go out later to eat if you like. Cadiz has a wonderful nightlife. We can have seafood tapas and sherry. I suspect that after the Sudan you might like to go out and have a good time."

Nick picked up the silver suitcase, and, since the beer had relaxed him, replied, "Actually, it would be nice to head out tonight. Let me know what time."

Malaga, Spain

The two large men in front of the bar glanced at Francis as he made his way from the taxi toward the bar. The smaller of the two was standing on the left side of the closed door and he stepped forward to confront Francis. The taxi driver had told Francis what he needed to do, and Francis didn't deviate from the instructions he had been given. He didn't speak or advance beyond a point about three feet in front of the door and had a 100 Euro note ready in his right hand, which he held out; as the man approached, he could clearly see it. The man took the note, and Francis turned around so he could be frisked and searched for any weapons. The larger of the two doormen hadn't moved and didn't look over as the smaller man checked Francis over thoroughly. In Spanish, the man asked for an ID, and he showed them his driver's license rather than his passport. Finally, the large man opened the door, pushing it open with his large hand and forearm. Francis entered as the smaller man stepped aside and continued to watch him until the door slammed shut behind him.

In front of Francis was a set of stairs, one going up and the other heading downward. The taxi driver had not told him about this, but he could hear low murmuring and music coming from upstairs, so he followed the sounds upward. As he made his way to the top of the stairs, he could smell cigarette smoke and the murmurs became more distinguishable as the sound of drunken men speaking Russian. Francis had no experience with the Russian language and felt completely vulnerable. He began to think the taxi driver might have set him up. Regardless, he pressed on and reached the landing and a doorway leading into a small crowded room with a long bar running down the left side toward a large window with a shade drawn. The men continued with their drinking, card playing, chess games, and smoking.

Francis immediately went up to the bar and stood at one end, trying to get the bartender's attention. The bartender finally noticed Francis and moved toward him speaking in Russian. Francis said in Spanish, "I would like to speak with the proprietor, please." The bartender recognized Francis was not Spanish or even European, but he also noticed the fifty Euro note in his hand, and, taking it, he replied in Spanish, "One minute, I will get him."

By now, some of the other customers in the bar had noticed Francis, and, realizing he was not Russian, became a little less boisterous, but continued drinking and playing games. The bartender brought over a bottle of vodka and two glasses, and, as he returned to his work, another man, well-dressed with glasses and balding, not exceptionally tall, approached Francis and asked in English, "Would you like a drink? My bartender told me you would like to talk to me."

Francis refused the drink and before he could talk, Leonid continued, "You look really out of place here, and I might add nervous. Why don't we head across the hall to my office?"

Francis considered his suggestion, but said, "I'm fine, but I will have a drink." Leonid poured two drinks and asked, "Now, what can I do for you? Do you have business in Spain?"

Francis kicked back the vodka and didn't sip it. He knew that would be frowned upon by this crowd. He extended his glass out, indicating he wanted another, and he said, "I need an address. I have the name of a doctor. He is Russian, and I would like to talk to him. I was told that you could help me."

"And what do you want with this doctor?" Leonid asked somewhat suspiciously.

"He has information about my brother, who I am trying to find. I haven't seen him for years. He is estranged from our father. Our father is gravely ill, and I really want my brother to know so that he can make his peace with him," Francis said.

"What is his name? I will see what I can do," Leonid asked.

Francis took another drink and said, "His name is Andrei Statnekov. He apparently lives somewhere on Calle Ayala."

"Yes, Calle Ayala. I am familiar with it. There are many Russians living there," Leonid said, "but the doctor you are looking for, he, he no longer lives there, he has moved. Actually, he still has an apartment there, but he is currently living elsewhere."

Francis felt Leonid was protecting the doctor for some reason. He held out his glass for another drink, and then reached into his pocket and laid three hundred Euros on the bar. Leonid filled Francis's glass and his own and then downed the vodka. Francis did the same. Taking the money in his hand, Leonid folded it and put it into his pants pocket. "Normally, I would ask for more, but, considering the situation with your father, I will give you a break. The doctor is nearby, just up the coast. He is in Cadiz. I will give you his address. I hope that he will be able to help you find your brother."

Francis headed out the front door, starting to feel the effects of the vodka. His cell phone rang, and he answered.

"Frank, I just wanted to talk to you, but I also have the DNA test results. They are a match; it was definitely Nick," Marina said.

Francis already knew that it was; the results didn't tell him anything new. "Marina I hit a dead end, but I have another lead. Everything went ok with the Mossad agent?" Francis asked.

"Well, he was only in jail for less than a day. The Israeli embassy got him released. Apparently, he had diplomatic immunity," Marina said.

This made Francis angry because he knew that Yitzhak had a better lead on Nick than he did. He would undoubtedly have to square off with him again.

The guards he had encountered when he first entered the bar nodded that he should move on, and Francis was more than willing to oblige. As he walked toward the intersection to get a taxi to the airport, he got another call. Looking at the display, he saw it was Reynolds. "Hey, Marina, I need to call you back. I have another call from the FBI," Francis said.

"Ok, sure. Be careful, Frank. I love you!" Marina said.

Francis answered the call. "Reynolds, you got my message?"

"Yes, yes, I did. Where are you? Are you still in Turkey? I confirmed the identity of the agent you met in Turkey. Now I think it's best that you come back home and let us handle this. Tell me what else you know and where you are, so I can send someone to meet you," Reynolds said.

Francis had always had pleasant conversations with Reynolds, but he could tell he was angry. It was a side he hadn't experienced before. Equally upset, Francis replied, "I'm close to my brother. I'll find him and call you when I do. If I turn it over to you, it will be too late."

Reynolds said, "You don't have the experience. You will jeopardize any future operations and, worse, you could get hurt or killed, and I don't want to see that happen."

"I'll call you in a day," Francis said.

Reynolds started to reply, but was cut off by his assistant who said in the background, "Mr. Reynolds we have a problem. There was a raid on an ammo depot in Idaho. There were..." Reynolds looked at him and nodded, he then returned to the call. "Francis you... Hell, I got something here. I have to go. You know I can trace this call, damn it!" With that threat, he hung up and Francis shut his phone off. He decided to rent a car since he couldn't see any better way to get to Cadiz quickly.

Cadiz, Spain

Nick hadn't expected to stay out as long as they had. He and the doctor went out around eleven the night before and didn't get home until seven in the morning. Contrary to what he thought in the airport in Madrid, Andrei wasn't at all like his father. For an old man, he knew some pretty hot young women, too. Mostly in their late twenties to early thirties, but far better than anything he had seen lately. Nick had to hand it to the doctor, the man knew how to live, that was obvious. They started the evening going from tapas bar to tapas bar eating seafood and drinking sherry, mostly Manzanilla. Nick hadn't had any sherry before, expect for cooking sherry, which the doctor explained was not at all the same. The dryness of the sherry and the saltiness of the shrimp, squid, crab, and other crustaceans seemed a perfect combination.

Nick was never big on eating well-prepared food, preferring grilled meat or fast food. He did enjoy crabs and, growing up, the family always had one or two crab feasts per summer with other families in the neighborhood, Chesapeake Bay blue crabs. The crabs at the tapas bars, while not quite as sweet, did bring back memories of the crab feasts. They spent almost three hours moving from one bar to another. Pretty soon the doctor had gathered a small contingent of female friends who joined up with them as they moved down the street. Nick noticed Andrei was very physical with them, and they didn't seem to mind, only occasionally scolding him. Hell he was doling out a lot of money, buying drinks for everyone. As the evening wore on, they eventually ended up at a club. By this time, the young ladies they had met at the tapas bars had moved on, or finally hooked up with their boyfriends, after partaking of the doctor's generosity. To Nick, it seemed such a waste, since the girls just wanted drinks. He supposed the doctor just loved the attention it brought to him.

Nick rolled over in bed and looked at the clock on the nightstand. It was almost 12:30 p.m. Sitting up in bed, he immediately settled back down, took a deep breath and yawned. He couldn't remember how much sherry he had drunk, nor could he remember how many glasses of cognac he had had at the club. Initially, he matched the doctor drink for drink, but later had to slow down. There was no slowing down the doctor though.

Nick sat up in bed and raised the shade, the kind that was built into the window frame; he had lowered it before going to sleep. It was slightly drizzling. The city was still silent, which was not surprising since it seemed most of the city had been out all night along with him and Andrei.

After showering and dressing, he went to the kitchen and found Andrei sitting, reading a paper, drinking coffee, and eating some pastries. He looked up from his coffee and said, "Great night last night, eh? Please, have something to eat."

Nick couldn't see how a man more than twice his age could do it. Maybe being independently wealthy and having a bevy of young female friends keep him in shape. Andrei turned to Nick and said, "Your associate called. He'll be here around two or two-thirty." Nick nodded, he felt like going back to sleep, but the doctor insisted he join him on a walk on the beach. Even though they weren't more than a few blocks from the ocean, Andrei insisted the two of them ride over on one of his motorcycles. It was a Harley, not unlike one of the bikes Olsen had back in Montana. Olsen never let anyone ride any of his bikes, but Nick had ridden before and had gone with a few others from the ranch to Rapid City, South Dakota, and other biker events.

They walked around the beach near the Cadiz lighthouse for about an hour, watching the sunbathers and the fishermen on the stone pier. When they finished, Andrei let Nick drive the bike back to the house. As Nick cruised through the streets of Cadiz with the doctor on the back, he almost forgot about what he had been doing for the last few weeks. That was until he approached the bungalow and saw Whitaker waiting outside the front door smoking a cigarette. Nick stepped off the back of the motorcycle as Andrei put down the kickstand and turned it off. "I wasn't expecting you until much later in the day," Nick said as he approached the house. The doctor, who had removed his helmet and walking next to Nick, extended his hand in order to shake Whitaker's.

Whitaker tossed his cigarette to the ground. "I'm John Whitaker," but he didn't shake the doctor's hand.

"I am Dr. Statnekov. Did you have a good journey? Perhaps you would like something to eat?" Andrei said. Whitaker didn't reply and walked toward the front door. Nick looked at the doctor and shrugged. Whitaker was never a big talker, but he was generally more personable; perhaps he had had a bad journey.

As they entered the house, Andrei headed toward the kitchen, and Nick started to head up to his room. Whitaker came up behind him and grabbed his shirt at the elbow and said, "Nick, listen, I need to talk to you. There is something we need to discuss."

Nick was starting to turn the corner toward his room, and, turning around, he said in a somewhat annoyed tone, "Sure, give me a minute. Go have a beer with the doctor. He's actually a pretty nice guy."

Still holding onto Nick's arm, Whitaker said, "Fuck the doctor. I need to talk with you, and I need to talk to you now. We have a problem, and it really can't wait."

Nick turned around completely to face Whitaker, and, looking at him, he could see he meant business. "Ok, come back to my room. We can talk there," Nick said. Once in the room, Nick closed the door behind him. He had left the silver briefcase on the floor between his bed and the nightstand. He looked over instinctively to make sure it was still there.

"Nick, I want to give you a chance. Hell, I'm just going to come out and say it. Since you've been gone, Olsen has been consumed with getting the damn virus. I just wanted to let you know I think it's all been a big mistake and a waste of time and money. We can do what we want without it. Time is running out," Whitaker said.

Nick didn't reply, but looked shocked that Whitaker would be second-guessing any decisions that Olsen had made. He had never shown any signs that he was anything but loyal to Olsen and the cause. Nick replied, "I think we're right on schedule, and after the shit I've been through, I'm not going to quit now. It will just get easier from now on."

Whitaker looked over at Nick. He raised his arm to gesticulate and make a point, and Nick could see the Glock nine mm in the holster on his belt. Whitaker caught him looking at it, but continued anyway. "Listen, those two guys that shot you up in Athens. Who knows who they are? I think you're risking too much. Maybe they've picked your trail up again." The strap on the holster was undone. Nick stopped and thought for a moment. All he had told Olsen was that he had run into some trouble. He had never said how many guys were involved. There was no mention in the news of the number of people involved, and he never told anyone he had been injured. He looked at Whitaker and said, "Athens. You knew I was hurt and that there were two men. The message I sent to Olsen never mentioned either fact. You're the one that made the call; you're the one who tried to stop me."

Whitaker took a step back and made a move for the sidearm. Nick caught him with a right upper cut to the chin, knocking him back into the dresser. Whitaker fell but was able to remove the gun from the holster, but he dropped it as he hit the floor. The gun slid under the dresser.

"You won't get away; I have some people outside. I wanted to give you a chance to join with me," Whitaker said as he lay against the dresser, rubbing his chin. Nick could see he was reaching around behind his back, probably for a spare gun or a knife, and without hesitating, he kicked Whitaker in the jaw. The contact sounded like a bat hitting a fat pitch, and this time he had knocked him out. He shoved Whitaker aside and reached under the dresser for the gun. He went to the bed and gathered his papers, including his passport and the briefcase and headed out the door.

He saw Andrei in the kitchen, and, against his better judgment, said, "We need to get out of here, and we need to do it fast. Give me the keys to your motorcycle." Nick knew he should have just left the old man there, and if he were anybody else he would have, but he knew what Whitaker's friends would do to him if they caught him alone. Andrei was accustomed to sudden departures and didn't hesitate, tossing the keys over to Nick. Nick opened a small screen on a window near the front door, and, looking outside, saw a car with three men sitting across the street from the house. There was a lot of traffic; Nick knew that he could use that to their advantage, and he saw his opportunity. A bus had stopped in traffic waiting for the light to change at the corner. Nick knew the light was not long so they had to act fast. Nick and the doctor, without helmets, made their way toward the motorcycle that was still parked where Andrei had left it. As Nick and the doctor sat on the bike, Nick looked up and saw that there was a lookout standing near the intersection. Nick had missed him. Drawing a pistol from inside his jacket, the lookout started making his way toward Nick and Andrei as he yelled into the microphone headset he was wearing. The bus had moved, and Nick heard the engine of the car with the three men start, but he did not look back. Nick took a swift left turn into traffic and used the bus as a shield from the lookout with the gun. He hadn't had time to secure the briefcase and was holding it in his left hand, making it difficult to apply the hand brakes evenly, but Nick had no intention of using the brakes anyway.

He was unfamiliar with the streets and could barely hear Andrei as he told him where to turn. First he made a left onto Calle Zorrrilla and gunned the engine, zooming past Plaza la Mina, reaching almost 60 mph.

"Take a left onto the next street, Calle San Pedro," Andrei yelled. The car had been slowed near the Plaza, but had managed to get within half a block of Nick and the doctor, before they had to make the left turn, almost missing it. By the time Nick and Andrei had gone down Calle General Luqua toward Plaza Espana, the car was right on their tail. Traffic had become heavier, and Nick had to slow to swerve between cars. The skinheads had turned on a flashing blue light, and cars began to get out of their way. Nick and the doctor made one loop around the Plaza, and, as they exited, made a right onto Avenida del Puerto.

The car was about a block behind, and Nick knew that they could now lose them on Avenida del Puerto, which led down the peninsula and onto the mainland. Within two blocks, they ran into two new problems: construction was blocking traffic in both directions, and they had gotten the attention of the local police. As Nick turned right onto Calle Rubio Y Diaz to avoid the construction, he could see two police cars were directly behind the car with the skinheads. The road was clear and Nick was able to get the bike up to speed again, but, following the instructions of Andrei, made a quick left turn onto Calle Rosario, followed by another left onto Calle Nicaragua. At the end of Calle Nicaragua, they came to Paseo de Canalejas. Nick gunned it across the park and back onto Avenida del Puerto. Now Nick had clear sailing toward the bridge that led out of Cadiz. He didn't stop for any of the lights and approached 110 mph. The sound of sirens disappeared.

Cadiz, Spain

Francis had knocked on the door and used the doorbell, but there was no answer. Maybe the doctor was out or out of town, or maybe he had been tipped off by the Russians in Malaga that Francis was on his way. Depending on how deeply he was involved with Nick, Francis could see the doctor might not want to stick around. "Damn it," he said to himself. He would have been there over four hours earlier, but he got stuck in traffic along A376. They were repairing the road, and traffic was stopped on the way to Cadiz. Traffic the other way was stopped because of a serious accident so he was screwed either way. On the map, it looked like the best route, since the route along the coast seemed longer. It was getting dark, and Francis looked in a window next to the door and saw there was a light on in the kitchen, and the refrigerator door was open. He tried the knob; the door wasn't locked. Something was up. In a city like Cadiz, they would lock their doors.

Francis entered the house and closed the door behind him. He looked into the kitchen and saw there were three open beers sitting on the counter along with an opener. The house was quiet. He thought maybe the doctor and the others he had been with had been abducted, or, worse, maybe they were somewhere in the house, incapacitated or murdered. Knowing what Nick had done in Turkey had him thinking Nick was capable of anything. All he knew was that he was unarmed, and, if Nick was still in the house, only God knew what he would do if they saw each other. The house had two floors with two rooms upstairs and one bedroom on the ground floor. Francis checked them all. In one room, the carpeting was pushed to one side, and there was a small stain that looked like blood next to the large dresser. Everything else seemed to be in order. He checked every closet and then finally went in the small office on the ground floor. The office had a computer and was filled with medical journals of all kinds, in several languages—Russian, English and German. There was also a small Dewar flask, or an insulated container for storing liquefied gases, on wheels, something Francis had never seen outside a lab. Opening it up, he saw it had a full supply of liquid nitrogen.

As he was closing it, he heard someone come into the house. Looking around the room for some sort of weapon, he found none. The hallway outside the office had become dark and the sun had set. He left the light on in the office, but slipped out into the hallway and behind the staircase. The staircase steps had openings between each level, and Francis was able to look between them toward the front door. Whoever had entered was in the kitchen. Francis could tell by the sound of his feet on the tile floor. It couldn't be the Russian doctor why would he be sneaking around? Maybe it was another Russian, one of the people Francis had seen in Malaga. God, he hoped not. He wasn't ready to take on the Russian mob. Maybe they had set him up in Malaga, perhaps the doctor didn't even live here. Alright Francis, let's stop doubting everything, he thought to himself. Paranoia was not his style.

The intruder came around from the dining area and was backlit by the light from the kitchen. Francis could see that he had a gun drawn in his right hand. The man began to move toward the staircase. Francis saw he had a flashlight in his left hand and reached over to turn it on with his right. If he stayed where he was, he would be seen so he swiftly and quietly moved back and toward his left, into the room with the bloodstain. Once he heard the man go up the steps, if he did go up the steps, he would make his way toward the kitchen. If the man didn't, he would have to confront him. Looking around, he grabbed a sculpture that was next to the nightstand as a weapon. The man came straight down the hallway with the flashlight shining in front of him. If Francis had stayed hidden where he was, he would have certainly been noticed. As the man started to turn into the office, Francis decided to make his move. He came up behind him, raised his hand and firmly hit the man on the back of his head. The man staggered, dropped the gun, and tried to turn around to face his attacker. As he did so, the light from the flashlight illuminated his face as he fell to the floor. Yitzhak. Francis grabbed the flashlight and pulled Yitzhak into the small bedroom where he had been hiding. Apparently, Yitzhak had known all along where the doctor was; the unexpected stay in the Turkish prison had just delayed him. This time he decided not to tie him up, but instead held him at gunpoint. He propped Yitzhak up in the bed and tried to revive him. He was out cold, and his breathing was extremely shallow. Francis didn't think he had hit him that hard, but he knew he had to keep him alive. Yitzhak knew more than he had told him before in Turkey, and Francis was at a dead end. Francis turned on the light next to the bed and tried one more time to revive Yitzhak. After about ten minutes he was conscious. His initial reaction was to try to get up. "I wouldn't try and get up. I have your gun," he said.

Yitzhak sat up, pulling himself into a sitting position on the side of the bed. He was still groggy and sitting up made it worse, but he toughed it out. "Mr. D'Abruzzo, Homeland Security. Don't you think you're out of your element? Put down the gun and leave this to the professionals."

"I'd say I'm doing just fine for a non-professional," Francis replied. "Now let's not waste time. I imagine if you had given me the information I needed, this could have been over already. Tell you what. I think that maybe we should call a truce. Maybe we should work together on this. I'm willing to give it a try—"

"I don't need your help. If you want to cooperate, give me the gun and go back to your desk job in Washington, D.C.!" Yitzhak demanded, moving to Francis's inside he grabbed Francis's wrist with his right hand and tried to push the barrel of the gun back toward Francis and release it from his grip at the same time. The room was small so Francis didn't have a lot of space to operate. Moving toward his left, he allowed Yitzhak to move his arm in the direction he was trying to, even allowing him to move the gun barrel back in direction where Francis had been. At the point where the gun was almost free from his grip, Francis grabbed Yitzhak's arm with his right hand, locked the gun in place with his left, and, using Yitzhak's motion and energy, extended his arm down and across his body to Francis's left, and, just as quickly, put him into a wrist lock taking Yitzhak's balance.

Francis had only intended to subdue him and regain control of the gun, he had not intended to injure him, but what happened next could have happened to either of them. The gun went off, one shot. By now, the barrel had been redirected toward Yitzhak. As he fell, the one shot hit him square in the chest, just to the left of his heart. As soon as the gun fired, Francis felt Yitzhak's one last attempt to gain control of the gun and then his grip loosened and he let go. He tried to get up and was able to partially stand, but then fell again to the floor.

Francis looked at the gun, and then at Yitzhak, "I should have tied you up. Why did you come at me?" he said. Yitzhak did not answer, but managed to push himself up and lean against the dresser. Francis set the gun down and leaned over to try and give Yitzhak some assistance, but he was waved off. Yitzhak was applying pressure to the wound with his right hand, but it was not helping very much and his clothes were quickly becoming saturated with blood.

"Listen to me," Yitzhak began talking, "There is nothing you can do for me. I should just tell you to fuck off, but it is more important that someone stop your brother. I have a phone in my jacket; there is a number for Ricardo Moreno. Call him. He can tell you what you need to know." He took one more breath, looked up at Francis, and slumped over, dead.

CHAPTER NINETEEN

Portugal

Nick and Andrei had made it out of Cadiz without any problems. The police didn't follow them, nor did any of Whitaker's friends pick up their trail. About five miles outside of town, Nick stopped and secured the briefcase in one of the side luggage containers. Nick didn't want to stop again, but Andrei convinced him it was safe to stop in Caceres, at least long enough to drop him off. It seemed the doctor had yet another house and a girlfriend there. He promised to give Nick some money he said he was in need of. Fortunately, the good-natured doctor took everything that had happened in stride, gave Nick five thousand dollars, and told him he would deal with Olsen as far as getting the rest of his money.

Nick left the doctor and headed west to Portugal. He made great time and only stopped once outside of Badajoz to refuel the bike and get something to eat and drink. By the time he made it to Lisbon, it was just getting dark, but he was able to find his way to the airport. Fortunately, he had stowed the counterfeit export documents in a side compartment of the metal suitcase, and he wouldn't have to worry about finding anyone to create some for him.

One thing he had to do was change his appearance; that was certain. The airport had a small shop, and he bought a disposable razor, some hair bleach, and some earrings. Nick was also able to find a store and bought a sweater, some different shoes, and a sports bag into which he put the metal briefcase. Finding a bathroom, he entered and went over to the sink, first shaving and then bleaching his hair. He didn't seem to attract much attention dying his hair, but he did get a few looks when he pierced his ears using only the sharp end of the earring itself. Some German tourists watched him and said something in German, but Nick, in German, told them to fuck off.

He drew some blood that dripped into the sink, but he winced only slightly. The pain was nothing; he'd felt much worse at the ranch in Montana. Olsen constantly tested his men, and he was particularly impressed when someone tolerated pain. Some of his favorite tests involved using tools, including vice grips and nail guns. Nick always faired pretty well in the sadistic tests Olsen liked to perform. Olsen had clenched onto Nick's earlobes with a vice grip not letting go for a good ten minutes.

The right earlobe went pretty easily, but the left one took a little more work. After three tries, he finally was able to pierce his ear. The earrings he chose were not too ostentatious, simple imitation diamond studs. He looked up into the mirror and saw his now clean-shaven face and blond head of hair looking back at him. He hoped there wouldn't be any problems with the passport, but he didn't look drastically different, just enough so he would probably not be easily recognized.

He had finished up and was putting everything in his bag when the cell phone he had purchased in Turkey, which he had forgotten about, rang. He was hesitant to answer, thinking it could be Whitaker, but didn't know the number though, nor did Olsen for that matter. He had given it to Andrei before he left him in Caceres, but he didn't think he would call him. He looked at the display, and there was no number showing. The phone rang again, and he answered. "Hola?" Nick said.

The voice on the other end said, "Oh, sorry, I must have the wrong number." It was his father. That bitch in Turkey must have given him the number, he thought. They must have traced the one phone call he had made in Turkey. The phone was obviously a liability; he would have to get rid of it.

The phone rang again. This time he looked at the display,

and there was a number from Spain showing. He suspected Andrei must have been calling him. He waited for the fifth ring and answered, this time in English. "Hello?"

"Nick? Nick? This is your brother. Where the hell are you? I'm in Cadiz. Nick, if you're in trouble, I can help you," Francis said.

Nick froze and listened to his brother talk. He didn't say a word. He was in Cadiz! Shit, he couldn't be too far off his trail. Nick didn't say a word. He turned off the phone, and, holding it in his right hand, smashed it down on the corner of the sink, shattering it.

Cadiz, Spain

Francis dialed the number again. He knew it was Nick. The voice was unmistakable. He looked down at Yitzhak's stiff lifeless body. He thought: Maybe I should at least call someone and tell the person he is here. Or I could call Reynolds and he could pass the info on to the Israelis, but after our last phone call, I think I'll let the local police know after I have left the city.

He also didn't want any more attention from the Israelis, all they had done was slow him down. He would certainly have caught up with Nick if Yitzhak hadn't gotten in his way. Francis paused and listened, thinking that he must have come with some backup. There was no sound, however, except for the city sounds and a few people walking by on the street. Francis next scrolled through the list of names on Yitzhak's cell phone and found the number of Ricardo Moreno. It was obviously a Spanish name, but when the phone began to ring, Francis could tell it was connecting with a long distance number. Finally a groggy sounding voice could be heard answering the phone. "Hola, Moreno."

Francis said in Spanish, "Mr. Moreno, my name is Francis D'Abruzzo. I am with the US government. A friend of yours gave me your number; he said I should call you. It is urgent. It is about my brother."

"I need more information than that. What about your brother and what friend of mine?" Moreno replied.

"The man that gave me your number is Israeli, Yitzhak. I don't know his last name, and he has been after my brother for a few weeks. He is carrying a very lethal virus," Francis said.

"First of all, Yitzhak was not a friend, let's just say that I helped his people find a few people here, and, second, he already spoke to me about your brother, and faxed me a description. There is really nothing that I can talk to you about. We have men posted at the airport. If he is on his way here, they will catch him. Are you calling from the United States?" Moreno asked.

"No, I am in Spain. I think I only missed my brother by a few hours. Where are you? Mexico?" Francis asked.

Moreno laughed, and said, "I am in Buenos Aires. I hardly think my accent is Mexican."

"Yes, Argentina. My brother has friends down there. I can't remember their names offhand, but he has been there before. I imagine he knows his way around," Francis said.

"As I have already said, we have the airport secure. There is only one way to get here and that is through the international airport in Buenos Aires. I have spoken with someone at the FBI, and they are sending a man down here to assist. Now, if you will excuse me, I need to get back to sleep. I have the day off tomorrow, and I have an early start planned," Moreno said.

"A day off! I don't think you understand the urgency of this. My brother is working with a terrorist network, and they have something awful planned. Who knows how many people could die from what he has with him!" Francis said loudly into the phone.

"Mr?" Moreno hesitated.

"D'Abruzzo," Francis replied.

"I am fully aware of what is at stake, and we have the situation under control. You really have no idea where he is or if he is coming here. Ask Mr. Izenberg, Yitzhak. He only had sketchy information. He also had information that he would be heading for Canada. Maybe you should be calling the Mounties and harassing them while they sleep?" Moreno replied.

"Yitzhak is dead. He told me to call you; he didn't mention anyone else. Based on that, I would say he was pretty certain that Nick was going to Argentina," Francis said.

The line was dead. Moreno had hung up, obviously feeling that the conversation was going nowhere. Francis thought he should call him again, but decided there was no point. He had to get to Buenos Aires. The only way to get to the airport by tomorrow morning was to drive straight to Madrid.

He looked over Yitzhak's body and found a passport and a wallet. He also found another gun tucked in a holster on his ankle. He thought about taking it, but there was no way he could get it on the plane, even with his government credentials, and, when he got to Buenos Aires, he was sure they wouldn't allow it. Francis started to dial his father's number, but stopped short and headed out the door to his car to begin the long drive to Madrid.

CHAPTER TWENTY

Buenos Aires, Ezezia International Airport

There were few people on the Lufthansa flight from Lisbon, so Nick was able to stretch out on the entire row of seats in the middle of the wide-body jet and slept really well. His earlobes felt numb, and on the back of one a scab had crusted over during the night. He had been awakened just before the plane was beginning its descent into the Buenos Aires metropolitan area, and immediately noticed the bag he had bought that had the metal briefcase in it was missing. Fortunately, before he tore the plane apart, the stewardess told him she had stowed it during the night after it had fallen off the seat to the floor. Nick gave her an insincere thank you when she handed it to him. He could feel the heavy metal briefcase was still inside.

The airport was not very busy, and Nick decided that was not a good thing; it was too easy to be noticed. He didn't know if Mossad had a clue where he was going, since he hadn't heard anything about them since the Sudan. Did Whitaker tell anyone down here? Did Whitaker know? He wasn't sure, and it made him unusually nervous. Nick could see there were a few more guards in the airport then the last time he was there, but, considering the hard times, he figured they were there to protect all the foreign visitors against petty theft and the ubiquitous scam artists. Nick followed the few people who were heading to the baggage area and then to the customs area.

He wished he had had time to come up with a better disguise. Even though he hadn't checked any bags, he decided to wait awhile by the luggage carousel and see if any other flights were coming in. The only other flight that had come in was from Japan, and he towered over everyone and couldn't exactly blend in with them. He waited about ten minutes with the few Germans who had come on his flight. He did look more European with his new hairdo and earrings and thought he could fade in with a group of about five young German men, but he hesitated. He looked around, and there seemed to be fewer guards then before, but he wasn't sure. Three of them were occupied at one of the customs' booths as they were collectively searching through the large bag of one of the Japanese tourists. He noticed that on the opposite end was a young female customs agent flirting with one of the German men. Ok, now's my chance.

He walked up behind the German man and had his passport open and ready to go. The German looked annoyed and turned around as Nick purposefully bumped into him, wanting to get a reaction from him. He turned and said something to him in German. The female customs agent touched the German man on his shoulder, and, speaking German, told him to relax. Nick handed her his passport and went around the German man's right side, keeping him between himself and the customs agent. She was obviously more interested in continuing the flirtation and stamped Nick's passport, waving him by. She didn't even ask him the customary questions about his length of stay and reasons for being there.

Nick was now on familiar ground and had a clear path to the exit and ground transportation. Nick looked over and saw there was an Internet café and realized he needed to warn Olsen about Whitaker, but that would have to wait. The airport was too risky. He walked outside, brushing aside all the offers from the independent cab drivers, scam artists, and thieves, and headed straight to the Manuel Tienda Leon bus line. He bought a ticket to Plaza San Martin and settled in for the thirty-minute ride into the heart of Buenos Aires. He looked around at the outlying communities and slums from the bus window as he made the way into town. Damn, this place looks like hell, he thought.

Fight from Madrid to Buenos Aires

Thinking back, he knew he had done the right thing. Francis had thought it was best to let the Israelis know about Yitzhak's death, and, along the route from Cadiz to Madrid, he stopped and made a phone call to the American embassy in Madrid, which he had on his cell phone, to get the number to the Israeli consulate and then phoned the Israelis themselves. Despite their requests, he gave few details surrounding the death of their agent, but he felt badly for the man's family and wanted them to get the body for burial. Right after he called them, Yitzhak's cell rang, and he figured it must have been the consulate staff. He transferred Moreno's number to his cell and tossed Yitzhak's phone into a trash can at a gasoline station.

When he had settled into the flight to Buenos Aires, he made another phone call. This time it was to his co-worker Jim. He hadn't heard from him since he had left, but it hadn't been long. He wanted to see if he had any more information on the Argentine doctor from Atlas Genetics. Jim didn't answer, so he left a message. He started to dial Reynolds' number, but, remembering what Moreno had said about the FBI already being informed, he thought he would wait. He hadn't talked to Marina since Malaga, but it was still early.

He didn't know what to expect, never having traveled to Argentina. Recently it was not a very safe place to be. He did remember his father had told him once they had some distant cousins there, but this was certainly no time to be looking up family, other than his brother.

Outside Buenos Aires, El Campo Polo Club

Nick had hired a car at the Hotel Plaza San Martin for the thirty-minute drive to the El Campo Polo Club on the outskirts of Buenos Aires, just past the town of Lujan. Dr. Zapiola's son, Ignacio, was to meet him there and give him some more liquid nitrogen for one final boost before he headed to the ranch to see the doctor. Nick knew Ignacio pretty well and considered him more of a brother than Francis. Hell, most of the Zapiola family were more like family to him than his own.

He had first met Ignacio at college when he was in graduate school and Ignacio was in veterinary school. He even dated Ignacio's sister, Veronica, for a short while when she was an undergraduate. He began to think back about how she looked—a tall redhead with a gorgeous figure. She wasn't butch or as trashy as some of the women at his university, and she dressed well. For the short time they were together, she really took care of him. It was hard getting her into bed since she claimed to be a pretty devout Catholic, but she finally relented, but only to anal intercourse. She said she needed to preserve her virginity.

Veronica was Nick's last real girlfriend, meaning someone he actually went out on dates with. He had even wanted to marry her, but she had told him she thought he was too angry, and there was something about him that made her uncomfortable. He laughed, thinking, I guess the bitch was right. I wonder what she would think of me now. The driver of the hired car overheard Nick talking to himself and looked back and said something, but Nick ignored him.

As they entered the club grounds, two armed guards approached the car and began to interrogate the driver. One guard motioned for Nick to step out of the car, but he knew they weren't the military or local police and wasn't worried. The times had necessitated that the club hire its own staff of security guards. There were too many things of value that the impoverished locals might want to steal or even eat, including the horses. The driver told the men he was not planning on entering the club. Nick stepped out and grabbed the bag that had the briefcase. He paid the driver and gave each guard a little bit for their troubles. They smiled and let him in after he told them he was there to meet Dr. Ignacio Zapiola.

The main building of the club was not too far from the gate, and Nick walked over quickly. He started thinking about Veronica again. She was into riding horses, and he wondered if she was here. Approaching the door, he was greeted by the smiling face of Ignacio, who extended one hand to shake, holding a mate gourd in the other hand. "Come in, it's cold. How was your trip? Here, please have some mate," Ignacio said, smiling the whole time.

Nick walked in and took the mate, drinking the entire batch of bitter tea as one was supposed to. "It was pretty good. I had the entire row in the plane to myself," Nick replied, setting his bag on the floor next to a desk that was in Ignacio's office.

"Is that it?" Ignacio asked, looking at the bag.

Nick was taken aback at first, and, remembering his cover, replied, "Yes, it's the bull semen your father told you about." Ignacio asked if Nick collected the semen himself, motioning with his hands as if Nick had to stimulate the bull's penis with his hands. Nick laughed, knowing Ignacio, a veterinarian, knew they used a teaser cow. "Do you mind me asking how much it's worth?" Ignacio said. "I mean, that's a pretty big case, how much could you possibly need here?"

"It's worth quite a lot. I really can't say exactly, but maybe your father could tell you. How is he doing?"

"He's great. I haven't seen him for awhile. He's been traveling for work, but I talked with him about two weeks ago," Ignacio said. "By the way, Veronica is here. She's about to go out riding. She is here with her... her fiancé." Nick didn't respond, but he did want to look at her again, and, for some reason, see the little prick she was going to marry. "Are you married?" Ignacio asked, sensing Nick probably didn't want to talk about his sister.

"No," Nick replied. "My job makes it difficult to date. I guess you still have your wife and one or two girlfriends on the side?"

Ignacio laughed. "By the way, I have some bad news. There's an airline strike for internal flights. It just started this morning. They're not sure when it will end, but I called my cousin, Jorge. He can drive you to Missiones. He said he was supposed to meet you there anyway. I'm leaving tonight for a conference in the United States." Nick looked pissed off, but knew he should expect such things in Argentina, especially these days. "Listen, it's no problem. He'll be here soon. I can give you the nitrogen, and you can leave either tonight or tomorrow morning."

Nick was about to reply, but was interrupted by a female voice. "Nick? How are you?" Veronica said as she entered the office. Nick felt his heart sink. He took a breath, turned around, and saw her standing there, even more beautiful then when he had seen her last.

"Good," he said. "Ignacio tells me you're getting married, congratulations." He wanted to get that out of the way and push aside any feelings he had for her.

"Yes, yes, I am, but we don't need to talk about that. Come outside, I want to hear about you and your family," she said as she took his arm and led him out the door. Nick smelled her freshly washed hair and body, and completely forgot about the briefcase. He didn't even hear it when Ignacio told him he would refill the container. Veronica always had that effect on him, always made him act like an idiot, a fool. "What have you done with your hair?" she asked.

"I needed a change. I thought I would look good as a blond. Women seem to like it," Nick replied, trying to get a dig in. As they walked outside, Nick could see a man standing over by a fence holding on to the bridles of two horses. He looked over at Nick and caught Nick's glare. "Listen, Veronica, I really don't have time to talk. Jorge will be here soon, and I have to leave. I have business. My father is fine, my brother, too."

"Nick, don't be mad at me. I really did like you, but you

216

know it wouldn't have worked out," she said.

"Trust me, I'm not mad at you, I just have a lot to do," Nick said. He kissed her on the cheek and turned to head back into the office, which now was empty. He looked on the floor and saw his bag was missing.

After about five minutes, Ignacio returned carrying the bag in one hand and the metal briefcase in the other. Nick gave him a look and Ignacio replied, "I added some more liquid nitrogen. That's a lot of bull semen you have. You could impregnate most of the cattle in Argentina." Nick didn't laugh and took both of the bags.

"Nick, man, you ok?" Ignacio asked.

"Yeah, no problem. Listen, I need to use your computer. I have to send a message to my boss."

"Sure, no problem, and, here, take this, it doesn't work in the US. It has my father's phone number in case you need it," Ignacio said, as he handed his cell phone to Nick. Taking the phone, Nick followed Ignacio into another office to use the computer.

Ezezia International Airport, Buenos Aires

Francis had gotten to Madrid in plenty of time to catch a flight. In fact he was about ten hours early. Since fewer people were traveling to Argentina from Spain, they had consolidated flights and moved them to the evening. He had never flown Iberia before and hoped he wouldn't have to again. It seemed there was no such thing as a non-smoking flight, and almost everyone, including the crew, smoked well into the late hours of the flight and then lit up first thing in the morning. Francis had smoked before, when he was a teenager, but it still wreaked havoc with his nasal passages, and made him queasy. Needless to say, it hadn't been the best of flights, and he was not feeling very alert.

Francis didn't have a bag so he made his way to the line for customs. He felt his nose running from the reaction he had to the smoke, and he sneezed vigorously. He had covered his nose and noticed some mucus had been expelled with the forceful sneeze. Stepping out of the line, he headed for a bathroom he had seen on the way to the customs area, right next to the baggage claim area. As he started to enter the bathroom, another man exited and momentarily kept him from entering.

In that brief instance, he felt both his arms being grabbed and heard the sound of the action being drawn on a large caliber machine gun. He recognized the command in Spanish to raise his arms and did so without hesitation. One man stepped to his left, with his sidearm drawn and pointed at Francis, as another man handcuffed him. The man who had come out of the bathroom and blocked Francis also raised his hands and was shaking. The man with the pistol pointed at Francis yelled at the shaking man to leave, which he did quickly. By now Francis was cuffed and held on to each side by a uniformed officer.

The man with the pistol finally spoke, standing close enough to Francis so he could smell the cigarettes on his breath. "Mr. D'Abruzzo from the United States, you are under arrest." Francis could only assume the obvious: Moreno's men had mistaken him for Nick. He didn't protest; he knew these men wouldn't listen; they had a job to do, and they felt they had accomplished it. Nothing was going to dissuade them from that. Much of the crowd that had formed when he had been detained were still glaring at the mystery man who had been taken into custody; others continued to go about their business.

Francis asked only one question as the men were putting him into a police vehicle, and, as he did so, saw the look of surprise on the man's face. "So how long until I get to see Ricardo Moreno?"

The ride to the headquarters of Argentine Intelligence

Service (SIDE) didn't take long as they sped down the motorway from the airport to the city of Buenos Aires. At one point, there was a parked car with its flashers on blocking the police vehicle, and the driver of the police car at first bumped the car and then pushed it further up on the curb to give them enough room to get by.

The car pulled up in front of the building near Plaza San Martin, and Francis was yanked out. He could hear one of the men proudly tell his compatriots he had caught the American terrorist they had been looking for. Francis shook his head. By now his sinus problem had gotten worse, aggravated by the exhaust smoke in the crowded city. He asked the men leading him into the government building if he could please get something to blow his nose. One of the men pulled out a handkerchief from his pocket and quickly wiped Francis's face. As they boarded the elevator, Francis could see a small crowd of uniformed men gathered to get a look at the terrorist. One was alternately looking at a piece of paper and at Francis, showing it to another man, who nodded his head in agreement.

They exited on the fifth floor and walked about halfway down the hallway. A guard walking ahead of the two who were escorting Francis opened a door to a small room with a table and four chairs. The escorts, without much concern for Francis's well-being, pushed him into one of the seats and took their places behind him, standing against a wall. The guard who had opened the door had not entered and closed it behind himself when the escorts entered. Soon a small man in a nice blue suit, smoking a cigarette, entered the room and sat down on the seat across from Francis. In his hands he had Francis's cell phone and passport, which the guards had removed from him at the airport as he was being cuffed.

The man looked at the passport and then at Francis. "You didn't have any luggage. Did you send the virus ahead? With another passenger? Do you have an accomplice?" he asked. The man's voice did not sound like the one he had talked to

219

from Spain.

"Let me talk to Moreno. You have made a mistake. I am not the man you want. Moreno can explain. I talked to him a few days ago," Francis said.

"Moreno? He is not here. So, did you get Moreno's name from your accomplices? How do you know his name? And, besides, you're dealing with me. My name is Juan Molino. Again, what did you do with the virus? Maybe you swallowed the test tubes, like a coke smuggler? How about if one of my men tries to extract them?"

The man continued throwing questions, but all Francis would say was, "You have the wrong man. You are looking for my brother. I need to talk to Moreno or someone from the United States."

CHAPTER TWENTY-ONE

Olsen Ranch, Montana

The message from Nick was brief: He was on schedule; he was headed to the third phase of his mission, and Whitaker had betrayed Olsen and his plans. It was late, so Olsen was alone in the control area. He had had his suspicions all along, and had thought there were others in his group who were disloyal, but Whitaker had never given any indication. Olsen knew the people who had shown more respect to Whitaker at times, three of them were sleeping in the small barracks area. The other men with close ties to Whitaker were located in Albany, New York, and Los Angeles, and he knew they could probably not be counted on for the planned attack on either area. The other group in Washington D.C. was definitely loyal to him and could be counted on.

Olsen sent Nick a brief reply, thinking maybe he needed some encouragement since he had been on the road alone for so long. Olsen sat back and wondered where Whitaker was at that moment. He hadn't called in, and, for all he knew, he was still in Europe, undoubtedly lying low with his skinhead friends, or, perhaps he had made his way to New York to join the crew there. He could be dealt with in time. Tomorrow, he would check with the nerds to see if Whitaker was trying to contact anyone on the ranch using the portal and instruct the nerds to lock him out. For now, he would assume the men here had not heard, or they would have left or tried something by now.

He stood and withdrew the Colt 45 from its holster and headed toward the barracks that had been set up just outside the cavern area. He covered the distance quickly and made his way to the first room where he knew two of the men were sleeping. The door was unlocked, and he pushed it open and stepped in. One man was sleeping on his stomach with his arms drooping off the side of the bed. The other man was sleeping in the fetal position with his face toward Olsen as he entered the room.

Olsen moved toward the man on his stomach, cocked the pistol, placed it at the back of his head, and fired. The other man sprung up in bed and reached for the holster he had hanging on the bedpost, but was caught in the chest with two shots fired off in succession by Olsen. Olsen could hear other men in the barracks getting up, and he could see the glow of lights coming out of some of the rooms.

Exiting the room, he was met by two men whom he knew were loyal to him. Behind them was the third man for whom he was looking, and, behind him, were some other men. Olsen stepped forward; the two loyal men stepped aside, and the man behind them looked into Olsen's eyes as he stepped forward with the gun pointed directly at him. The man didn't flinch. "I never would have followed him in the end. I always believed—" A small hole appeared in the center of his forehead. Olsen looked around with the gun still raised and yelled, "Anyone else care to come forward and let me know where their true loyalties lie?" There was silence and the men all lowered their guns. "Very well, get these assholes out of here."

Washington, D.C.

The Computer Analysis and Response Team had called Reynolds earlier in the day and left a message on his voice mail. He didn't understand why they hadn't called him on his cell if they had something important to tell him. Returning their call, Reynolds got hold of a junior technician in the laboratory. The others had apparently gone out for a late lunch. He was furious, and the tech knew it. "Listen to me, I need the results of the analysis of case number FBI-678654321," he said. The tech replied that he was not authorized to give the results, and he would have to wait.

"Listen to me again. I am giving you authorization," Reynolds said, "and if your boss finds out, I really don't give a damn. Now tell me what you've found, and I will see to it that you have a long and prosperous career with the FBI."

"Ok," the tech said. "It seems that the website that was found on their computer is a portal of some kind. We've found an encrypted communication system that can be accessed via the various images and attachments that are on the site. We've not yet been able to break into it or intercept any messages that have been sent by the system. As far as the website itself, it's hosted by a small service provider in Michigan. We've not contacted them because the guy that runs it is a well-known militiaman. We're ready to shut it down whenever you give us the signal."

"We can't do that yet, it will make whoever is using it suspicious. Anything else? What about the people who purchased the computer, have they been linked to anyone? Were there any e-mails or deleted files on the computer of any interest?"

"No, the hard drive had been purchased recently, and there were no files of any real significance, just the usual racist crap and anti-Jewish material. There was a story that had been downloaded about an incident in Montana. It was about some kid that got stabbed at a university in Bozeman," the tech said. Reynolds was silent. "Mr. Reynolds? Is there some significance to that file?"

"Maybe, maybe there is. How long before you think you can break into the communication package? And what are the risks? For instance, will they be able to tell that you're accessing the system?" Reynolds asked.

"We don't know for sure yet, but we'll let you know. Did you want me to send you that file that we found?"

"No, no, I have it bookmarked on my computer. Thanks for your help," Reynolds said. Next he called the FBI office in Denver. "Matt? This is Jim Reynolds from Washington. I need you to do me a favor. I need you to go to Bozeman and see if you can find out the whereabouts of Michael Olsen. This is really important, and we need something fast. Call me when you have any information."

CHAPTER TWENTY-TWO

Road to Puerto Iguazu, Missiones Province, Argentina

Nick had slept most of the night and woke up as he and Ignacio's cousin, Jorge, were just outside of Posadas. Jorge, with a mate gourd between his knees, looked over at Nick and said, "I am going to pull over so we can get something to eat. I need to get some gas and some oil, too." Pulling off the highway they drove for a few miles until they came to Posadas.

Sitting in the car while Jorge was filling the tank, the cell phone Ignacio had given him rang. He answered the phone and said hello. "Nick, this is Ignacio." He sounded weak, and his breathing sounded labored.

"What is it? Are you in the States?" Nick said.

"Yes, yes. Listen, I'm in my motel room in Arlington. I was going to tour around Washington before heading to the conference, but I feel like hell. I can hardly move, and my chest and stomach hurt. Have you seen my father yet? I wanted to ask him about a doctor he knows here. I don't want to go to the hospital. I would rather see someone my father knows. I tried to call him, but couldn't get in touch with him," Ignacio said.

"Well, we're pretty close to Iguazu. I'll try and call him. You know, the hospitals there are really good."

"Hey, man, listen, while I have you on the phone, I have a confession to make," Ignacio said, this time sounding worse, his breathing even more labored.

Nick waited and then said, "Ignacio? What confession? What are you talking about?"

Nick heard what sounded like vomiting or gagging and then again heard Ignacio's voice, weak and very low. "Nick, I looked at the samples you brought. I was going to take one; I thought you had plenty. You know times are tough. I thought I could sell it. The containers were large, and what the hell was it? It didn't look like bull semen. It was a powder. Was it some kind of drug?" Ignacio spoke, his coughing and wheezing making him difficult to understand. Nick knew right away what had happened.

"Nick?" Ignacio said. Jorge had come back to the car and saw Nick was on the phone. "What room are you in and what motel?" Nick asked Ignacio.

"I'm at a Homewood Suites on Columbia Pike, room 301. Why?" Ignacio asked. "I'm going to the hospital. Just tell my father that I'm sick."

"NO, no," Nick yelled, getting Jorge's attention. "Listen to me, I have a friend in Arlington who's a doctor. He's really close to your hotel. I can have him come by and look at you—sounds like the flu. I'll call him, and he can come by."

"Nick, really, I'll just call the front desk and have them get an ambulance. You don't, have..." Ignacio's voice trailed off.

"Ignacio?" Nick asked, but only heard the sound of gagging and then silence.

"What's going on?" Jorge asked. "Were you talking to Nacho? Is he ok?"

Nick looked over at Jorge. "He's sick; he wants me to call his father. Let's get going. I want to get there as soon as we can." He dialed a number on the cell phone and waited for the answer.

"Hello?" the voice on the other end said. Nick wanted to make the call brief and certainly didn't want to reveal too much of what was going on, but he needed someone to get to the hotel and take care of the room fast. The last thing he wanted was to have the virus start to spread prematurely. Everything had to be on schedule.

"Hey, I need a delivery done," Nick said, not using his name, but instead using the code. "Phoenix said that you are reliable."

"Yes, what is it?"

Nick gave the man on the line the name and room number of the hotel room. "We need the cleaning fluids sent over. You can let yourself in and leave them inside," Nick said. He knew the man would know what to do. He turned off the phone and looked over at Jorge, and said, "Let's get going."

Puerto Iguazu, Missiones, Argentina

About midday, Nick and Jorge entered the town of Puerto Iguazu on the border with Brazil. The town looked like all the other towns on the way there—dirty, with ratty feral dogs running loose, and dusty dry red soil. All the towns looked depressed. Nick asked Jorge if he had been to the town before, and he replied he had; he even had a few friends there. "We're going to stop by their house. They can make the fake tourist visa that you'll need to get into Brazil. They're really pretty good and inexpensive, too. Why didn't you just get one before you came?"

Nick gave him a look that said, don't ask, and Jorge obliged. They drove on through town toward the highway that led to Brazil, and at the intersection with the highway, two policemen were standing, talking, outside their car. They watched as Jorge and Nick drove up, and Jorge waved and smiled at the policemen. They didn't return either the wave or the smile and simply continued looking at the approaching car. This pissed Nick off. The last thing they needed was to get the attention of some corrupt small-town cops.

Just before they got to the intersection, Jorge made a right-hand turn into a small cluster of houses, many of which looked abandoned. The others were not particularly well made, and, again, the feral dogs and a few pigs were walking freely around as some children played a game of soccer on a

227

side street with a tattered half-inflated soccer ball. It was hot, and Nick wondered how the virus was holding up in the back seat. They approached one of the better-looking homes at the end of the road. It was surrounded by a fence and had a closed-in porch on one side. Parked out front were a nice-looking car, a pickup truck, and a motorcycle. The house, while not outstanding, was quite a contrast to the others they had passed on the way in.

Jorge stopped the car. "Wait here, I'm going to see if they're in. Their other car is not here, so maybe they went out." Jorge got out of the car, opened the gate in the fence, and went up to the house. He knocked, but there was no answer. He turned around, shrugged his shoulders, and started heading back out the gate. He leaned into the passenger side window and said, "We can wait. They know we're coming. I'm sure they'll be here soon." He motioned for Nick to grab the bag of food, and, more importantly, the container of mate and the thermos of hot water, saying "Want some mate?"

Nick shook his head no. What he really wanted was to get to Foz on the Brazilian side. They waited for about an hour, eating some of the food they had bought in Posadas, and Jorge drank mate.

Nick got out of the car and walked around the side of the house to take a leak. He didn't know why he was being so discrete; the entire place was filthy. Walking back into some undergrowth, he undid his fly and began to pee. He heard the sound of a car approaching the house rapidly. Great, Jorge's friends are finally here, he thought. Zipping his zipper, he started to return to the car only to see it was not Jorge's friends who had arrived, but the police they had seen earlier, along with another car. Jorge was up against the car on the passenger's side; in one of the police cars were two other people, undoubtedly Jorge's friends. Nick could hear them asking where the other man was, probably meaning him.

He ducked down below the fence and listened to see if Jorge would give him away, but Nick could hear Jorge say he didn't know.

Nick thought he should try to approach from the other side and surprise the police, but then thought better of it. There were four of them, and they had guns, cocked and ready to be fired. Jorge was cuffed and put into one of the police cars. Nick didn't really give a shit, as long as he had the virus. He could find another way across the border or just bribe someone. But one of the police officers got into the car they had come in from Buenos Aires, started it, and began to turn it around to follow the other vehicles that had already begun to make their way out of the neighborhood.

Buenos Aires, Argentina

Francis couldn't remember a more miserable evening. Most of the day they spent questioning him, giving him only water, and, once, some weak tea to drink. He couldn't understand why the FBI had not showed up. Moreno had said the FBI had been told; you would think they would have a man in Buenos Aires, or that the Argentines would at least have gotten someone from the embassy. Before being taken to the holding cell, he remembered asking them to at least be allowed to make a phone call to the US Embassy or to a family member. He was granted neither. The following morning, after finally falling asleep at around three a.m., he awoke in the dimly lit cell to the odor of cigarettes and coffee. He hadn't eaten much on the plane and was starving, the coffee whetting his appetite even more. Sitting up on the bench that passed for a bed, he cleared his throat; he was still suffering from the effects of the cigarette smoke on the airplane.

He heard a voice from outside the cell say, "Mr. Francis D'Abruzzo. Please accept my apologies. Mr. Molino can be a bit overzealous. Trust me, you will not be dealing with him anymore. I am Ricardo Moreno. I believe we have spoken to each other before."

Francis, though groggy, was furious and stood up and faced Moreno, looking at him through the iron bars of the holding cell. "Yes, I believe we have, but I also remember you telling me that you were prepared to catch my brother and bring him in. I don't recall you telling me that I would be afforded such wonderful Argentine hospitality. Where are the FBI guys you mentioned?"

"Mr. D'Abruzzo, I understand that you are upset. Please, again, accept my apologies. I am going to let you out. We need to talk more about your brother and any associates he may have in Argentina," Moreno said, opening the door to the holding cell and motioning for Francis to exit. As they walked together down the hallway toward Moreno's office, Francis saw Molino smoking and talking with some associates. Their gazes met, and Francis simply glared at the man, who, somewhat to Francis's surprise, averted his eyes and looked away. Perhaps Moreno had severely reprimanded him. They entered the office, and Francis sat down in a plush chair across from Ricardo's desk.

Moreno sat in his chair and said, "First things first, would you like some coffee? Something to eat? I will ask my secretary to bring something in for us. Next, here are your things." He handed Francis his cell phone and passport. Francis turned on the phone and saw there were two messages waiting for him.

"Did you wish to make a call?" Moreno asked.

"Maybe in a minute or two. What do you know about my brother's friends here? Anything? All I know is that the company he allegedly works for, Atlas Genetics, has an Argentine working for them, a Dr. Zapiola. Also, when he went to school, he met some Argentines. I think he even dated a women from Argentina briefly," Francis said.

"He is your twin brother?" Moreno asked in a somewhat puzzled voice, as if to ask why Francis seemed to know so little about him.

Francis, picking up on the tone of his voice, replied, "Yes, we haven't been particularly close in the last couple of years, but that's not important." Fumbling with his cell phone again, he checked to see who had called him and recognized the first number as Jim's, his co-worker. He looked at Moreno and said, "Let me check this call; I have a co-worker looking up information on Dr. Zapiola." Checking, he found Jim had left him information concerning the doctor, giving him the names of his two children, Ignacio and Veronica, and that they lived in the province of Buenos Aires. The next message was from his father, but he didn't check it. He passed on the information about the Zapiolas to Moreno.

"Good," Moreno replied, logging on to his computer. Calling up a national database of phone numbers, he looked for all listings under Zapiola and found over fifty. He did a subsearch for Ignacio and found three listings, Ignacio A, Ignacio B, and Ignacio L. He checked for Veronica and found one listing in the Recoleta neighborhood of the capital.

Francis was positioned behind Moreno as he searched the computer sites. Honestly, he thought, after the third-world treatment he had received from Molino, he didn't expect they would have any advanced computer systems.

Moreno dialed the number, and the two of them anxiously waited for a reply. A woman answered, but Moreno quickly established it was not Veronica. He explained who he was, and she offered a cell phone number. Moreno dialed the number, and Veronica answered. "Hola?"

"Ms. Zapiola, this is Ricardo Moreno of SIDE. I need to ask you some questions. First and foremost, do you know an American named Nicholas D'Abruzzo?"

"Yes. Is there something wrong? Did something happen to him?"

"We are trying to establish his whereabouts; we need some information from him. Have you seen him recently?"

"Yes, I saw him a few days ago, just for a moment. He had

231

some business with my brother and cousin," she said.

"So, he is here in Buenos Aires?" Moreno asked excitedly.

Veronica replied, "No, he left with my cousin. I'm not sure where they went—they didn't say. Perhaps my brother knows. I can give you his cell phone number."

"Yes, please do, and if you should hear from your brother, Nick, or your cousin, I want to advise you not to let them know that I am asking questions. It is very important. And if you should hear from them, please call me at this number," Moreno said, giving her his cell phone. "Please, what is your cousin's name?"

Veronica gave Moreno the information, and they hung up. Francis asked, "Where is he? Is he here?"

Moreno replied, "He was, but he has left. We need to check on the woman's cousin. It seems Nick is with him, or at least that's the last person he was with." Moreno called up another database and typed in the name Jorge Cabiniera. "We can look for any credit card transactions, airline ticket purchases, etc. We have it cross-referenced with different police databases around the country as well."

Again, Francis was impressed and saw that there were about ten hits, mostly credit card transactions. Nothing was recent, however, at least not since Nick had been in the country. "This boy has been in trouble many times before, mostly for drug charges and some petty crimes," Moreno said. Moreno moved his mouse to the last posting in the listing. "It seems that Jorge has been arrested recently. He is being held in a jail in Puerto Iguazu. That is up near the border with Brazil. We can call the local police chief on the way."

"On the way?" Francis asked.

"Yes, we can take a government plane there. It will only take about one hour and forty-five minutes. He was the last one to see your brother; he must know where he is."

"What about the FBI?" Francis asked.

Moreno smiled. "Sure, we can call them, too, if you like." As they left and got into a government car, Moreno dialed Ignacio's cell number. Someone answered, and Moreno asked, "Mr. Ignacio Zapiola?"

Nick quickly snapped back, "No, wrong number."

CHAPTER TWENTY-THREE

Arlington, Virginia, Homewood Suites Hotel

The firefighters and hotel staff were amazed the fire had been contained to only a few rooms. The blaze was intense, and some kind of accelerant had been used. Thank God for the sprinkler system, most of the hotel guests were saying to themselves. Chief Fulton of the Arlington County Fire Department had informed the staff crime investigators there was only one body in the room, and that the room was registered to an Ignacio Zapiola of Argentina. It seemed he was in town for sightseeing and had mentioned to one of the waitresses in the restaurant he was a doctor attending a conference. She also mentioned she had declined his invitation to join him for an evening of partying, having noticed he was wearing a ring on his finger.

To the chief it seemed, at first, that it could have been a suicide, but the position of the body and the point where the blaze began did not coincide, so it was either a terrible prank or someone just didn't like the poor fellow. Chief Fulton made certain to place a call to the attaché at the Argentine Embassy and inform him. It seemed to be a murder, and they would have to retain the body for quite some time to complete their investigation.

Puerto Iguazu, Missiones Argentina

Nick had waited behind the house for a good thirty minutes before venturing out. He wanted to be sure there were no police left waiting for him and to see if anyone else had showed up. Perhaps he could still get a fake visa without Jorge. No one showed up, neither Jorge's friends or the police. There were just the dogs wandering around and sleeping in the shade. The only thing he had that he had

234

taken from the car was Ignacio's cell phone. He went to the address book to look for Dr. Zapiola's number. Finding it under Papa, he hit dial and the phone rang.

"Hola?" the man said.

"Pablo? This is Nick. I have run into some trouble. I am in Puerto Iguazu, but Jorge was detained before we could get the visas. I think the police have his friends as well. Do you know anyone else who can either get me across the border or can get a visa?" Nick asked.

"What about the samples? Do you have them?" Pablo asked.

Lying, Nick said, "Yes, yes, I do. That's not a problem." He would have to find the car and see if they were still there. He certainly didn't want to have to take on the entire police force.

"Can you bail Jorge out? What was he taken in for?" Pablo asked.

"Not sure, but I didn't hear them asking about me. Even so, I don't want to risk it, and besides, it's probably for making the fake visas," Nick said.

"Very well. Do you remember the park, Parque Nacional de Iguazu?" Pablo asked. "We went there with Veronica and Ignacio when you came here to visit."

Nick replied, "Yes, of course. What of it?"

"I can meet you there, later in the day, around 5 p.m. I will meet you by the snack bar. I will work on getting some visas. If not, we can cross into Paraguay another way. The contacts in Foz will have to come and meet us there instead."

"Ok," Nick replied, "I'll meet you there. By the way, this is Ignacio's cell phone. If you need to call me, you can reach me at his number."

"Have you heard from Nacho? How is he getting along in Washington?" Pablo asked.

Nick hesitated. "Yes, he called me when he got there. I think he met up with some other people from the conference and is sightseeing. Sounded like he was having a good time."

"Good," Pablo replied. "I will see you later today."

Nick hung up the phone and thought about Ignacio. He hoped he had been taken care of.

Nick had to find the police station and get to the car. He found a hat on Jorge's friend's porch and decided to put it on to hide his blond hair. He also took out the earrings, put them into his pocket and headed into town. He pulled his shirt out of his pants and unbuttoned the top three buttons. The town was small, centered mainly around the bus station, which had a few restaurants and some tourist agencies. There were a number of small hotels in town, a municipal building, and a church. Next to the municipal building, Nick saw a military outpost and next to that the police station. He walked past and tried not to make eye contact with any of the men milling outside the barracks. Shit, that's a lot of firepower, he thought. There is no way I can get past them.

He continued walking up the dusty red street, passing a few restaurants and a small hotel. He decided to go back to one of the restaurants and sit out front, drink some mate, and continue to watch the station and barracks for any opportunities. It was just past noon, so he had five hours to get the case and get to the park in time to meet Pablo.

The waitress came out, and he ordered an empanada and some mate. He had been sitting there for a good ten minutes, slowly eating the empanada and drinking, when he saw it. Across the street from the barracks and the police station was a small auto repair and tire store, like so many others in Argentina. Under the brightly colored words on the sign, Gomeria, he saw the chain-link fence and the gate. Behind that, shaded by some low-hanging tree branches, he could make out the shapes of automobiles and quickly recognized the right front tire of Jorge's car. The hubcap had been painted, and the tire itself was a faded white wall. All this time, he figured the police had a yard behind them and the military barracks, when, in fact, it was just across the street.

He didn't see anyone sitting near the gate, but periodically he could see the figure of a dog, or perhaps two, stroll by and peer out through the chain link. A dog? Not a problem, he thought. He paid the woman and pocketed the silverware she had given him for the empanada. Nick decided it was best to continue walking away from the police station toward a road that cut off to the right and then turned and ran parallel to the one he was on. He had seen it through the trees as he walked by the repair shop earlier. He took the turn and started heading back the other way, looking out for anyone else that might be loitering. It was hot, and most people seemed to be indoors. There was no one walking around except for a few children and the dogs, more dogs. He turned and dashed through the trees and brush that he knew would come up behind the chain-link fence of the impound yard.

He approached slowly, but still caught the attention of the German shepherd that was inside the lot. There was only one dog, at least one that he could see. The dog, growling low, stood his ground and looked in Nick's direction. Nick took his hat off and set it on the ground. He quickly scanned the fence to look for any openings or areas, which could be scaled quickly. The fence seemed well maintained, but the dog had done some digging, and there were areas where the bottom of the fence had been raised above ground level. Nick could see that in one of these areas, where the fence joined a pole, the fence was pulling away and seemed to be tied with cord or rope.

He stepped to the side and looked over at the barracks. There weren't as many men in front, and one of the police cars that was there before had left. He went back and stood in the woods in front of the area of the fence that was loose. He would have to act quickly. Not even sure the bag was still in the car, he knew he had to check here first and then, if necessary, would have to somehow get it from the station. He would rather take on the dog right now.

He took off his shirt and wrapped it around his lower right arm, securing it in place with a strip he had ripped off from it, and then, moving toward the fence, he withdrew the knife and tried to cut the cord that was holding the fence in place. The knife, while not very sharp, easily cut through the cord that had deteriorated in the tropical heat and rain. The fence had been pushed out a few inches, so Nick, using all his force, pulled it back, opening a space just big enough for him to get through if he knelt down slightly.

By now, the shepherd was barking and covered the distance to the opening rapidly. Nick had made it through and stood as the dog jumped to get hold of his arm. Nick let the dog take his right arm, which he had held out parallel to the ground. As the dog did so, Nick wrapped his other arm around from behind the dog's neck and lifted him into the air. The dog clamped down tighter on his arm, with the shirt providing only minimal protection. The dog did not ease up on the grip, but was at least silenced by Nick's arm in his mouth. With his left arm securely around the dog's neck, he then lowered the dog just enough so he could get the dog's lower torso between his legs. This provided the leverage he was looking for, and, with a quick jerk and twist to the side, he snapped the dog's neck. The dog was not yet dead, but would not bother Nick anymore, so he dropped him and moved toward the car.

He tried the driver's side door, which was locked, as were all the others. Looking in, he saw the satchel was still shoved under the front seat on the passenger's side. He really couldn't believe his luck, guessing maybe it was what Jorge knew, and not what he had, that was important to the police. He couldn't see any way they would make a connection between Jorge and himself, so he thought he was safe in that regard.

He went over to the passenger side that was up against a

fence that was overgrown with vines. The car was on a slight uphill grade, and Nick had just enough room so he could use the same arm he had wrapped with his shirt and break open the window in the back. It took more than a couple of tries. The glass sprayed into the backseat and on top of the satchel. Nick broke away the remaining glass that was still in place on the lower part of the window and reached in for the satchel. The weight of the bag told him what he really wanted was there, the metal briefcase. Perfect, he thought, and headed back out through the fence the way he had come in. He headed to the bus depot where he knew he could buy a t-shirt and catch a late tour to the park, just in time to meet Pablo.

Skies over Puerto Iguazu, Argentina

The military plane was very comfortable, and as Ricardo and Francis made their approach into the airport at Puerto Iguazu, they took a long right-hand turn from their flight path along the Parana River, skirted the Iguazu river heading east, and then turned southeast toward the landing strip. Looking down, Moreno pointed out the junction of the three borders of Argentina, Brazil, and Paraguay, known as the Tres Frontieres or Three Frontiers. Ricardo had mostly talked business on the way there, comparing notes on how their different governments functioned and also expressing his displeasure at sometimes being treated like a retarded stepchild by the FBI.

As they made the turn, he pointed out the city of Foz in Brazil, lamenting the fact that the Brazilian side was much better off economically, and then directed Francis's attention to a billowing cloud of what looked like steam rising up over the green forest below. "That is Las Cataratas. If you are ever here again, I recommend you see it. It is well worth the trip. No offense, but it puts your Niagara Falls to shame," Moreno said. Francis said that he had heard of it, and that it had been used in the movie *The Mission* with Robert De

239

Niro, one of Marina's favorite actors. He hadn't talked about Marina, but he did think of her as he talked about the movie.

They were met on the tarmac by a military car. The trip into town was quick, the traffic not very heavy. Few cars or buses came the other way, only one small van with a few passengers and a pickup truck heading toward the park.

They came into town and pulled into the garrison next to the police station. Ricardo said on the plane that he had met the local police chief before. There were always problems with drugs here, but, much to Francis's surprise, he said they had been dealing with some local al Qaeda activity as well. Most of the problems were in Foz and Paraguay, which was also very close, but Argentina had at least been attempting to get a handle on the problems. Paraguay didn't seem to care one way or another.

They entered the station and were greeted by the chief, and, realizing the nature of their work, he led them straight to Jorge. Jorge was cuffed, wearing a dirty tank top and sitting in a chair that had been turned around, so he was leaning forward with his chin on the back of the chair. He looked up and was only puzzled for a moment. He knew who it was. He had been to the United States to visit Nick once and briefly met his family when they dropped Nick off at the airport.

Moreno took the seat across from Jorge and told him to sit up. He also asked the chief to take the cuffs off and give him something to drink and eat. Francis remained standing and leaned against the wall behind Moreno, watching the smooth professional man at work. He had to admit he was very suave.

"Mr. Cabiniera. I don't know what the local police have been asking you, and I really don't care," Moreno said. This caught the local chief's attention, and he laughed, knowing Moreno was not entirely serious. "What I have to ask you is much more important, and, if you cooperate, I'm sure the local police will look favorably upon it. It seems they owe me a favor. Many favors, to be exact."

"I need to know where Nick D'Abruzzo is, and I already know you were with him, so don't lie to me about that. He has something that is very important for Argentina, and for the rest of the world. Now, did he come with you to Missiones?"

Jorge, feeling at the areas on his wrists where the cuffs had left abrasions, looked over at Francis. "Yes, yes, he did. We got here this morning." Continuing with some pride in his voice, he said, "He was no more than five meters away from me when the cops got me. He was peeing in the bushes. If they had stopped yelling at me, I'm sure they would have heard him peeing."

Moreno smiled. "Very well. Do you have any idea where he may be, or where he was going? Did he have anything with him?"

Again, Jorge laughed. "If you're looking for the briefcase full of bull semen, it's in the backseat of my car. One of the cops drove the car here." Moreno jumped up and grabbed Francis. He quickly asked the chief where the car was, and, at the same time, told another officer to bring Jorge along with them. A burly junior officer with a crew cut rehandcuffed Jorge and dragged him to his feet, following the three other men out across the road to the impound lot. They got to the gate, which was on the left-hand side of the repair shop, and the local chief quickly opened it. Walking the few short feet toward the car, they couldn't see the damage to the left-hand side. As the chief opened the front driver's door, Moreno said to Jorge, in a not-so-friendly voice this time, "Where is the semen?"

Jorge was, by this time, laughing again and pointing. "The window, the window. Nick has already been here, man. Look at the window."

Francis ran around to the other side, looked into the broken window, and saw there wasn't anything on the backseat, or under the passenger's seat. Nothing. He returned to the other side, looked at Jorge and then at Moreno, and knew Nick had been here. By now, the chief began apologizing; knowing his men had really screwed up by not checking the car, but Moreno knew they didn't know what it contained.

As they stood still, the burly officer who had cuffed Jorge appeared from further in the impound area carrying the lifeless body of a guard dog. Jorge, realizing they were looking for something more important than bull semen, said in a rather carefree manner, "You know, I do have his cell phone number. Why didn't you ask me that earlier?"

Moreno stepped forward, and, losing his cool, grabbed Jorge by the neck. Francis, knowing they had lost precious time and would lose even more time without the number, intervened, as did the burly cop. Jorge stood up and spoke the numbers as Moreno entered them into his cell.

The phone rang twice and Nick answered cautiously, "Hola?"

Moreno held the phone to Jorge's face and whispered to him to say he had been let out and wanted to know where he was. Francis was skeptical, knowing how paranoid Nick had become, but it was worth a shot. The phone was placed near Jorge's face, and all that Nick was heard to say was, "Hey, man, I told you before, wrong number."

Jorge looked at Ricardo. "He said you have a wrong number."

Francis asked, "Any way to trace the call?"

Moreno shook his head. "Not up here, but he must be close by. We need to get out a description to all the local jurisdictions and to the border guards quickly, he must be laying low somewhere."

As they walked back to the police station to regroup, Moreno got another call, this time from his office in Buenos Aires.

"Yes. We wanted to let you know. Someone in Washington called," the secretary said. "It seems that an Argentine citizen has been murdered in a hotel in Virginia near Washington D.C."

Moreno replied, "Listen, I can't handle it right now. Give me his name. I'll call Molino; he can handle this one."

"Yes, sir, his name is Ignacio Zapiola. And one more thing, they're not releasing the body as yet. They have discovered some abnormalities with it. I can call Molino if you like, sir," the secretary said.

"Yes, yes, please do," Moreno said. He pulled Francis aside, and said, "Remember Ignacio, the man that Nick met with in Buenos Aires? They found him dead in a hotel near Washington, D.C."

CHAPTER TWENTY-FOUR

Buenos Aires, Argentina

"Papa? Papa?" Veronica asked, getting an answering machine. "Papa, if you are there, please pick up the phone," she continued between sobs, sighs, and blowing her nose. Someone picked up, and in Spanish heavily accented by some foreign tongue, said, "Your father is not here at present, but I will go and get him, so hold on." By now Veronica had contained herself, but her fiancé continued to massage her back, hold her hand, and tell her things would be fine. She looked up at him and smiled, appreciating his tenderness greatly, especially after she had received the terrible news. She called him first, because he was close and she knew, before she could tell her father, she would have to somehow get hold of her senses.

"Veronica?" the voice came over the phone. "What is the matter? My assistant said that you were crying. Please, precious, did something happen? Are you ok? It's not Juan, your boyfriend?" Pablo asked.

"Papa, please, no. I am alright, but I have some terrible news. I wish I could be there to tell you. Papa, Nacho is dead!" she said, only managing to get out those final words before breaking into uncontrollable crying again. Juan let her cry and took the phone. "Dr. Zapiola, this is Juan. Your daughter called me when she got the news from the United States," he said.

Juan heard Pablo's harsh breathing mixed with cries of deep pain. Then Pablo cleared his throat, and asked, "Please tell me what happened."

"Sir, I'm sorry to have to tell you this, but it seems that Ignacio was murdered. The room in which he was staying was burned, and the fire was intentionally set. The police in the United States are sure of that." Again Juan heard labored breathing and the sound of sobbing continued. "Sir, Agent Molino of the SIDE called to tell us. He also indicated that the body is being held because the coroner found some abnormalities. They are not sure—"

Dr. Zapiola interrupted and said, "What kind of abnormalities? Where? With what part of his body?"

Veronica had contained herself again and took the phone. "Papa, Nacho seemed to have some kind of infection. They're not sure if it is a virus or bacteria. They have quarantined the body until they can decide if it is harmless or not."

"Carina, please, tell me when they get back to you. I will try to make some calls to see if I can speed up the return of his body. You will be ok?" Pablo asked.

"Yes, Papa. Will you? I can't believe he is dead!" Veronica said, breaking into tears again.

"Neither can I, sweetheart," Pablo said. They said their goodbyes, and, as he hung the phone up, Dr. Zapiola collapsed to the floor on his knees, his head in his hands. Crying and saying over and over, "No one was supposed to get hurt, not my Nacho! No one! That bastard Nick, this is his fault! I should not have let him talk me into this. I shouldn't have let him get Ignacio involved."

The man who had answered the phone had entered the room, and Pablo caught his look and told him to get out. He stood and went to a gun cabinet that had rifles, shotguns, small handguns, and a few machine guns. He grabbed the first shotgun and took a handful of shells and put them in his coat pocket. Next he found a 9-mm Beretta handgun, stuck it in his coat pocket, and did the same with a case of bullets. Again the man entered the room and saw Pablo had armed himself. "Doctor? What has happened? Perhaps we should talk."

Pablo, fuming, said, "Someone has hurt one of my children. I need to take care of the person that did this. I am sure a person like you could understand."

"Who is this person, and where is he? I thought you were getting ready to make contact with the carrier and bring him across?" the man asked. Pablo did not answer and clutched the shotgun even tighter, continuing to glare at the man. "When did you last talk to the carrier?" the man asked, trying to get the doctor to focus on the task at hand.

Still Pablo fumed, but this time he stepped forward, clutching a gun in each hand. "Perhaps you should call him since I don't think you will make it there at the designated time," the man continued.

"Yes," Pablo said as the man handed him a cell phone. Pablo set the gun down and started to dial Ignacio's number, only managing to get in six numbers. The man looked at him, and he finished dialing.

Nick answered, and Pablo hesitated until he heard Nick say, "Doctor? Is there a problem?"

"No, of course not. I just wanted to tell you that I'm getting off to a late start. I should not be too late. I will see you soon." Pablo hung up, handing the man the phone. He left, leaving the shotgun where he had set it down, but he still had the 9mm in his jacket. He wasn't certain how he would get it across the border, but he had to figure out some way. He was finished with this project. He was finished as soon as he learned of his son's death. The money did not matter now. No amount of money could replace his pride and joy, his number one child, Ignacio.

Driving over the border into Brazil from Paraguay was not a problem; he was well-known by the border guards. He continued driving around the outskirts of the city of Foz and on toward the Argentine crossing. As he drove, he thought about how to perform his task. Images of Nick flashed through his head. He imagined walking up behind him and shooting him in the head, watching his head explode.

246

Simple, easy, and it would certainly make him feel much better. Next, he imagined a gut shot and then kicking Nick as he lay in a fetal position, bleeding and moaning.

He had reached the border between Brazil and Argentina. To be on the safe side, he had hidden the gun and the bullets under the driver's seat. He still had the shotgun shells and put them under the seat as well. There seemed to be a greater number of guards at the crossing than usual, but he had no trouble getting through. He was only a twenty-minute drive from the park and from his revenge.

Puerto Iguazu

Moreno took over command of the local police station. The first order of business was to canvass the town and ask if anyone had seen a man fitting Nick's description, the new description that Jorge provided. Francis felt helpless sitting around and offered to help in the search, but Moreno insisted he remain close to him so when they got a lead they could act quickly. It didn't take long to find someone who had seen Nick. The man was brought into the station and related how he had driven a man fitting Nick's description to Parque Nacional de Iguazu.

Moreno looked at Francis and said, "That is very close; he must be waiting there. Let's go!" Francis jumped up and followed Moreno out the door. The local chief came along and threw Moreno the keys to his car. Francis got into the front passenger side. As they left, Moreno said to the chief, "Call the park, ask them to see if there is anyone around there fitting Nick's description, but tell them not to do anything until we get there. Make sure the people at the entrance know, and if he tries to leave before we get there, they should try to detain him. Otherwise, they should simply wait." The chief nodded his head affirmatively. Four other cars full of local police and military staff had joined up with them, and they quickly made their way toward the park.

Parque Nacional de Iguazu

The man at the entrance to the park told Pablo they would be closing soon, but Pablo replied he still wanted to enter and paid the fee. He drove quickly to the area just above the falls and parked his car. He reached under the seat, and, finding the 9mm, picked it up, and set it in his lap. He was more nervous then he had expected and fumbled with the shells, dropping a few on the floor as he tried to load the magazine. He finally managed to insert the fifteen bullets needed to fill the magazine and jammed it in. Taking off the safety, he chambered one round. Approaching the outdoor snack area, Pablo scanned the faces of the few people who were sitting there and did not see Nick among them. He went up to the bar and was going to ask the bartender if he had seen anyone that looked like Nick, but the bartender was busy, and Pablo became more nervous. He looked around again and went into a small gift shop, but the only person there was the woman behind the counter, and she only seemed interested in closing the shop.

Pablo walked outside again and saw Nick. At least the man's profile looked like it could be Nick, but his hair was blond. He was on a bench parallel to the trail that led down to the gorge below the falls. He had a bag on the bench next to him and was busy feeding some coatimundis. Pablo approached with his hands folded behind his back, the gun in his right hand. Nick heard him approaching and stood to greet him; he saw the expression on the doctor's face was not a welcoming look.

The doctor was about fifteen feet away when he pulled the gun out from behind his back. "I know what happened to Nacho. I know that you made him sick and then tried to cover it up. That wasn't supposed to happen." Nick froze, thinking about his options. Pablo fired the first shot, hitting Nick about eight inches above his left knee. Nick winced, but stood his ground, and began to speak. "You knew the risks. You suggested that he could give me the nitrogen. You were going to give him and his wife part of the money you made from this."

"Fuck the money! My children mean more than money!" Pablo yelled and tried to fire another round, but it jammed in the chamber. As the doctor fumbled with the gun, trying to unjam it, Nick moved forward and nailed him in the face with a quick left hook, dropping him where he stood. The shot had attracted attention from the snack bar, including that of a security guard who had been standing near the museum for the last half hour. The guard had drawn his weapon and was calling for someone else on his radio.

Nick bent down and picked up the 9mm the doctor had been fumbling with. He removed the jammed round quickly, chambered another, and was moving forward to take out the guard when he saw them, a large group of armed men approaching from directly behind the guard. There were local police, men in military uniforms, and two men in suits. One he did not recognize, but the other, the other was his fucking brother, Francis. He was pinned up against the falls and was not about to give up. Not now, not to his brother. He guessed he had at least thirteen more rounds, but that was not nearly enough for the twenty or thirty men who were approaching.

He had only one option: Head down into the gorge toward the raging falls and rapids of the Iguazu River and hope the tour boats were still there. First the poor doctor, who was slowly regaining his senses, would have to be taken care of; he was a liability. Nick stood over him and saw that his eyes had just opened; he was shaking off the grogginess. Nick put a bullet into his forehead. Ignoring the pain in his left leg, he bolted down the trail toward the stairs that led to the boats. A few people were heading up the trail, and even fewer were heading the same way as Nick. Nick bumped into one person, knocking him to the ground and ignored his protests as he continued to make his way toward the boats. He could hear the sound and force of the water and feel the mist as he came toward the top of a set of stairs that led down to the stone path toward the river. He could not yet see the lagoon under the falls, but could see some of the more than two hundred cataracts that made the two-hundred-plus foot plunge to the river below. Nick made his way down the slippery steps and could see the lagoon and the area where the boats came ashore to let their passengers off. There were two boats, each about thirty-feet long, at the landing; one had some passengers debarking. The other was empty, tied to a wooden pole. Now, mingled in with the powerful sound of the waterfalls, Nick could hear the sound of voices approaching and yelling, telling the tourists to clear the area. Nick had not looked back since he had made his initial approach toward the security guard. There were other people, about ten, waiting on shore for the last trip under the falls on the Argentine and Brazilian sides. The last part of the trail was the most difficult; it was narrow, and the rocks were slippery, and the people that had unloaded began to make their way up the trail, getting in Nick's way.

By the time Nick made it to the boat, the people waiting began to board. Nick had shoved the gun into his pants, and now withdrew it, and yelled in Spanish for them to get out of the boat. The driver looked up and didn't hesitate; he and the remaining passengers quickly got out. The driver left both of the powerful engines running, and Nick jumped in, holding the bag tightly.

Nick quickly put a bullet into each of the engines of the tied-up boat, and told the driver to untie it, and then push it out into the water. Nick pointed the gun at the driver, and the boat slowly moved out into the calm waters near the shore after the driver gave it a shove.

Nick first heard, and then saw, bullets striking the water around his boat. One or two hit his boat near the gunnels, causing an explosion of fiberglass. His boat had floated out into the lagoon and was facing up river, toward the Argentine side. Nick gunned the engine and headed out into the lagoon in the direction of San Martin Island. He would have to make a big left-hand turn and head the boat down river. He had taken the tour before and knew the boat drivers avoided the major eddies and rapids, pretty much hugging the Argentine shore. More shots came; some of the military men had made it almost to the boat-landing area.

Nick was about to gun the engine and make the move that would position him for the downriver run, but he saw another boat coming from the Brazilian side start to make the move back across the main current. The boat he had disabled had caught the current and started to float downstream, but became hung up near the left side of the main channel, the side he needed to pass through. He knew if he waited much longer he would be a sitting duck. Shots were whizzing over his head and hitting the water next to the boat.

He decided to slip in just behind the boat coming from the Brazilian side, using it as a shield, and try to squeeze his way past the other boat hung up on the corner. He gunned the engine, skirting the shoreline of San Martin Island, made a sharp left turn, just behind the boat from the Brazilian side, as it began to make its way toward the docking area. The combination of speed, the turbulence of the water, and the wake of the boat launched Nick's boat into the air and he came down hard. He was able to maintain control, but the boat he had just passed made a move to try and avoid him and almost turned over. They overcorrected, turned sharply to their left, and ended up crashing into the rocks along San Martin Island. Nick was able to slip by the disabled boat and avoid the large rapids on the right side. This was his most vulnerable point, and, as he gunned the engine, Nick took cover deep inside the fiberglass hold, because, as expected, the men following him had taken up positions along the shore and let off a huge barrage.

Nick tried to remember the trip he had taken years ago with Pablo and Veronica. He thought there were at least four major sets of rapids. He slowed after clearing the corner and making his way through the first set. Huge waves churned and turned back onto themselves on the Brazilian side. After clearing the rapids, he gunned the engine and scouted out the river ahead for the next set. Unexpectedly, a cloud of fiberglass kicked up off the right side of his boat, and he caught sight of another boat. The boat he had shot had obviously been recovered and was not disabled by the bullets. It was already coming up behind him fast.

Nick quickly approached the next set of rapids and decided it was best to take them down the middle. The boat following him was not more than three boat-lengths behind. There was a longer stretch without any rapids, and Nick gunned it, but the other boat, shooting at him, followed almost directly behind. Nick knew they would just continue to follow him; he had to stop them now. He could already see another set of rapids coming up. The Argentine side looked clear with the bulk of the bigger waves on the right. In the middle, Nick could see an exposed rock and directly to its left was an even bigger one.

Nick headed straight toward this part, slowing down to let the other boat catch up. When he was about two boat-lengths from the target area, Nick took a quick turn to his right, and, with just barely enough room, skirted the Brazilian shoreline and headed back upstream, turning his boat back around to face the other boat. It worked.

The chase boat wasn't swamped, but Nick could see smoke coming from at least one of the engines. They had either hit the rocks and stalled or damaged their engines somehow. Nick looked back upstream and did not see any other boats. The stalled boat was still out of control. He saw Francis and another man by his side looking over at him. He figured they could float through the remaining rapids successfully, but he didn't care. Gunning the engine, he shot past them on the Argentine side of the river.

Francis couldn't believe there was only one oar in the boat, and it wasn't that big. Hadn't these people ever had engine problems before? While Ricardo was yelling back and forth with some of the policemen in the boat with them, Francis took the oar and tried to keep the boat headed straight down the river. Despite his best efforts, they took one set of rapids sideways. Ricardo wanted to get back to the Argentine side, near where they launched the tour boats at Puerto Descanso, but Francis saw an opportunity to land the boat on the Brazilian side. Ricardo pointed frantically to the Argentine side, but Francis turned around, glared at him, and said, "We're landing here. Now call the Brazilian police and have them come and get us."

Ricardo looked embarrassed and disappointed all at once, but he knew Francis was right. The sides of the gorge were fairly steep, but if they worked their way back upstream, they could get to a point that would take them to the Brazilian park. Ricardo had already tried his phone in the gorge to try and get some backup downriver, but it didn't work. Making their way along the bank was difficult, but they finally came to a spot that had a cut, through which they could make their way to the top. About halfway up, Ricardo got his phone to work and contacted the Brazilian police chief in Foz.

Speaking in Portuguese, Ricardo said, "This is Ricardo Moreno of SIDE. I was pursuing a fugitive in the Iguazu River and had an accident. Could you send some of your officers to pick us up? We're going to be in the Parque Nacional de Iguacu in about thirty minutes." Next Ricardo called the military base back in Puerto Iguazu and told them to get a helicopter up in the air to search further down the river.

"Nick has had plenty of time to get to the Parana River and could even be in Foz by now. I should have had backup down river," said Moreno to Francis, "but didn't anticipate that Nick would take a boat. Not on this river! The man has balls. I really thought we had him trapped, with his back against the wall."

Francis looked over at him. "I couldn't see my brother doing this either. Anyone else would have given up or gone out shooting. I thought we had him, too. I really did. He must be going to Foz, I mean, isn't that where the al Qaeda groups are?" They had reached the top of the gorge and had found the road leading into the park.

Ricardo, catching his breath, said, "Yes, Foz, he must be going there. It's not a big city, not like Buenos Aires or Rio de Janeiro. We will find him."

Francis had utmost confidence in Ricardo from their initial meetings, but now he really didn't believe they would get Nick. As a Brazilian military vehicle approached, Francis got a call on his cell phone; it was Reynolds. He really wanted to ignore it, but decided it was best to answer. He spoke with him for a few minutes and then said, "That was my contact with the FBI. He's insisted that I go back to Buenos Aires and meet with the FBI there, and then return to the United States."

"Are you going to go?"

"He said they need me back in the States to do my job, and that's to protect the country from bio-terror attacks. He's going to send up some FBI guys to take my place, or professionals as he put it," Francis said. "He also said that if I don't come voluntarily that you have authorization to arrest and detain me. In fact, your superiors have insisted that you do so anyway. Apparently, they weren't happy that you didn't wait for the FBI and that you took me along."

"Ok, then," Ricardo said. "We can drop you at the border, and one of my men can meet you there and take you to the airport. It was good to have worked with you. We'll find him."

CHAPTER TWENTY-FIVE

Airplane from Buenos Aires to Washington, D.C.

Once Francis was settled on the flight to the US, he decided he needed to talk to Marina.

"Hello?" she answered.

Damn, it was good to hear her voice, he thought. "Marina, it's me, Francis."

"Frank, where are you, did you get Nick?"

"I'm on my way back from Argentina. I saw him! I was no more than thirty yards from him. We thought we had him trapped, but he got away. Then the FBI ordered me back to the United States. We were so close; we should have gotten him. We think he's in Brazil in a city called Foz. There are a large number of Muslims there and many suspected al Qaeda."

The FBI guy looked over at him and said, "Who are you talking to? Don't tell her that. I would think you would know better."

Francis did know better and began to talk of more mundane things. "Didn't you tell me that you're going to a conference in the United States?"

"Yes, Frank. I'll be in San Diego for a few days visiting friends and then I head to Baltimore for a meeting. You'd better come and see me. I'll be staying at the Marriott in the Inner Harbor. Do you want to go to the Mall in D.C. for the Fourth of July? I haven't seen it for awhile, and I love being downtown. I called your father after I hadn't heard from you in awhile, and he said that he might come up and meet us there. What do you say?" she asked.

"Sure, sure, that would be great. Call me when you get to Baltimore, and we can go to Sabatino's," Francis said.

"I love you, Frank."

"I love you, too," Francis replied.

Parana River near Tres Frontieres

Nick ran through a few more minor sets of rapids, after he left the other boat behind, and then passed under the bridge near Puerto Iguazu before he made it to the Parana River. He crossed over to Paraguay, disembarked, and set the boat adrift in the river. He had only a vague idea of where the ranch was, but he knew it was close to Ciudad del Este. He knew it had a name, and tried to remember it. He went through the alphabet in his mind, seeing if any of the letters would spark his memory. Damn it! He should have asked Ignacio before he left Buenos Aires. It was just that he really expected this part of the trip to be a breeze. Shit! Francis, my fucking brother was here. I should have shot him back in the park or when he disabled their boat.

Nick wasn't sure how he would find the ranch and could only imagine what would happen if some Paraguayan police found him. He still had the Beretta 9 mm. Nick walked for about forty minutes and finally came to a road. He turned to his right because he knew the city was north of where he landed. As he walked along the road with the metal briefcase in his grip, he continued to try and remember the name. Ignacio had mentioned it when they had visited this part of Argentina before. Carina! That was it, Carina! Pablo had named it after Veronica; he always called her that.

Nick heard the sound of a diesel engine coming in his direction from behind. When he turned to look, he saw it was a bus. He flagged it down. Nick approached, entered, and looked at the few people who were riding the bus. He didn't have any guarani, but he did have dollars. He held out a hundred, and said in Spanish to the bus driver, "Have you ever heard of the Carina Ranch? I will give you this now and another one when we get there. Can you take me there now?"

The bus driver smiled a semi-toothless smile and took the hundred. He assured Nick he knew where it was. He told the passengers, a woman and two children, that they would be taking a short detour. He closed the door, and Nick took his place in the seat behind the bus driver. He didn't look at the old woman or the kids, and he forgot that he had the Beretta stuck in his pants. He overheard the woman and the children whispering about him. He heard the words "spy," "policeman," and "CIA" as they were speculating about who he was.

It took about forty minutes to get to the ranch. It wasn't really much of a ranch, just a small farm. It was set far back from the road, and there were no signs indicating its existence. There was a small house and two outbuildings, one much more modern and made of metal. The other was made of red block, as was the house. The metal building had a fenced-in area attached, which had about fifty head of Brahma bulls. Nick asked the driver to drop him off on the road and not pull in, but the driver insisted and took him all the way up the driveway, even honking the horn.

Two men came out of the building, walking toward the bus. Nick could see the second man was holding a gun, an automatic weapon of some kind. Nick was furious, but gave the driver the promised hundred-dollar bill and told him to leave. The man smiled and waved, and, as the bus left, Nick could see the old woman and children looking at him from the back of the bus.

The men did not look like they were South American, and Nick immediately realized they were al Qaeda. He approached, and, looking at the first man, introduced himself. The man looked angry about the disturbance and Nick could understand why. Nick said, "Dr. Zapiola is no longer working for us. In fact, he is dead. I think it is best that we get to work immediately, so I can make the last leg of the trip as soon as possible."

The lead al Qaeda introduced himself. "I am Al-Hawadi bin

Saud. What happened to the doctor and your leg?"

Nick had decided to leave the bullet in his leg for now and not try to dig it out until he was heading back to the United States. Nick sighed. "He came to the meeting point and wanted to kill me. He shot at me, his gun jammed, and I took it from him. I wasn't going to kill him until I saw the police right behind him. The doctor must have changed his mind. I had no choice."

"I got away from the police, and I'm sure they have no idea where I am. The boat I took is probably halfway to Buenos Aires by now, but I think the sooner we get to work, the better. Are you going to help, or am I on my own again, like in the Sudan?"

Looking at Nick's leg again, Al-Hawadi replied, "We've already prepared the carrier compound and the containers. We've made arrangements in Buenos Aires for your transport. All that is left is to crystalize the virus, mix it with the carrier, and pack the containers. Follow me."

It sounded to Nick like they had everything ready to go. Entering the metal building Nick could see it was set up much like the tent in the Sudan except the walls were made of plexiglass and there was a more elaborate negative-pressure air system. He and the other man, the one with the gun, put on the protective suits and entered the laboratory area. The roundish containers were stacked in boxes by a bench, and the carrier compound was in large plastic boxes in a glass-covered freezer.

Nick opened the briefcase with the containers and virus and removed the first large plastic container. The al Qaeda handed Nick a metal spatula to begin dissolving the dried viral material in a liquid to begin the process of creating viral crystals. The laboratory was much more advanced then the one in the Sudan and had all the equipment needed to create stable crystals. As agreed upon, Nick gave the man one of the containers of virus, and he stored it in a liquid nitrogen freezer for future use. After the crystallization was complete, they mixed it with the carrier compound and packed it into the containers. Nick thought, at least now he won't have to worry about getting any more liquid nitrogen, as the virus could now be kept at higher temperatures, as found in a common refrigerator.

Nick was only in Paraguay for one day, long enough to get the virus loaded into the containers and into a small refrigerator that was in a truck. He and a man named Jose drove the truck from Paraguay across the border at Posadas and back into Argentina. Driving all night and half the next day, Jose made it to the Port of Buenos Aires. They were silent the entire trip, only speaking when it was time to eat or stop to go to the bathroom. The traffic coming into Buenos Aires on Route 9 was a mess; the weather was cold and rainy which didn't help matters. Nick recognized the familiar sight of the soccer stadium for the team known as River. They drove by the Jorge-Newberry airport that was next to the Rio Plato and got caught up in a sea of yellow-and-black taxis that were everywhere in the city, driving around like some kind of nervous bugs.

Finally, they made it to the turn near the bus station and headed into the port area. There were two guards at the gate, but they waved Jose and Nick through. They headed toward the ship Al-Hawadi had made arrangements with, the *Andalucia*, which Nick recognized as the region in Spain where he had been recently. Ironic, he thought. Let's hope that I have better luck than I did there. He looked at the flag flying on the ship and recognized it as Greek. Again, he thought about the taxi drive in Athens and laughed at the coincidence. If there is a Turkish crew with an Iraqi doctor and a Sudanese cook, I'm in trouble. Jose looked over at Nick who was smiling, something he had not done for awhile, except for the one night out with Andrei. Jose stopped the truck at the end of the ship.

It was a medium-sized container vessel, and there were five

crew members standing around smoking as the dockworkers loaded on a few more containers. The plan originally was to stow the bug in one of the containers, along with Nick, but he said that there was no way he was going to spend fifteen days in a box, so Al-Hawadi made arrangements for Nick to become a temporary member of the crew. The plastic boxes with the virus in the containers with the carrier agent would be brought on board with the refrigerator. They ran the risk of the containers being discovered if there was an inspection, so, once on board, the containers were to be put into cardboard boxes with oranges and grapefruit placed on top. Nick was to maintain his Irish identity and was given an official position as a cook, although he wasn't expected to actually cook. Al-Hawadi had gone so far as to have the logs faked so that it indicated Nick came on board in Amsterdam.

Once the refrigerator was on board, Nick and Jose grunted their goodbyes to each other, and Nick climbed the gangway and boarded the ship. Despite his title, his plan was to sleep and relax as much as possible for the next ten days, but, before relaxing, he made sure the refrigerator was secure in his office/quarters. Once inside, he locked the door behind him and fell onto his bed and went to sleep, forgetting about the bullet still embedded in his thigh muscle.

Foz, Brazil

Ricardo, working with the local police in Brazil, rounded up a number of Islamic men in the city of Foz, some suspected terrorists, others not. They knew the ones who were terrorists would probably not talk, but the others, who were more timid, may have heard some rumors in the community that could prove useful. Ricardo, still upset about the missed opportunity at the park, knew they had a big job ahead and little time to work with few leads. Nick's boat had been found miles down on the Parana River, well inside Argentina, and Ricardo's superiors requested he return, insisting that the attempt to get into Brazil was a ruse, or perhaps a temporary stop for a meeting or some other contact. They wanted him to continue his search inside Argentina, but Ricardo knew better.

He knew the meeting in the park had some significance; that Dr. Pablo Zapiola was connected somehow and was to provide assistance; at least he was until his son died after meeting with Nick. Moreno and his men had worked nonstop for nearly two days and had not generated anything. Not one of the men admitted knowing the doctor or Nick. The Brazilian police were bowing to pressure from the Islamic community to back off. Ricardo was furious, but knew there was nothing he could do. The FBI agents who were to come up and assist him had been delayed in Buenos Aires and were then called back to Washington.

Ricardo was left all alone. The Brazilians had given up; the Americans were focusing their attention elsewhere back home. His bosses wanted him to come back and work on some other cases that had come up since he first left for Missiones with Francis. Ricardo returned to the Argentine side of the river and went back into the town of Puerto Iguazu. He went to the restaurant next to the police station to have a cup of coffee before being driven to the airport for the flight back to Buenos Aires.

Sipping his coffee, he set his cell phone down on the table and thought about the last couple of days. Someone had been paid off; someone knew something about Nick and Zapiola and was protecting the whole group of people up here. He knew he was never going to get the answers he needed. Too much filthy money in this part of the country, too many places to hide, and too many people willing to hide you for the right price. He took another sip of his coffee, and his cell phone rang. He picked it up and answered in Spanish.

"I'm sorry, I don't remember too much of my high school Spanish. This is Jim Reynolds of the FBI, calling from Washington. I want to apologize for the fact that our guys never made it up to where you are. Listen, I wanted to see if

261

you had some time to come up to Washington, maybe brief us on the situation down there."

Ricardo replied, "I was in Washington two months ago. I have run into a wall here. I'll get some of my men to continue the search here, but I think your man has already left the area."

"Well, that's what we'd like to talk about. When do you think you could come?"

"In five days, most likely. I'll have to clear it with my boss, but it should be ok," Ricardo said.

CHAPTER TWENTY-SIX

Bozeman, Montana

The man sitting across from Matt Jacobs in the booth in the bar looked frightened, really tired and frightened. As Special Agent Jacobs looked at him again, he realized he wasn't a man, but a frightened kid, maybe nineteen or twenty. The kid had simply come down from the hills and walked into the local police station. As they sat at the bar, eating soup and bread, Jacobs continually scanned the room and talked in a very hushed tone. "If it makes you feel any better, we can talk in my car or even back at the hotel. I just thought you might want something to eat."

The kid put down his spoon. "I am pretty hungry. I hiked for more than a week, eating some grubs and some almost rancid carrion I found along the way. As for talking, I think I'll wait till we are back to the hotel, unless you're in a hurry."

"No, I'm waiting for some others to come, so we have some time. Tell me about yourself, if you like. Do you have any family?" Jacobs said, making small talk to kill time until Reynolds and his men arrived, which he figured would be about two hours.

"Yes, yes, I do. I actually have a wife and some kids. They live in town here. I haven't seen them for about a year. My parents are retired in Arizona," the kid said. Jacobs just nodded, and then asked him if he had ever been to this restaurant before. "No, I haven't, but I think some of my friends may have," he said.

Jacobs was about to respond when his cell phone rang. "Matt, this is Reynolds. We were able to get an earlier transport. We'll be arriving in about thirty minutes. Take the kid back to the hotel and start to get as much info from him as you can. We need to take care of Olsen quickly,"

Reynolds said.

Jacobs acknowledged his superior, threw some money on the table, and said, "Grab what you can take, kid. We're going to the hotel." The young man grabbed the rest of the bread and some crackers and followed Jacobs out the door. Walking across the street, they headed toward a small five-story hotel at the end of the block. Once inside, Jacobs locked the door and said, "Ok, now, tell me where you were, how you got here, and everything you know about where Olsen is and what he's doing."

The kid, finishing a piece of bread, swallowed and started talking. "I can tell you where I hitched a ride with a semi. I'm not sure I could retrace my hike, but I can tell you some of the landmarks along the way. I really don't know much about what Olsen has planned; I wasn't in the inner circle. I was there to protect the compound and do other grunt work. I know he has something big planned, but I can't say when or what."

"Does he know that you're gone?"

"I would have to say yes, but I expect that he would never have guessed that I could make it back to civilization. I mean without a weapon or water or nothing, but I can't say for sure."

"Ok, I have a map. Show me where you hooked up with the semi, and let's see if there are any landmarks on the map that you can recognize," Jacobs said.

"There, right there off of Route 287. I came out of the forest on the north side," the kid said, as he scanned the map for any recognizable landmarks. "I'm pretty certain that I headed almost due south. There! There! I know I passed a lake; I walked along the edge of the lake. The ridge line on the west side of the lake, if you follow that, will take you straight to Olsen's compound. It's more like a cavern," the kid said as he pointed at the map excitedly. "I don't know what or who your friend is bringing with him, but it better be a small army, because that place is a fortress." Jacobs looked over at the kid and smiled.

Reynolds wanted the element of surprise, but, since they only had a vague idea of where Olsen's hideout was located, they would have to do some reconnaissance first. The Montana National Guard was at his disposal, as was an elite team of FBI counter-terrorism agents. After three days of night flights with Black Hawk helicopters equipped with listening devices and night-vision video, Reynolds and his team were fairly certain they had the location. To be certain, they had a military satellite take photos of the surrounding area. Much of the area was undisturbed, but there were definitely signs of human activity. They could see the shooting range and some craters that were left by the mortar practice, which the informant confirmed had taken place.

The Black Hawks had picked up some communications, most of which was small talk, but one that mentioned Olsen specifically. As Reynolds stood outside the Black Hawk, with its rotors turning overhead, ready to board, he said to Jacobs, "This is going to be a rough couple of days." Jacobs nodded and boarded the helicopter with Reynolds.

The flight took less than two hours and was set to coincide with daybreak. All together, there were twenty helicopters with about one hundred and fifty troops armed with assault rifles, grenade launchers, and fifty-caliber machine guns. The troop-carrying helicopters were armed with Hellfire missiles and were supported by three Apache helicopters. The Montana Air National Guard was being held in reserve if an air strike was needed.

The helicopters made their way toward the compound from the east with the rising sun at their backs. The plan was to drop troops along the ridgeline to the south and avoid the areas beneath and to the north of the compound. Once the troops were in place, the Apaches were to begin an aerial assault to soften up the target. Reynolds, the Special FBI team, and the National Guard troops repelled to the ground from the Black Hawks since there was no room and no clearings for them to land in.

Despite the early attack, it was likely the Olsen group had heard the incoming choppers, but, to be honest, Reynolds wanted to draw their fire to gauge their strength. The informant had been brought along to point out any unknown hazards as they made their way toward the compound. It was no more than a minute after he had repelled to the ground, and the Black Hawks had pulled away that Reynolds heard the first of the Hellfire missiles explode against the target. It was immediately followed by more rockets as well as return fire from the compound, which sounded to Reynolds like fifty-caliber machine guns and shoulder-launched rockets.

Perhaps anticipating that any attack on the compound would come from the south end of the ridge, mortars began exploding in and around where the troops had landed. Reynolds grabbed the informant and dove for cover behind a rock outcropping. He looked back and saw Jacobs had not been so lucky. While still alive, he had a severely injured leg and was yelling as the searing heat of the shell fragments burned inside his wound. More mortars landed nearby, and Reynolds could hear the chatter on his radio; the commander of the ground troops began to coordinate with the Apaches and Black Hawks to try to eliminate the mortars. He listened and heard as one, then two, and then three of the unknown number of mortars had been silenced. It seemed Olsen's men were moving around to different positions, either by tunnels or well-camouflaged trails.

In the midst of the chatter, he heard an explosion come over the radio, followed by the acknowledgment that one of the Apaches had been hit by small arms' fire and had crashed on the east side of the compound at the bottom of the small cliff. The informant said, "Like I said before, they're not going to engage in hand-to-hand, at least not at this point, but they can keep moving around and keep up the enfilading fire on the east side of the compound. I know of one tunnel that comes out beyond their perimeter, but you can bet that they've either blown it up or have it ready to be blown up." The mortar fire had become much more sporadic and was mostly overshooting their location since they had moved forward about fifty yards. The small arms' and machine guns' fire and the sound of helicopters could still be heard off in the distance.

Then Reynolds heard the call. The choppers were to pull back, and the men were to take shelter. They had called in some laser-guided munitions to further soften the target. Reynolds again found shelter against some rocks and waited along with everyone else for the strike. He believed that Olsen and his men knew something was coming since the government forces had backed off. The wait was shorter than Reynolds had expected. The booming sound of the explosions was quickly followed by the concussion against his body. He had never felt anything like it. He could see the informant was equally stunned. Next he heard a sound that, at first, he didn't recognize, but he then recognized the sound of large rocks falling and breaking away from the mountain side, crashing to the ground below. He heard on the radio from one of the Black Hawks that had taken position in front of what was now a gapping hole in the side of a mountain. "Hell, it looks like we just cracked open an anthill," the voice of one of the pilots said. Reynolds heard the telltale sound of mini-guns as the Black Hawk began to take advantage of the stunned and dazed enemy.

"Let's move out," rang in Reynolds's ear. He and the informant jumped to their feet and began to negotiate the ground between their position and the now smoldering and disabled compound. The informant had helped lay the mines and had already given Reynolds instructions on how to get through the field.

Olsen, sitting in his chair deep inside the cavern of the bunker, listened to reports coming in from his various lieutenants. Only four of the ten remained, and, of those four, only two had any significant number of men at their disposal. Olsen looked at the nerds who were cowering in a small natural alcove. He rose from his chair, withdrew his revolver, and, before they could react, he put a bullet into each of their heads. He went over to the computers and the other equipment in the control center and turned on the self-destruct sequence that would ignite incendiary bombs that would destroy them.

Nick and the others would still carry out the plan, of that he was sure. He needed to guarantee that it would. He looked at the control center one more time and then ran out the back, toward what he imagined would be the on-rushing government troops. With revolver in hand he ran into battle, having no intention of being taken alive. If he could kill any government soldiers or agents, all the better.

CHAPTER TWENTY-SEVEN

At Sea on the *Andalucia*

On the ship, Nick had stayed in his room, and, when he did leave to eat or shower, he made sure the door was locked behind him. The trip was uneventful. Nick had thought he would get seasick staying down in his room for so much of the time, but he didn't. Only once or twice was he bothered and that was by a young Turkish crewman who was anxious to improve his English. Nick obliged only because he seemed to come around at the times when Nick was the most bored. He asked about the refrigerator, and Nick joked that it was full of beer. The kid reminded him of the teenager he had killed on the beach. Nick, for the first time since sitting in the café in Athens, thought about all the people he had killed. The last name got to him, and he felt sad. He had spent many good times with the Zapiolas, and Pablo was always very good to him.

When the ship entered the Chesapeake Bay and passed by the Bay Bridge Tunnel, Nick began to spend more time on deck. As a kid, he had spent many summers at various beach resorts around the bay and the northern neck of Virginia and he knew the place well. There wasn't much to see in regard to the landscape, but there were many watercraft that passed by, including powerboats and sailboats. About midway up the Chesapeake Bay, near the mouth of the Potomac River, a Coast Guard cutter passed them. It came very close, and Nick thought they were going to board and perhaps search.

The one thing Nick had not been doing since leaving Argentina was accessing the communication portal. It was not for lack of an Internet connection; the ship had a very modern computer room. Olsen had specified there would be communication silence from the time he left until the fifth of July. Al-Hawadi had apparently sent a message through his communication network. Nick had not really endeared himself to the al Qaeda he had met along the way, and he had insisted on making the communiqué himself, but had finally acquiesced.

They came to Craighill Channel Lighthouse, and Nick knew his mission would soon be over. Olsen had not given him any indication of further activities. He knew he wasn't going to return to the ranch, at least not for some time. What he really wanted to do was spend some time at a beach, and he had made some plans. Before leaving for Europe, he had purchased a Harley and stored it in a facility near the port in Baltimore, along with some clothes and much of the money he had been given before the trip. Nick looked out at the lighthouse and started thinking about driving down to Padre Island, Key West, or even New Orleans. The only thing was, after the shit that was going to happen in D.C. on the fourth, he really wondered what state the country would be in. Hell, he didn't care, he just didn't care.

As night approached, the ship made its way past Old Harbor Tunnel and into the Port of Baltimore. Guided in by a tug, the ship was moored at South Locust Point, and the engines came to a stop. They had already been boarded well outside the harbor earlier in the day and were thoroughly checked out by the U.S. Customs Service. Nick didn't speak much when they were on board, but made sure his Irish accent was more authentic this time around.

Nick was to transfer the containers to the men who would actually do the dirty work. He hadn't met any of them, but he was told before he left that they would meet him at the ship. He was not to try and contact anyone; he was just to wait. The other men had since gotten off the ship and headed into town for a night of drinking, but Nick stood on deck, smoking and waiting. It was getting close to midnight, and nobody had approached yet. The only activity around the moored ship was the occasional watchman and countless rats scurrying about looking for food.

Nick was reaching into his shirt pocket for yet another cigarette when he saw a van approaching. It was a fairly new white van, a regular-sized one, not a mini-van. Nick had already had some of the other men help him bring the refrigerator up on deck and had it plugged in with a long extension cord. The van slowly drove up to the side of the ship, stopped, and left its engine running. Three men got out, one from the driver side and two from the passenger side. Nick had considered asking them for a ride to his storage unit, but knew it was not part of the plan and thought better of it. The gangplank leading up to the deck was raised, and Nick, extinguishing his cigarette, went over to the controls and began to lower it so the men could board. No one spoke.

Two men came up and the other remained at the base of the gangplank, periodically scanning the area near the van. The lighting was dim, but, as the men approached, Nick saw they were not what he had expected—the men he had trained with back in Montana, men with crew cuts, blond and brown hair, green and blue eyes, wearing Levi's and black t-shirts. While the men were wearing jeans, they all had the telltale dark skin and dark eyes of the Middle East. Something didn't feel right to Nick.

The two men approached, and Nick pointed to the refrigerator. "The stuff is in there. It's all ready to go. I guess you'll need help getting it down to the van." One of the men, who seemed to be in charge, a tall, thin, but rather impressive man with a stern look said, "Yes, you and my assistant here can carry it down, and please be quick about it."

Nick laughed and thought to himself, what a way to greet someone, but he knew this was all very serious business. He had taped the refrigerator shut with duct tape, and it was still chained shut. It was out of his hands now, but he still wondered if they had a power source in the van to keep things cool. He took one end and the other Middle Eastern man took the other. They tilted it so they could carry it flat, with the door facing upwards. Nick went down last, and the

271

other man walked down backward, toward the already open van doors. They slid it in and left it on its back with the doors facing up. Shutting the door, the two assistants got back into the van while the other man waited. Nick looked at him and said nothing.

The man looked at the van and then at Nick. "Thinking back, we should have done this ourselves. You were a bumbling jackass."

Nick didn't say anything and turned to leave. The man pulled a gun from his jacket, leveled it at Nick and fired, hitting him in the lower right abdomen. Nick was stunned, but was still able to run instinctively back toward the gangplank. If he got to his room, he could get his gun. Damn, he thought, I should have brought it!

He was almost at the gangplank when he heard the second shot. This one caught him in his left shoulder and sent him off balance. Grabbing for the handles on the gangplank, he lost his footing on something at its base. He slipped and fell, hitting his head hard against the ship. The next thing he felt was his body hitting the water. He was still alert enough to pull himself under the pier and into the pilings that supported the structure above. The water was cool, but began to feel warmer. Blood ran from his belly wound and from his shoulder. He heard the van speeding away.

Sabatino's Italian Restaurant, Little Italy, Baltimore

"Frank, what's wrong?" Marina said as she looked across the table at Francis. "You seem preoccupied. Are you going to be like this all night?"

Poking at his manicotti and sausage, he looked over at her and didn't speak at first, then said, "I think you know what it is. They couldn't find him after we lost him at the park. I keep thinking that maybe he died, maybe he crashed and fell in the river, but they never found a body, only the boat."

"What if he's dead? How would you feel about that? I mean, after all he did. I don't mean to be callous, but..." she said, reaching over to take hold of his hand.

"You have to understand that most of my memories of him are good. I really didn't know him in the last couple of years, and I feel guilty. Maybe I could have made a difference," he replied.

Marina just looked at him. She wished he were happier. They only had one more night together before she had to go back to Turkey.

Changing the subject, she said, "I told your father last week that we would be spending the fourth up here, but he seemed so disappointed. We can meet him later, near the Lincoln Memorial. We should probably just take the train down. What do you think?" Francis was still down, and was looking around the restaurant. They had come back to Sabatino's again to relive some of the good memories they had from when they had first met.

Francis didn't want to bore Marina with the details of the work, but he was concerned about the threats to the United States lately. Despite the fact they knew Nick was carrying an unknown virus, the Department of Homeland Security was certain there was no intention of using it anytime soon. The intelligence they had gathered gave no indication of any plan. And, since the FBI had killed Olsen and his men, they felt any threat from Olsen had been neutralized, at least for the time being, with the possibility that he had some other cells lying in wait and that there was an established chain of succession.

Now that al Qaeda had the virus, it was another matter. Along with the CDC and USAMRIID, Francis had been charged with trying to identify whatever it was. He was set to go back to Spain to try and find the mysterious Russian doctor. Ignacio's body had been cremated and tissue samples collected from his body had not, as yet, revealed anything about the virus.

He looked back over at Marina, smiled and started talking about the time she had spent in San Diego. He watched her talk, but at times, he wasn't really listening, just smiling and nodding. The feelings that had welled up again in Istanbul were starting to come to the surface now. She hadn't let go of his hand, and he gave hers a little squeeze. They were eating early, and planned to walk back toward the Inner Harbor to Marina's hotel, and then head to Washington, D.C.

When they left the hotel, the crowds were just beginning to gather and take their places along the harbor to enjoy some pre-fireworks entertainment. Francis took a sip of his wine, Montepulciano d'Abruzzo, from the Abruzzo region of Italy. He enjoyed the wine's strong robust flavor. He finished the last of the wine in his glass, and Marina poured him another from the bottle sitting on the table. Feeling the effects of the wine kick in, Francis almost didn't notice the phone in his pocket, which he had set on vibrate. He thought about not answering, but had promised his boss he would be available throughout the holiday weekend. Grabbing the phone, he answered, expecting to hear his boss's voice. "Francis D'Abruzzo."

"Mr. D'Abruzzo, this is Reynolds. Where are you?"

"I'm in Baltimore. We're eating dinner. What's going on?" he said, hearing the tension and excitement in Reynolds's voice.

"I thought you'd mentioned that you'd be in Baltimore for some reason. Listen, we have him! Your brother, Nick, is in a hospital in Baltimore, the Maryland General Hospital. He was in ICU, but his condition was downgraded. He's in room 506b," Reynolds said.

Francis stood up, looked at Marina, and spoke into the phone, "Is there anyone there? How do you know?"

"I've called the local police, and they're sending a squad car. He's been shot. Someone found him on the docks at the

South Locust Point harbor. He didn't have any ID, but they ran prints on him since he'd been involved in a shooting. His prints came from Interpol. Seems the Turkish are looking for him as well. Are you close?"

Francis said, "I'm on my way."

He hung up the phone. "Marina, Nick is at Maryland General Hospital, here in Baltimore. If you think you can keep up, I'm going to run over there now." She jumped up, threw down some money to cover the bill, and dashed out the door with Francis as the other patrons and the waiters looked on curiously.

Marina and Francis quickly headed down Fawn Street, took a right on President, and then a left onto Pratt. The hospital was just past Marina's hotel. The sidewalks and streets were even more crowded now. Pratt Street had the usual backup of cars as people coming late were trying to find parking. They ran in and out of the crowds on the sidewalk, with Francis finally deciding to jump a barrier and run against traffic in the street, which was easier. A traffic cop tried to stop him, but Francis didn't stop or say anything; he pushed him out of the way. He knew the cop couldn't catch him, even if he wanted to. Marina had fallen a few steps behind, and she jumped over the cop as he lay in the street, dazed from the fall.

They continued their run down the street toward Green Street and the hospital. Francis had moonlighted in the emergency room there and at the University of Maryland Hospital nearby to get some experience at the world-renowned shock trauma unit. He knew the hospital well. Marina had caught up with Francis and was running with him, stride for stride. Another policeman tried to stop them, and, again without hesitation, Francis knocked him out of the way. This one was not quite as incompetent as the other and quickly jumped to his feet and drew a weapon. Francis could hear him yelling stop, but he knew the crowds were too dense and the cop would be foolish to discharge his weapon.

When they made it to the intersection of Pratt and Paca, the light had just changed, so the cars began to move through. Francis and Marina stopped and saw the cop with the gun was not far behind, so Francis took out his badge and held it out for the officer to see. "This is a matter of national security. I have to get to Maryland General Hospital; that's why I couldn't stop for you. Come with me, you may be needed," Francis spoke between gasps for air.

The cop still held his gun out and stepped forward to look at the badge. Yelling, he said, "You could have just showed me that earlier—" cutting himself short. "Ok, let's move." He put his whistle in his mouth, began blowing and moving out into the intersection at the same time to stop the traffic. All three of them crossed over Paca and made their way to South Green Street. The cop again stopped traffic, and they crossed over and headed up the few blocks to the hospital. The three of them entered the hospital, ran past the front desk and to the elevators.

There was already a City of Baltimore policeman outside Nick's room when Francis, Marina, and the traffic cop got there. Francis was relieved; at least he was still where Reynolds had said he would be. Composing himself, he showed the officer at the entrance to the room his badge. Marina stayed outside the room, as did the other officer, who excused himself and apparently returned to his street duties. Marina thanked him for his help, and he nodded a reply.

Francis, stepping into the room, heard the all too familiar electronic sounds of monitors and an IV pump. Looking at Nick, he could tell he had been sedated and was not all together there. Nick had a lump on his head and a bruise on the side of his face. It looked like he had taken a beating as well as being shot. Francis stepped closer and looked at Nick's chart. As suspected, he had been given Demerol, but it had been awhile ago, so he thought maybe Nick would be semi-conscious, not that Francis expected him to say much of anything even if he were. Francis didn't know what to think. He was angry at what his brother had been involved in, but, at the same time, he was happy to see him again. He knew if he were to get anything from Nick, he would have to curb any familial feelings.

Moving to the left side of Nick's bed, the side to which his head was leaning, he pulled a chair up next to the bed and placed his head close to Nick's. "Nick? Nick? This is your brother. It's time you told me what's going on, so we can stop whatever it is you're involved in."

Nick's eyes opened, and he jerked his head back. Taking a deep breath, he closed his eyes again and muttered slowly, "Fuck you, Francis."

At least Nick knew who he was, Francis thought. He was not as doped up as he had been. This time, Francis put his hand behind Nick's head, pulled it forward, and said, "Olsen's dead. The FBI shot him full of holes. I'd say whoever is in charge now couldn't care less about you since this is the way they treated you. As far as I'm concerned, as soon as you're better, I might just take you back to Turkey myself to face murder charges, or perhaps Argentina. I'll have to see who has worse prisons."

Marina had entered the room, and, when she heard Francis getting angry, she gave him a look that said, "That's not going to get you anywhere." He knew she was right, but Nick had always been stubborn, and Francis didn't see any other way.

Nick had woken up, and, though groggy and somewhat queasy from the Demerol, he could probably speak clearly. He pulled himself up in bed and looked over at Marina.

Francis stepped back. "Nick, you're going to spend the rest of your life in prison, one way or another. Or you might even get the death penalty. If you cooperate, I'm sure the Attorney General can work something out with Turkey and Argentina. Olsen is dead; it's over. Al Qaeda used you! It's obvious to everyone, but you."

Nick didn't speak; he simply took some labored breaths with his mouth hanging open, some drool forming in one corner. Wiping away the drool, he looked at Francis and said, "Where's Dad?"

Francis replied, "He's in Washington. We're going to meet him on the Mall. Why? Did you want to talk to him?"

Nick laughed. "I heard they always have some really good fireworks. You know I'm not going to tell you anything, so you might as well go have a good time with Dad. Now tell the nurse to get me some more Demerol and get the fuck out of my room."

Francis pulled out a card, and said, "Nick, the FBI will be here soon. I'm sure they're not going to be as fair with you as I've been. Here's my card. Call me if you change your mind." Nick tossed the card on his nightstand.

Francis left the room, took Marina by the arm, and said in a hushed tone, "We need to get to D.C. fast." To the police officer standing by the door he said, "I need you to call the state police. I need to use their helicopter. It's a national emergency."

The officer talked into his radio and said, "Sir, they want to know under whose authority?"

"Tell them I'm from the Department of Homeland Security, and I've been working with the FBI. I really don't have time to explain!"

"Francis, what is it?" Marina said.

"The way Nick told me to enjoy myself on the Mall and how the fireworks were expected to be good, just gave me a hunch."

Francis took out his cell phone and tried to call Reynolds, but he didn't get through. Next, he called the District of Columbia police and started to explain what he thought was going on. As he was talking on the phone, the officer tapped him on the shoulder. "The chopper will be here in ten minutes. It will land at the hospital helipad."

Washington, D.C.

On the flight down to Washington D.C. from Baltimore, Francis got hold of Reynolds. As it turned out, he and Ricardo, who had finally made it to D.C. for the debriefing he had talked to Reynolds about, were eating at a restaurant on M Street in Georgetown. There were extra flight restrictions in place due to the holiday festivities, and the only place where Reynolds could get permission for the chopper to land was on the street in front of the entrance to Arlington National Cemetery. The road through the cemetery and up to Fort Myers was closed to traffic, so it seemed like a good place to land, being close to the National Mall as well. The helicopter had to skirt sensitive areas and made its way down through Bethesda and Wisconsin Avenue. The no-fly zone around the Naval Observatory had been extended to the west, so, before coming into that area, the chopper had to make a turn to the right and cross the Potomac River just west of the Georgetown reservoir. Off in the distance, Francis could see that some fireworks displays had begun in Arlington and possibly Alexandria.

The view from the helicopter was certainly one of the better vantage points he had ever had. Francis could see the tall buildings of Rosslyn, as they flew over, and then felt gravity take hold as the chopper dropped low over the Iwo Jima Memorial, finally coming down just in front of the Virginia State trooper cars and Park Police that were posted at the entrance to Arlington National Cemetery. Francis stepped out of the helicopter, thanked the pilot, and gave a hand to Marina as she descended. He stopped quickly to ask her to call his father and see where he was, if he had gotten to the mall yet.

Reynolds and Ricardo were standing just a step behind him. "Francis, are you working with anything definite? What did your brother say exactly?" Reynolds asked.

"Nothing specific, but I know him. You have a brother? A sister? You know when they're lying or when they're hinting at something, right? Trust me, it's not because he's my twin or anything like that. I just know whomever he was working with, they're here, or have set something up," Francis said. "We just have to figure out how they plan to release the virus, assuming that they haven't already."

Both Reynolds's and Ricardo's faces registered skepticism. "Ok, if they try to come by air, they'll be shot down. We have patriot missiles, and we have men posted on buildings with handheld anti-aircraft. Let's just assume that an air assault can't be what they have planned," Reynolds said. They all got into a black sedan, Reynolds sitting in the front passenger seat and the other three, Ricardo, Marina, and Francis, in the back. Reynolds turned around and continued talking. "After you called me, I called the Park Police and the D.C. Police, and they're flooding the Mall, looking for any suspicious vehicles or people. Francis, what would someone need to disperse this virus?"

Francis said, "A mister of some kind, something akin to a leaf blower, but not as large. Or they could have an explosive device planted somewhere. They would typically release it in the morning before the wind builds up, but I would guess they're counting on increased exposure due to the large crowd." The sedan was heading over the Memorial Bridge and to the area around the Lincoln Memorial. As usual, for the Fourth of July on the National Mall, crowds had formed along the Virginia shoreline and families, couples, and people of every sort were walking across the bridge toward the Memorial.

Marina said, "What about the boats? I mean, there are a lot of boats in the water. Couldn't they release it from there?"

Francis looked out the window at the boats. He had briefly considered that scenario. They could expose a lot of people, and, even though the shore was packed and the prevailing winds blew toward the Mall area, Francis thought it was not the most likely delivery means. Still he wasn't sure. Just in case, Reynolds was trying to get the local Coast Guard detachment on his phone and have them begin searching for suspicious watercraft. No, Francis thought, it had to be somewhere on the Mall itself.

"Marina, I think it's more likely they would disperse it over the Mall," he said, answering her question.

The sedan was allowed through the barriers that were set up along the road that skirted the Lincoln Memorial. The driver parked on the south side, just next to the steps leading into the Memorial. Reynolds pulled out a handful of papers and split them into four groups and handed one to each person. "Ok, this is what I got from the Park Service about all the support groups that have been hired to set up the concessions, the sound stage, and the ground clean-up crew. I trust that they had everything all cleared and booked in advance. I'm not sure what we're looking for." They began to scour the documents, looking for anything that stood out, but it was mostly as expected: simple work descriptions, including employees' names.

Nothing stood out, and Francis was getting anxious. Marina looked at him, but knew there wasn't anything she could say that would make any difference. As they continued to pour through the documents, there was a knock on the window of the sedan. Marina opened her door and saw the elder Mr. D'Abruzzo looking back at her. She and Francis both got out and gave him a big hug. "Did you see Nick?" his father asked.

"Yes, yes, I did, Dad," Francis said. He paused, not knowing what else to tell his dad about his twin. Clutching the papers in his hand, he looked down at them as Reynolds and Ricardo got out of the car.

Ricardo said, "What's this? There was some work done today on a new memorial that's going up—the World War II Memorial. To me, it looks out of place. I mean this is the

Fourth of July. Is there anything that important that they wouldn't give the work crew the day off?"

Reynolds took the paper. It looked in order, but the work description was vague and mentioned something about securing the work zone. "That's just at the other end of the reflecting pool," Reynolds said. "The Washington Metropolitan Police have surveillance cameras all over the Mall as does Homeland Security. We should be able to get some still photos from the time period when the work was allegedly completed."

"I don't think there's time," Francis said. "Call them and let them know to start looking, but we should go check it out now." All five of them made their way through the thick crowds ringing the reflecting pool, Francis in the lead, followed closely by Ricardo. They came to the construction site, and there was no one in the area, but it was surrounded by the orange construction fence meant to keep people out.

The memorial had stone pillars in semi-circles at each of the ends that were parallel with the side of the reflecting pool. Reynolds caught up and produced a flashlight. "Again, I would look for a tube. This time maybe something as big or bigger than the tube of a leaf blower. They have to aerosolize it, so that people can breathe it in."

Francis tore away at the orange fence. Reynolds, flashing his badge to a Park Police officer who had approached the group, asked him for his flashlight. As they made an opening big enough to get through, a cheer went up from the crowd as the first of the fireworks was set off from the area between one end of the reflecting pool and the road that ran between the Washington and Lincoln Memorial sites. The crowd noise became almost deafening as the Marine Corps Band began playing the National Anthem and some people cheered as others screamed or sang along.

They decided to split up. Francis, Ricardo, and Marina took one side as Reynolds, the senior D'Abruzzo, and the Park officer took the other. The site was filled with the equipment and trash one would usually find in a construction area—discarded soda cans, pieces of wood leftover from the frames for the concrete, as well as a compressor, a generator, and other assorted small tools had been left. They moved along the perimeter of the memorial; earlier scans of the interior part with the flashlight didn't show anything.

Francis stopped. There it was. He could just make out the round object through the clear plastic that had been put up to conceal it. From a distance, it looked the size of a small end table, but less than half as tall. He held his hand out to stop Ricardo and Marina, and yelled over to Reynolds. Reynolds and the Park officer came quickly, and Francis, using the flashlight, showed them the object, pointing out the set of car batteries on the one end.

Ricardo said, "It looks like, like mortar tubes," which he recognized, having been in the military.

"It must be on a timer. Do you see anyone in the crowd that may have a remote-control device?" Francis said.

"Fuegos artificiales?" Ricardo muttered. Francis knew he was thinking fireworks. It seemed an unlikely dispersal mechanism, but the angles of the tubes told Francis they planned to launch them with a low angle, just high enough to get it over the heads of the main crowds, the large group in and around the Washington Monument, and the people crowding the area around the Lincoln Memorial. "Ok," Francis said, "I suspect they have it set to go off if we mess with the power supply. Maybe that's just a decoy."

"Have you ever dealt with anything like this?" Reynolds said. Francis turned to the Park Police officer and said, "You have a decontamination team, right? Get them here now!"

Reynolds said, "Francis, let me call the bomb squad."

"There's no time; they must have this set up to coincide with the fireworks. We have to take care of this now," Francis yelled.

Ricardo stepped forward and said, "I have some experience with things like this. I did some demolition in the Argentine military. I can help." The others stayed, but stepped back to give Francis and Ricardo some space. Reynolds noticed a small crowd had seen the activity in the memorial and were curiously looking through the hole in the orange fence. He motioned for the Park Police officer to handle it.

"Where do we begin?" Francis said.

"The problem I see is that if we mess with one, and we don't do it right, it could just launch all of them at once. Also, if they're smart, they probably set it up so that if it moves or is, say, tipped over, they'll go off. I'm not sure how sensitive it is to motion either, but I think if it was set up for that, considering all the people and noise, it would have gone off already," Ricardo said.

"You take a look at the wiring near the power supply, see if you can do anything there. I'll look at the base of one of the tubes. Maybe we can disable the firing mechanism," Francis said.

Ricardo carefully pulled aside the plastic and began his inspection of the battery, as Francis slipped under the plastic and tried to look into the bottom of the first tube in the rack of six, but it was plugged with concrete and he could not see inside.

Ricardo rose to his feet and said in a frustrated voice, "The battery could just be a decoy, but I can't tell, and if I cut the power, each one of these could have their own power and that would set it off. I think the control unit is in one of these tubes."

Francis stood up, hands on his hips, exasperated. He saw a truck for the decontamination team making its way through the crowd from 17th Street, the street running between the reflecting pool and the Washington Monument. The fireworks were still going off, and it seemed like the grand finale was near, as the frequency of the blasts intensified, but he knew the show would be going on for another twenty minutes or so. Francis looked for an answer. There. A sledgehammer and a stack of large slabs of stone about two by two feet and six inches thick. "We need to plug the tubes so that when they go off, they'll blow up here," Francis said to Ricardo. "I'm going to break these up, and you grab as many pieces as you can and start jamming them down the tubes!"

Francis and Ricardo grabbed one stone after another and went around putting two to four stones into each of the tubes, trying to fit them in as snugly as possible, until they had all of them blocked.

Francis still didn't feel that was enough. The explosive devices could blow the tubes and still spread the virus, forming a plume that would start to spread. By now, the decontamination team had arrived. The clearly marked truck and the activity in the construction area set off a panic in the crowd. With the fireworks still going off, people began to get up, screaming and running, back toward the Lincoln Memorial and toward the fireworks and the Washington Monument. As the decontamination team moved into the construction zone, the first of the six tubes went off. Francis heard a click and the sound of the explosive charge igniting. Smoke from the propellant filled the area as it was forced out the top of the tube, but the projectile did not emerge. Francis grabbed Ricardo and ran toward the hole in the fence and his father, Marina, and Reynolds.

The first charge exploded some five seconds after the propellant had burned out, sending a plume of what looked like smoke out about ten feet into the air. Another tube went off, followed in quick succession by another. The decontamination team had arrived with their suits on, which, while fortunate, was probably the reason for the sudden panic in the crowd. By the time the fourth tube had gone off, the second charge had exploded, sending out not only a plume, but the stones as well. First, the decontamination team placed a hard four-sided tent-like structure over the mortar tubes. Next, they attached a hose from their truck and filled the structure with thick, heavy foam that, once the tube was disconnected, flowed out of the top slightly and began to harden.

The wind was still now, but Francis felt unsure about whether the virus had been contained and told the others to move further away. Carefully, they made their way through the panic-filled crowd, upwind toward the Tidal Basin and the famous cherry trees that lined it. Reynolds was on the phone the entire time. Francis couldn't tell to whom he was speaking, maybe other neighboring jurisdictions or agencies. Waiting along the walkway, they looked back at the fireworks that were still going off to the sound of "Stars and Stripes Forever."

Francis turned the other way, and, facing the lighted Jefferson Memorial, took a deep breath and prayed this was the only attack. His mind was flooded with memories of he and Nick as children and the times they had gone to see fireworks with their parents. Marina put her arms around him, hugging him from behind, as he leaned over the railing with his head in his hands, knowing he didn't want her to see the tears in his eyes.